DRUMMER GIRL

BRIDGET TYLER

templar

A TEMPLAR BOOK

First published in the UK in 2013
by Templar Publishing,
an imprint of The Templar Company Limited,
Deepdene Lodge, Deepdene Avenue,
Dorking, Surrey, RH5 4AT, UK

www.templarco.co.uk

Cover design by Will Steele

First UK edition

FSC
www.fsc.org
MIX
Paper from
responsible sources
FSC® C020471

ISBN 978-1-84877-692-0

Printed and bound by CPI Group (UK) Ltd, Croydon, CR0 4YY

DRUMMER GIRL

To Janice, Nicola, Menaka, Jane,
Amber, Reece and Dana – a girl couldn't
ask for a better collection of BFFs

TRACK LIST:

INTRO : NEON HALO

Lucy Gosling had imagined a lot of different ways that her friendship with Harper McKenzie might end. One of them had involved Harper being locked up in the Tower of London for the crime of being the most heinous bitch that Britain had ever seen. Another had involved Lucy using her drumsticks in a way that would have impressed a ninja. None of them had involved finding Harper's dead body in a swimming pool in LA.

But there she was, floating face down in the bright turquoise water. A cloud of blood wove itself around her, tangling with the chlorine and the orange rays of dawn sunlight to wrap her body in a halo of neon pink.

Harper would love that colour.

Lucy marvelled at the stray thought as it sank through her brain. What was wrong with her? It wasn't as though she'd spotted a nail varnish she thought Harper would like.

It was blood.

There was so much blood.

"Is this Harper McKenzie?" asked Detective Hernandez, the LAPD officer in charge of the scene.

"Yes," Lucy said. She felt as though a thin layer of cotton wool was wrapping itself around her, filling in her ears and nose and mouth, making it difficult to breathe.

Harper was dead.

No, she wasn't just dead. She'd been shot.

What happened, Harper? Lucy raged silently at the girl she'd never get the chance to bicker with again. *What did you do? I was your best friend. Why didn't you talk to me?*

Lucy looked down at the single charm that dangled from her wrist. The little half heart read *BFF*. Best Friends Forever. She couldn't see it from where she stood, but Lucy knew that Harper still wore the other half.

The charms were silly. Kids' stuff. She had laughed at Harper when she'd insisted that Lucy dig out the tiny relic from their childhood, but it really had been lovely to wear it again. To feel like it was true again. And despite everything that had happened that summer, neither girl had taken the charm off.

Lucy felt the first tear slip down her cheek.

Detective Hernandez was asking questions, but Lucy couldn't hear him. She couldn't seem to focus on anything but the single sentence that was playing on repeat inside her head.

Harper McKenzie was dead.

EIGHT MONTHS EARLIER...

1. I LOVE YOU, I HATE YOU

Lucy settled into her usual, solitary table in the corner of the dining hall at St Gabriel's Girls' School. First day back from the Christmas holidays and her brain was already sloshing with maths and French and loads of other things she was sure no normal person could be expected to cram into their head all at the same time.

She popped in her earbuds, cranked up Electric's latest album, *Swing*, and dug into her fish fingers and chips with a sigh of contentment. A little quality time with Trent Eisner's midnight-blue voice was exactly what she needed. She must have listened to *Swing* twenty-five times in the three days since she'd downloaded it, but she still liked it as much as she had the first time.

She'd worked her way into a respectable musical wallow when Harper McKenzie dropped into the chair across from her, unplugged Lucy's headphones and stole one of her fish fingers.

"I hope you know a hot girl who plays bass, because we've got a guitar and drums... and obviously a lead singer." Harper gestured to herself with the half-eaten fish finger. "But a real rock band needs a bass."

Lucy stared at Harper. The tall, blonde American girl had been her friend once. Her best friend, in fact. But they hadn't said a word to each other in nearly two years. Lucy wasn't sure Harper had actually acknowledged her presence on planet Earth in that time. Now she was sitting at Lucy's lunch table, eating Lucy's lunch.

"We might need something else too. Not a violin, that's too 1994, and not in a good way. We need something cutting edge but, like, classic. I want Crush to be more what you'd get if Katy Perry had a baby with The Clash and then let Madonna circa 1989 raise it. You know?" Harper asked in her Californian twang.

"I mean, I'm totally right. Right?" Harper tried again.

"Crush?" Lucy said, still trying to figure out what Harper was on about.

"Our band. Crush. We're going to rock *Project Next's* world."

"We?"

"You, me, Robyn Miller – she plays the guitar – and our TBA bass player. We've got two months before the deadline to turn our demo in to *Project Next*, but we really need to get practising, like, yesterday. Do any of the girls in orchestra play bass too? I guess we can audition—"

"Harper," Lucy cut in. "You do realise you haven't spoken to me in ages, right?"

"So?" Harper said, dipping a chip into the ketchup on Lucy's plate and taking another bite. "That was your parents' idea, not ours. That doesn't mean we're not friends any more, does it?"

How was Lucy meant to answer that question?

Her first impulse was to say, "You got drunk at my fifteenth birthday party and smashed my mum's car – with me in it – into a tree. Then you completely abandoned me to being grounded for six months, on crutches with three pins in my leg, while you were busy becoming the most popular girl in school because Rafe bloody Jackson thinks being a daredevil makes you sexy. So yes, that's absolutely what it means," which would only make her sound like a stuck-up, grudge-holding cow. Even if it was true.

Lucy settled on, "Um, I don't know."

Harper shot her a brilliant grin. "Well I do. We are friends. We always have been and we always will be. And Crush is going to be brilliant!"

As Harper chattered on, Lucy contemplated reminding her that she'd never agreed to be in a band, or to try out for a reality show like *Project Next*. Not to mention the fact that Lucy's parents were unlikely to allow it, even if the whole thing hadn't been Harper's idea.

That was the kiss of death, though. The 'Harper's idea' bit. Because the Gosling Parental Ban on Harper McKenzie had most definitely not expired. But the longer Lucy let

Harper chatter on about costumes and lyrical themes, the less she wanted to put an end to her friend's delusion. Harper had been the reason Lucy had learned to play the drums in the first place, after all. If she hadn't forced Lucy to actually go into the music shop and try out the drum kit she'd been ogling through the window, Lucy might never have picked up a drumstick. It only seemed fair to hear her out.

Besides, if she was being honest, Lucy knew she didn't want to say no.

She wanted to say yes.

"Toni and I sat next to each other in chemistry last year," Lucy explained to Harper later that afternoon as they pushed through the heavy glass doors of Bella, the elegant Italian restaurant that Toni Clarke's grandparents owned in Greenwich.

"Her granddad was a jazz musician when he was young. I guess he was quite famous. Her mum was a pretty well-known model before she died, on the cover of *Vogue* and whatever. Toni's always been keen to be famous as well. She used to play with Josie Hartcourt's band, Spitfire, but they broke up last year. I'm sure she'll be interested."

It was freezing outside and chucking it down, but Harper looked like she had just been made-up to shoot a romantic rain scene in a Hollywood film. Lucy, on the other hand, was quite sure she looked like a drowned porcupine. But then that was the difference between being

Lucy Gosling and being Harper McKenzie, Lucy supposed.

"Of course she'll want to join Crush," Harper said, pushing a twist of wet blonde hair from her eyes. "The question is do *we* want *her*? I mean, sure, she's pretty. And Spitfire wasn't tragic, so I guess she can probably play. But she was on the hockey team with me last season and she was such a stuck-up brat that I almost had to kill her then. I can't imagine having to rehearse with her every day."

"I like her," Lucy said, "and she's really very good on bass. Who said we were rehearsing every day?"

"Maybe she's awesome," Harper replied, ignoring the question, "but if the two of us end up murdering each other we'll be short a bassist *and* a lead singer – and then where will Crush be?"

Lucy giggled and craned her neck, looking for Toni. "We'll have to see if she's interested before you decide whether or not you'll have to kill her. Where is she?"

Toni Clarke ducked into the break room, tossing her apron into the laundry and grabbing her oversized shoulder bag on her way to the kitchen.

"Elaina," Toni called to the short, sour-faced waitress who was waiting for a round of orders. "Granddad wants you to cover for me this afternoon. It's a slow day, so he thinks you can handle the floor alone."

"I bet he does," Elaina snapped. "All his idea as well, was it?"

Toni grabbed table nine's cappuccino and returned the older waitress's dagger-sharp glare with a bright grin.

"Thankyousomuch," she sing-songed as she pushed into the dining room.

Toni didn't know why Elaina always had to be stroppy about it when Toni ducked out early. She made loads in extra tips when she didn't have to split the shift's takings. Besides, Toni wasn't even a proper waitress. She only worked at Bella because her grandparents wanted her to know the family business from the ground up. Not that Toni ever intended to run Bella. There were a lot of things Toni planned to be famous for but pasta wasn't one of them.

She skimmed to a stop at table nine, tossed her curtain of black hair over her shoulder and flashed a charming smile down at the perfectly gorgeous specimen that sat at table nine, furiously thumbing his Blackberry.

"My shift's finished," she said, "but I wanted to make sure that you got this."

"Aren't you sweet?" Perfectly Gorgeous drawled, looking up from the Blackberry with a slow smile.

"Occasionally," she chirruped back.

"Why don't you—"

"Hey, Toni!"

What had surely been an invitation to sit down was cut off by a bright feminine voice from across the room. Two girls in St Gabriel's uniforms were sitting at table twelve. One of them was waving madly.

Toni shot the interrupters a death glare and returned her attentions to Perfectly Gorgeous.

"You were saying?" she said encouragingly.

"Toni! Over here!"

Someone was going to die. Painfully.

"Hold that thought," Toni told Perfectly Gorgeous, covering her irritation with a sparkly smile. Then she spun on her heel and stalked towards table twelve.

She was on the verge of shredding the pair of them when she recognised the smaller girl's wild curls.

"Lucy Gosling?" she said. "I haven't seen you in ages. What are you doing here?"

"Luckily, she's not here to eat," said the blonde sitting across from Lucy. "Fifteen minutes we've been sitting here and not even a menu to show for it."

She looked awfully familiar. But why... A flash of memory flooded Toni's brain. Skidding across a patch of rough mud in a hockey skirt whilst that set of perfect blonde waves beat her to the goal. Then she knew.

"Harper McKenzie," Toni said, eyes narrowed. "Since when do you eat carbs?"

"I don't," Harper shot back. "I told you, we're not here to eat. We're here to talk to you."

"I'm just leaving, actually."

"We'll be quick," Lucy said, ignoring Harper's eye roll. "Promise. We're putting a band together and we need a bass."

"Band?"

"A rock band," Lucy said. "We need a bass player. We're calling ourselves Crush."

"Great. Good for you. I don't have time to mess about in someone's basement, pretending we're going to be The Beatles. I have an actual job." Toni waved towards the restaurant behind her for emphasis and caught sight of Evil Elaina handing Perfectly Gorgeous his bill. "And a life. Which, at the moment, you are ruining."

"Oh please," Harper said. "You're not talking about that guy you were batting your eyelashes at, I hope. He's ancient. And wearing a ring, by the way. As in married. If that's what you call having a life, we may have to find another bass player."

Toni shrugged. "Some of us have more sophisticated tastes than others. Now, if you'll excuse me..."

With that Toni marched straight past Perfectly Gorgeous towards the front doors, ignoring his hopeful expression. Married? And flirting with her? Only in his dreams.

Toni was almost to the door when Harper called after her. "We're going to be on *Project Next*. And we're going to win."

Toni stopped. She'd heard of *Project Next*. It wasn't going to be like any of the other tired talent competitions on TV. Bands on *Project Next* would actually play gigs and record an album in America. Then the winner would go on an international tour. They would be truly, properly famous. If Lucy and Harper had a band good enough to win *Project Next*...

No. Harper was too annoying to live. Not even starring in *Project Next* was worth that.

Famous.

Toni found herself turning back.

She dropped into the seat beside Lucy. "How can you be so sure you're going to win?" she asked Harper.

"Because I don't lose."

The next afternoon, Robyn Miller sucked in her stomach and turned sideways, examining herself in the warped full-length mirrors of the St Gabriel's music practice room where she was waiting for Harper and the new additions to Crush. Even when she sucked it in so hard that she couldn't breathe, she was too enormous for words.

No wonder Ryan had found another girl. A prettier, thinner university girl who probably knew every move in the entire *Kama Sutra*. In French. How could a deathly pale Sixth-Form virgin who was roughly the size of a whale compete?

It wasn't fair. Somehow Harper had turned being ditched by Ryan's best friend, Rafe Jackson, into an occasion for dropping a stone, writing an LP's worth of perfect break-up rock and starting a band that might just be good enough to win the *Project Next* competition.

Robyn, on the other hand, had used being ditched at the exact same time as a golden opportunity to get bigger. And blotchier.

At least Harper had let Robyn compose the music

for the Crush songs, even if it was only because Harper needed someone who knew how to harmonise a melody. Robyn had always liked making up little tunes on her guitar, and composing to Harper's lyrics had been simply brilliant. Robyn had loved every second of it. She desperately wanted to hear her music played by a full band.

Of course, she was also positively rigid with terror that the others would hate the music she'd written. What if Robyn was completely delusional about her musical abilities? What if she was actually a crap composer who should never be allowed to scribble a single note ever again?

Robyn twisted to check that her bum hadn't grown since the stack of chocolate biscuits she'd inhaled at lunch because she was so depressed over Ryan George and his bony university girl. That was the last time she'd let Ryan make her fatter. She swore it was. She was better than that, wasn't she?

"You *are* better than that," she told the mirror, then she looked around her, suddenly sure Harper and the others were just outside, watching her and laughing.

They weren't, but she definitely wasn't alone in the music centre. A soft, winding melody was beginning to find its way through the thin walls. Someone was next door, playing Chopin – and playing Chopin rather brilliantly.

The music swelled into thunderous, driving arpeggios filled with so much emotion that they nearly made Robyn's hair stand on end. Whoever was playing was pissed off

– the way they were bashing out the notes was quite rock and roll, despite it being a classical piece. A sudden image of Chopin with a battered leather jacket and black-varnished nails shot into Robyn's brain, making her giggle.

Robyn slipped out of the practice room and silently padded down the hall to peek into the room next door. When she peered through the viewing window, her jaw dropped.

Izabella Mazurczak sat on the piano stool, completely absorbed in her music. Izabella was possibly the shyest, quietest girl in their year. Yet here she was, creating a wave of violent emotion with the piano keys.

"Sorry, Robs, I know we're late," Harper called as she hurried past Robyn to the Crush practice room. With her was Lucy Gosling and a tall brunette who Robyn recognised as Toni Clarke, their year's resident wannabe supermodel, in her wake.

Lucy stopped beside Robyn at the practice room window.

"Bloody brilliant, isn't she?" Robyn whispered.

"Better than brilliant," Lucy said, beckoning Harper and Toni back to join them. "Come here."

"What?" Harper asked.

"Shush and come here," Lucy said. "We've found her."

"Found who?"

"Our fifth member."

"No," Toni said when she caught sight of Izabella. "Absolutely not. We're not making Izabella Mazurczak part of Crush. We'll have a four o'clock curfew."

"But listen to that," said Lucy. "Nobody's going to confuse us with a Disney Channel act if we've got a baby grand on stage."

"Maybe," Robyn said, mulling over the possibilities. She could already hear how she'd weave Izabella's piano into the melodies she'd written. Delicately sometimes, and pounding like a drum in others. It was so spectacularly perfect that she had to stop herself running back to their practice room for her pad of music paper and pencil.

"I mean, adding piano variations for the songs would be brilliant, actually," Robyn said, containing her excitement so that she didn't look completely daft in front of the others. "But Toni's right; we wanted Iza to accompany the musical last year but she's literally not allowed out of the house after dark. How would we even rehearse, let alone deal with being on the telly or going to LA for the whole summer if we win?"

"When," Harper said, a smile spreading across her face as she listened to the percussive passion of the piano ringing through the walls of the music centre. "*When* we win."

Izabella Mazurczak had never been so wildly, incredibly, disastrously embarrassed. Ever.

She still couldn't believe that Miss Littleton, the headmistress, had actually called her mother in for a conference to discuss Iza's social life – or rather lack thereof. Listening to them talk about her "*challenged interpersonal skills*" being a "*serious obstacle at the Cambridge interview*" would have been bad enough, but her mum's English was so useless that Iza had needed to translate the entire humiliating conversation into Polish for her.

Iza had wanted to scream. Really, really loudly. She wished she'd done it too, or at least tried to stand up for herself, but Iza had always found that the angrier she was, the harder it was to get the words in her head out of her mouth. And Iza had been very, very angry.

When it was over, Iza had practically run from the office to the practice room. She hadn't wanted anyone to see her crying, it would just make things worse. Though she didn't know how things *could* get worse than her mother and the headmistress spending three-quarters of an hour discussing what a pathetic, friendless loser she was.

In here, wrapped in the music, she didn't have to think about it. She didn't have to feel lonely or wonder if Miss Littleton was right and the fact that she hadn't made any friends since the Mazurczaks had come to London five years ago meant that something was wrong with her.

Things had been so much easier in Warsaw when she was small. Or even in Cambridge, where Papa had been on a teaching fellowship before he'd been offered the Classics chair at University College London. She'd had friends there. Not a lot of friends, but enough. So what had changed? Had she got uglier? More awkward?

Had she spent so much time playing the piano that she'd forgotten how to talk properly?

Knock. Knock. Knock.

Iza nearly jumped out of her skin. She looked up to find Harper McKenzie and Lucy Gosling waving at her through the observation window.

Lucy pushed the door open. "Mind if we come in, Izabella? It is Izabella Mazurczak, right?"

Great. They had two subjects together this term, but Lucy could hardly remember Iza's name. Iza really must be socially retarded. Or possibly invisible. Perhaps that was it. Perhaps she was actually acquiring superpowers and it just seemed like she was 'under-socialised' and 'troublingly introverted'.

"Oh no, have I pronounced your name wrong?" Lucy said.

Suddenly Iza realised she hadn't actually responded to the other girl's greeting.

"I'm so sorry, I'm always mangling things," Lucy continued, growing flustered. "My mum says I sound as though I learned to speak from wolves, which makes no sense now that I think of it. But she's right, I'm rubbish with new words."

"No," Iza finally managed. "I'm sorry, I was just surprised. You pronounced it right. Most people just call me Iza, though," she added.

"Ah. Iza. Right. That's lovely," Lucy said. But then she didn't seem to know what to say next. Neither did Iza.

"Stop hovering in the doorway, Luce!" Harper pushed past her friend into the room. "Hi, Iza! You're in my further maths class, right? Mr G is a nightmare, isn't he?" Harper flashed her a warm grin that made Iza feel as though they were the best of friends, and that they always had been.

Iza felt herself smiling back; it was impossible to do anything else. "Yeah, I guess so," she replied.

"Rather you than me," Lucy jumped in. "I hate maths. I'm just glad I dropped it after GCSE. I don't know how you two manage *further* maths."

"It's not so hard," Iza said. Then she wished she could take it back. She sounded like such a geek.

Harper broke the awkward pause, taking control of the conversation. "We're totally sorry to interrupt, but we were in the practice room next door and we heard you playing."

"Was I too loud?" Iza asked. Of course. They'd come to complain. Why else would they bother to talk to her? "I'm so sorry."

"Oh no!" Lucy said. "You were amazing. That's why we're here. We need your help."

"My help?"

"We've just started a band," Harper said, "and we were hoping we could convince you to join us."

"A band? Like, a rock band?" Iza said, confused.

"Absolutely," Harper replied. "It's called Crush. It's going to be awesome, but it'll be even better if you decide to join us. We've written some really killer songs and adding a piano to the mix will make us totally stand out on the show. We're going to enter *Project Next*, you know – the new reality show? After we get through to the final, we'll get to go to LA for the summer and record an album and do gigs and everything."

"And even if we lose, it'll be a blast to try," Lucy said.

"We're not going to lose, Lucy." Harper shoved the smaller girl playfully. "Stop being such a downer."

"I am not a downer," Lucy shot back. "I'm just realistic, that's all. But that doesn't mean Crush won't be fun. And totally worth—"

"I'll do it," Iza said, before she had the chance to talk herself out of it.

"You will?" Lucy looked surprised.

"Yes. I will. Definitely," Iza repeated. "Absolutely. No question."

If Mum and that awful Miss Littleton wanted Iza to be social, then she'd be social. And if her mum didn't like the fact that she'd chosen to do that by joining a rock band that would suck up hours of study time with practice and might take her five thousand miles away for the summer, then that was just too bad.

"I'm in."

Lucy still wasn't quite sure how Harper had talked the Mazurczaks, who had to be the most overprotective parents in London, into allowing their daughter to join a rock band – and Lucy had been there when she'd done it. Somehow, with a little smooth talking, Harper had managed to convince them that Crush would be a 'wonderful educational experience' for their precious daughter and that being on a hit television programme would 'look great on the UCAS form'.

Too bad Lucy's mum and dad thought Harper was the devil in teenage form. She could have used Harper's help in convincing them that Crush wasn't going to completely wreck Lucy's life.

Lucy had mentioned the vague possibility of joining a band at dinner the night before and her mum had forbidden it straight from the off. "You need to focus on your studies now. You can join a band once you're at Oxford."

Mum talked of nothing but Oxford these days. She was obsessed. That was John's fault, of course. Since Lucy's big brother had gone up, her mum wasn't about to settle for anything less for the rest of the Gosling brood. It didn't matter that Lucy didn't particularly want to go to Oxford or that she hadn't got the grades or brains to get in. Mum would still ground Lucy for the rest of the year if she found out Lucy had joined a band instead of swotting for hours every day in a futile attempt to match John's achievement.

Lucy sighed and looked up at the poster above her bed. It was a blow up of Electric's first album cover, with the band rocking out, their backs to the camera.

A drummer's eye view, Lucy thought. A view she'd give anything to have. A view she'd never see if she didn't get moving. They were rehearsing at Harper's house today and Harper would murder Lucy if she was late.

Her mum would find out eventually of course. Lucy knew that. Nina Gosling's children never managed to put one over on her for long. But Lucy had already survived being grounded for six months after her fifteenth birthday party fiasco. She wasn't about to let the prospect of a little more time in solitary confinement keep her away from something that had already changed her life for the better in just a few days.

It wasn't just the music. Crush was more than that. Today, when first Toni, then Robyn, and then Harper – dragging Iza along from their shared fourth period maths lesson – had elbowed their way into her lunchtime bubble, Lucy had felt something she hadn't experienced in a long time. She'd felt like she belonged.

Studying at the library, back half six, she scribbled and stuck the dishonest little note to the fridge with her mum's *Yellow Submarine* album cover magnet. Then she yanked her drumsticks from her rucksack and fled out the front door to Harper's house.

An hour later, Lucy decided she didn't have to worry about how her parents would react to Crush after all.

Crush would never actually make it to *Project Next*. At this rate they wouldn't survive their first full practice...

Toni had been fifteen minutes late. Then Iza's keyboard stand fell apart halfway through their first attempt to actually play. Even after they'd finally reassembled the stand, they could barely finish a song without Harper stopping to snipe at Toni for missing a chord or Toni stopping to suggest an alternative harmony – or, after a while, stopping just to point out that Harper was off-key. All the bickering had Iza so nervous she could barely play.

Robyn leaned back to Lucy. "Do something. We'll never get anywhere like this."

"Do what?" Lucy asked. "Harper doesn't listen to anyone and neither does Toni. And Iza looks like she's about to faint."

"I dunno, lady. You're the drummer," Robyn said.

What did that have to do with anything? Lucy doubted that hitting Harper or Toni over the head with a cymbal would be productive, even if it sounded like a bloody good idea.

She looked longingly at the marked-up copies of their songs clipped to the stand in front of her. The downbeat was right there. If only they could get playing.

Suddenly, she realised what Robyn meant. Lucy was the drummer. She called the beat, or at least she was meant to. If anyone could get this medley of disaster moving, it was the drummer. The others probably wouldn't pay any attention... but it was worth a shot.

Lucy raised her sticks and beat them together.

"One... Two..."

With a glare at Toni, Harper stepped back to her microphone. Toni glared right back as she shifted the strap of her bass on her shoulders.

"Three..."

Iza set her hands to the keys.

Robyn shot Lucy a grin as she gripped the fretboard of her guitar.

"Four."

And then, as one, they started to play.

2. Everything is impossible

"And... we're out," the producer yelled. "Three minutes, ladies and gents. Contestants, stay put, please!"

Lucy kept her toes glued to the X of tape that marked her spot on the massive *Project Next* stage. Robyn stood beside her, looking a bit green, and Iza was practically bouncing out of her skin trying to contain her excitement. Toni and Harper were too busy flirting with the guys in Dead Kitten Mambo – semi-finalist band number three – to be bothered with being nervous.

Lucy didn't know why she was nervous. They weren't going to win. Crush had come a long way in the past six months. They'd had to eat, sleep and breathe their music, but none of them had minded. Each weekend had been a whirlwind of rehearsing, trawling for costumes in vintage shops or bickering about choreography... and it had been the best six months of Lucy's life. But they would still lose. She was sure of it. Even if Toni and Harper had suddenly, after two months of never being quite in sync, discovered how perfectly their voices blended if they just sang together. Even if Robyn had written positively brilliant piano solos for Iza into 'Emotional Bloodbath' that made Lucy want to cry in the best possible way. Even if Lucy could feel the music pumping in her veins like fire every time they played. None of that mattered. Five schoolgirls from Greenwich who'd only been playing together since January were not going to trump bands who'd been playing the club circuit for years. Black Tuesday even had an album out on an indie label. Crush would never beat them. Lucy just hoped the others wouldn't want to quit once they'd lost *Project Next.*

Crush couldn't win anyway, because if they did, Lucy would have to tell her parents that she'd been lying to them for months and that she was disappearing to California for the summer.

How they'd actually managed to get this far without her mum and dad catching on, Lucy had no idea. She had never got away with anything in her entire life, but somehow she'd managed to get away with this. Her mum had even congratulated her on "being so devoted to her daily study sessions", which were, of course, Lucy's crap excuse for getting out of the house. The time they thought she spent at the library was really spent practising at Harper's.

Lucy really had meant to tell her parents the truth, particularly after Crush became semi-finalists. She'd been terrified they'd find out on their own; *Project Next* was everywhere, after all. But still Lucy had put it off, and somehow her parents had managed not to notice that their middle child was on TV. Of course, her mum and dad had never been much for telly. They didn't read entertainment magazines and Dad insisted that the only programmes worth watching were BBC nature documentaries.

It was after the Miracle of the Answerphone that Lucy had given up on trying to come clean altogether. A few weeks prior to the *Project Next* UK semi-final, Dad's weird cousin from Wales had noticed Lucy's name in an article about the show and called to congratulate them.

Fortunately, he'd called while Mum and Dad were out and Lucy was babysitting her little sister Emily. Unfortunately, Lucy had been helping Emily hunt for her guinea pig, Pippa, who had chosen that moment to go AWOL, so she'd let the call go to answerphone.

Lucy had debated what to do with the message for a long time. Just when she'd decided that actually erasing her parents' messages was a step further than she was willing to go, Emily had raced by in hot pursuit of Pippa and sent the answerphone flying. It had been thoroughly smashed, and Lucy's secret had been safe once more.

That was when Lucy had decided that it was fate. The universe obviously wanted her to be on *Project Next.*

Who was she to argue? Besides, all of this would be over soon. It wasn't as though Crush was going to win.

The flashing red light above the stage, which signalled that live recording was about to resume, brought Lucy back to the present.

"We're back in five... four... three... two... and—" The producer pointed at Liam Michaels, the international host of *Project Next* and mouthed, *One.*

"We're back, gang!" Liam said. "It's been an quite an evening, hasn't it? So many brilliant performances! So many special moments. Our semi-finalist bands have played their hearts out for a chance at a place in the final. They're packed and ready to fly to Los Angeles for the summer, but sadly we can only take two of these fantastic bands with us to the land of movie stars and sunshine. I don't know about all of you, but I'm just dying to find out who's coming along!"

The audience hooted their agreement.

Lucy was so intently focused on Liam that she nearly jumped out of her skin when Harper reached out and grabbed her hand, squeezing it tight. The two girls grinned at each other. Lucy could feel Harper's BFF charm pressed against her palm. Harper had insisted they wear them tonight, even though it'd taken Lucy a solid hour to find her half of the set. Harper thought the charms would be good luck. Lucy had teased her friend for insisting that they wear the silly little puzzle-piece hearts on their cheap silver chains, but she had to admit, if only to herself, that she'd been pleased Harper wanted to wear them again.

"This is it!" Harper whispered, grinning at Lucy.

Poor Harper, thought Lucy. She'd be so disappointed when their name wasn't called.

"Ready... steady..." Liam called, shooting his made-for-television-grin first at the audience, then at the contestants. "And..."

He made a flourish of presenting a stiff red envelope to the crowd. He started to tear it open but then, just to wind everyone up a bit further, he stopped.

"Now, just to remind you, our Top Ten UK bands came tonight with their bags packed. Our two finalist bands will be whisked straight from our studios to Heathrow and put on a jet headed to Los Angeles, California to join our two American finalist bands. They'll live there, each in their own fantastic *Project Next* mansion, while they record an album with Catch-22's top producers and hone their performing skills with management teams handpicked by Sir Peter Hanswell himself – and you'll get to watch them every step of the way on our *Project Next* specials and online. Then, in August, they'll face off with the American finalists in a UK versus US fight to the finish in our big finale show – live from fabulous Las Vegas! You won't want to miss a single minute."

The crowd roared.

"Are we ready?" Liam asked the crowd.

They cheered harder.

"What about you, top four?" he said, turning back to the bands. "Are you ready?"

No, thought Lucy. *I'm not ready for it to be over. I'm not ready at all.*

"Well, ready or not, here we go!" Liam looked down at the slip of paper again, then up at the camera that had swooped down from the ceiling to focus on his face. "The *Project Next* UK finalists are... Dead Kitten Mambo and... Crush!"

Harper grabbed Lucy's hands and whirled her around in a circle. "Oh my God, Lucy! We're going to LA!"

Oh my God, Lucy thought, *Mum and Dad are going to murder me.*

Lucy was still shell-shocked when the girls were finally led back to their dressing room.

"We actually did it!" Toni crowed. "I never thought we'd pull it off. You're a bloody miracle worker, you cow," she said, throwing her arms around Harper.

Harper laughed and hugged Toni back. "We couldn't have done it without you, you silly tart."

Lucy marvelled at the strange sort of friends that Harper and Toni had actually become after about a month of constantly bitching to Lucy and Robyn behind each other's backs. Toni convincing her grandfather to help them make a professional demo had done wonders to help Harper decide she wasn't so horrible after all.

"Have you spoken to your parents yet?" Robyn asked Lucy, sounding nearly as worried as Lucy felt.

"No," Lucy replied. The very thought of that conversation made it hard to breathe. "I was going to tell them, but then... I knew they wouldn't let me do the live show. And I figured we wouldn't win so..."

"That's what you get for not believing in us!" Harper said, throwing an arm over Lucy's shoulders. "Don't worry so much, Luce. You're seventeen, there's nothing your folks can do to stop you. They'll flip, sure, but they'll get over it. And even if they don't, what can they do about it really?"

Disown me for life, Lucy thought miserably.

"Hello, Crush!" A rich voice spoke from the doorway of the dressing room. "I'm thrilled that you did such a brilliant job tonight. I'll confess, I've been a fan since callbacks!"

A tall, whip-thin man with thick blonde hair and a craggy smile stepped into their dressing room. Lucy thought she might faint. Sir Peter Hanswell – *the* Sir Peter Hanswell, rock star turned music producer turned international media mogul – had just confessed to being a Crush fan.

"Sir Peter," Harper said smoothly. "So good to see you."

"You as well, Harper," Sir Peter said, leaning in to kiss her cheek. "I always knew you'd be big news some day. If only some of your ambition had worn off on Rafe." He shook his head. "Hopefully having you in town will inspire him – he's in LA now, you know, at USC."

Rafe? Lucy gaped at Harper. There couldn't possibly

be two boys named Rafe that Harper knew well enough to have 'worn off on'. Sir Peter had to be speaking of Rafe Jackson. The same Rafe Jackson who'd dared Harper to drink three shots of peach schnapps and drive the Gosling's Volvo around the block at Lucy's fifteenth birthday party, then run off after Harper had wrecked both the car *and* Lucy's leg. The very same Rafe Jackson who'd ditched Harper because he was leaving for university. Apparently the University of Southern California, to be exact. In LA.

Oh, bugger.

Harper had told her once, years ago, that Rafe's dad was someone famous, and that Rafe went by his mother's name since his parents had split when he was four and his father had moved on to his second – or was it his third? – family.

So Rafe's father was Sir Peter Hanswell. Now it all made sense. Harper wasn't in this for the music; she was in this for Rafe bloody Jackson.

"Oh you're so sweet!" Harper simpered up at Sir Peter while Lucy stared, agog at the scheme that was unfolding before her eyes. "We're just so lucky to have got this far."

"Rubbish," Sir Peter declared, turning to share his broad smile with all of them. "If I know anything, I know the next big thing when I see it. We're just pleased Catch-22 and *Project Next* found Crush in time to be able to take some of the credit. Now, you girls don't have to be at the airport until six a.m. *Project Next* will take care of all your luggage – I suggest you go out and celebrate!"

And with that he was gone.

"He's right, we should hit a bar. There's no point in trying to sleep or anything," said Harper.

"I dunno," Iza said doubtfully. "I'm not sure how I'm going to convince my parents I need to need to stay in town for a plane they know doesn't leave until the morning... They're nervous enough about me going."

"We'll tell them we're having a sleepover before the flight," Toni said. "I bet my grandmother would even call and ask if you can stay. Come on, she's waiting for us out the front with Granddad – we'll get you sorted."

"I've got to deal with my parents," Lucy sighed. "You probably shouldn't wait for me. I may have to go AWOL just to make it to the plane."

"I'll go with you," Harper said. "I forgot my favourite white wedges anyway. If you're not out in an hour, I'll come in after you."

Good. Lucy needed to talk to Harper alone.

"Why don't we meet at Bella in three hours?" Robyn suggested. "I need to say a proper goodbye to the parentals, but I'll be there after."

They split up at the backstage door and Lucy and Harper flopped into the back of the black car Catch-22 had provided for them as contestants. The wide passenger door snapped closed and the girls sat in silence for a long moment.

"This is all about Rafe, isn't it?" Lucy blurted. "The whole bloody band and everything. It's always been about

Rafe Jackson. It's some sort of elaborate scheme to get him back."

"What?" Harper said, as though she were utterly flabbergasted. But Lucy knew she wasn't. "How could you say such a thing? What kind of pathetic moron would go halfway across the world for—"

"The kind who'd write a song called 'I'll Cross the World', then use it to win a reality competition that just happens to be produced by her arsehole ex's dad and just happens to be taking us to the same city where the tosser is going to uni," Lucy said quietly.

Harper winced. Lucy had clearly struck a nerve.

"Look, Luce," Harper said. "I know you have good reasons not to trust me when it comes to Rafe, and I deserve that. But I'm not doing this because of Rafe Jackson. I actually started this whole thing – Crush, *Project Next*, everything – because of you."

"What?" Lucy said, the bottom dropping out of her temper. "Me?"

"Yeah... I didn't mean to tell you any of this. It makes me sound totally pathetic, but... whatever. I'd rather look pathetic than have you think I'm using you to get to Rafe. The truth is, I decided to try out for *Project Next* because I thought it might be a good way to be friends with you again. I missed you."

Harper actually sounded sincere.

"I mean, I'm not going to say that forcing Rafe to stand on the sidelines and watch us win this thing and get rich and famous wasn't part of the appeal, but that's just gravy." She smiled hopefully at Lucy.

Lucy studied Harper. She didn't want a thing to do with this if it was just a scheme to get Rafe Jackson back. But if it wasn't... Lucy wanted to believe that Harper was telling the truth. She wanted to go to LA. She wanted to keep playing with Crush. She wanted her best friend back. But when it came to Rafe Jackson... could Harper really be trusted?

"Home, girls," called the driver. "Congratulations, by the way. *Project Next* finalists! Imagine!"

"Thanks." Lucy opened the door. "Wait for us, will you? Harper at least will be going back soon."

She climbed out of the car, Harper on her heels.

"You're not going to let Rafe Jackson stop you from following your destiny, are you?" Harper said. "Because this is your destiny, Lucy. This is what you're meant to do. More than any of the rest of us, you belong up there on stage, on the drums. I can see it, and I hope you can see it too."

When Lucy didn't respond, Harper shrugged. "Go talk to your parents. I'm going to go find my wedges and freshen up. Come over when you're done. If you're coming."

Lucy turned to face her house. Mum and Dad were going to be so angry. She'd been lying to them for ages and now she was basically running away to LA with a couple of hours' notice. They might never speak to her again.

Was it worth it?

She'd thought it would be. When she was on stage tonight, feeling the music pump through her veins like lightning and starlight and molten lava all mixed together, she'd been positive that she would do anything to do it again. But now she wasn't sure.

She pushed open the front door.

"She's back!" Emily called cheerfully from the top of the stairs, where she'd clearly been lying in wait in her pyjamas. "You're in trou-ble, Lucy."

"What? I am not," Lucy said, crossing into the family room. "You are. You're meant to be asleep, brat."

"Yes, you are," Emily assured her, grinning. "We saw you on *Project Next.* Mum is going to axe murder you."

"LUCILLE ELOISE GOSLING!" Mum shouted from the kitchen. "Get in here this instant!"

Lucy blew out a long breath and then walked into the blazing light of the kitchen and the burning stare of her parents.

"Well?" Mum demanded. "What do you have to say for yourself, young lady?"

"I'm sorry!" Lucy blurted. "I meant to tell you, I did. Every day for weeks. I honestly didn't think we'd get this far, so I didn't think there'd be any harm done. It was only meant to be for fun. But did you see us? We were drop-dead brilliant and we deserved to win and I just have to go to LA and see if we can go all the way."

Neither of her parents spoke, so Lucy pressed on.

"Please, please, please may I go? You're always telling me to set goals and apply myself to them and I have done! And it's just the summer. We'd be back in time for the autumn term, and I'll be totally focused on my A levels then. Please?"

Mum and Dad looked at each other in that silent, secret parent-speak they had for a long time. Then Mum stood and handed Lucy a folded sheet of paper. "Read that out to us, Lucy."

Lucy didn't have to unfold the paper. It had to be her mocks results, and going by the look on Mum's face, they were worse than Lucy had expected. Crush were doomed.

"Did you study at all this year?" Mum asked very, very quietly.

"I did! I—"

"I wish I thought you weren't lying to me again, Lucy," Mum said, her voice dripping with disappointment, "but I think you might be. I think you've been hanging around that American girl instead of studying and that's why your predictions are so wretched. I think you didn't study one bit."

Outraged tears burned Lucy's eyes. "I did study! I stayed up all night revising to make up for the time I took to practise with *Crush*. If my predictions are rubbish, it's because I'm not that clever!"

"That's not true, Lucy," Dad put in, but Lucy was too furious to let him finish.

"It so is true – I did so badly you think I didn't study

at all when I really did. I did! I just couldn't give up the opportunity to be part of *Crush* on the chance that a few more hours revising would get me better grades. You don't understand."

"No, I really don't," Mum snapped. "Why don't you explain it to me?"

Lucy shook her head. Mum had no clue what playing real music was like, otherwise she'd know there weren't any words for it. In fact, that was the whole point of music, wasn't it? To say things that couldn't be said with words alone. There was simply no way Lucy'd be able to say the right things to make them understand. And even if she could, Mum and Dad were making it clear that the whole thing would be impossible. Sitting there, arms crossed, matching dubious expressions on their faces; they'd obviously already decided she couldn't convince them to let her go.

Lucy crossed her arms too and glared right back at her parents. If they weren't seriously going to listen, then why should she bother trying?

Finally, Mum shook her head. "You've been messing about all term rather than studying properly and you can't even say why. If you're going to wreck your life over something, you should at least know why you're doing it. But you don't, do you?"

Lucy had never seen Mum this angry. Not even when Lucy had landed in hospital after her disastrous fifteenth birthday party.

"I don't understand why you don't take your education seriously, Lucy," Mum continued. "It's so important. After Oxford, you can do whatever you want, but you're going to get a decent degree first, like your brother."

"I know you feel like your band and this programme are the most important things in the universe right now, pet," Dad said in a gentler tone, "but someday you'll be glad you have a degree from Oxford. We're not going to let you give up. If you'd got decent enough predictions this term, we might have considered letting you go to LA, but your mother and I really believe you need to stay and have some tutoring over the summer."

"Aside from your grades, Lucy, letting you go to Los Angeles on your own like this requires trust," Mum snapped, still fuming. "You lied to us. For months! And you spent time with *her* after we specifically told you that was not permitted. You could have been killed because of that girl. She got drunk and drove our car into a tree to impress some boy. Did you forget that? Do you really think you can trust her? Because I know you haven't forgotten the three operations on your leg or the weeks you spent in hospital because of her. I don't think we're being unreasonable asking you to stay away from her."

Do you really think you can trust her?

Lucy had thought the very same thing not ten minutes before, but hearing her own doubts coming from her mother's lips was more than she could bear. Mum saying it made it a real doubt somehow, and it couldn't be real. Lucy had to trust Harper. If she didn't, then everything she'd wanted, everything she'd been so pleased to have all term, was a lie.

"That was years ago, Mum," Lucy said, near tears. "Harper's different now. But this isn't about her. This is about me. I want this."

"We're sorry, Lucy," Dad said, "but we're not going to let you follow Harper McKenzie off a cliff. You can't go. That's final."

Harper resisted the urge to look at the clock again. It was bad enough that she was literally watching the front door, waiting for her parents to come home. This was getting pathetic.

She hadn't been all that surprised when neither of her parents had claimed their tickets for the *Project Next* semi-final. They had important, busy jobs. She had learned a long time ago she couldn't expect them to drop everything just to cheer her on. Not that it bothered her. She could cheer herself on just fine. She always had.

But she still wanted them to come home in time to say goodbye.

A key turned in the lock.

"Mom?" she called. "Mom, we're finalists! We're going to LA!"

"Sorry, babe, it's not Mom," her father said as he pushed through the door. "Just me. But that's great! Happy for you." He didn't even look up from his Blackberry as he added, "Congrats. Really."

Harper ignored the sharp bite of hurt feelings. It was just Dad being Dad.

"Where's Mom? When is she getting home?" Mom would want to celebrate, even if Dad wasn't impressed.

"She had to fly to Zurich this afternoon," Dad said. "I thought she was going to call you to wish you luck."

Harper shook her head.

"Oh. Well, I'm sure she's sorry she's going to miss seeing you off," he said. "When do you leave, by the way?"

"We leave in the morning. The finale is August twenty-eighth, so we'll be back before the new school term starts."

"That's good stuff, kiddo. Why don't we—" The Blackberry in his hands buzzed. "Oh, hang on." He clicked on his hands-free. "Bill? Thanks for getting back to me. We need to talk about this dilution clause... Hang on, let me grab my laptop."

He hurried towards his home office. At the end of the hall he turned and called back to her, "Text your mother when you land!"

Then he was gone.

Harper sighed. At least she didn't have to worry about her parents being crazily overprotective like Lucy's were. What if they stopped Lucy from coming to LA? Or worse, what if Lucy decided that she was just being used to get to Rafe again and didn't want to go any more?

Harper would never admit it to anyone, but she didn't think she could do this without Lucy.

A knock at the back door sent a charge of adrenaline up her spine. That was Lucy. It had to be.

"Please be coming, please be coming, please be coming, please be coming," Harper whispered to herself as she crossed the kitchen and flung the door open.

It was Lucy, all right. Harper's heart deflated when she saw the tears running down her best friend's face.

"Oh no," Harper said. "They're not letting you come, are they?"

Lucy shook her head. "No."

That was it. Crush was done for.

But then, to Harper's surprise, her friend straightened up and scrubbed the tears from her eyes.

"They've forbidden me to go, but I don't care," Lucy declared. "I'm going to LA and they can't stop me."

3. I'll Cross the World

Lucy stretched and yawned as the pastel light of morning at thirty thousand feet washed over her. She felt great for about twenty seconds, and then the hot ball of anxiety in her stomach flared to life again.

Lucy had been light-headed with exhaustion, fury and tears when she and Harper arrived at Bella the night before. Toni had taken one look at Lucy's splotchy face and declared that they all needed shots, ASAP.

There had been shots. And champagne. And they'd got into clubs full of cute boys to dance with. And thanks to the dancing, champagne and cosy upper-class sleeping pod she'd been led to on the plane, Lucy had been able to sleep.

She hadn't thought she would. She'd never fought with her parents that way, and she'd certainly never walked out of the house and boarded a plane to another country against their explicit instructions. What if they never forgave her?

"I can hear you worrying from here, Luce," Harper said, from her pod. "Stop! Your parents will get over it, and we'll win *Project Next* and sell a bajillion records so you can buy them a matching set of new Volvos to say you're sorry."

Lucy shook her head. "I know, I know... I just... I wish it didn't have to be this way, that's all."

"I know you do, lady," Robyn said, walking up the aisle from the loo. "But you had to do what was right for you. They'll come round. And in the meantime, we're about to be surrounded by movie stars! Cheer up!"

Lucy thought it would be impossible, but she felt her spirits lifting as they exited the plane into the international terminal at LAX. Even the airport in Los Angeles thrummed with energy, like the sound box of a guitar being tuned, about to burst into song.

"Isn't someone meant to be picking us up?" Toni asked as she scanned the milling crowds.

"I think so," Robyn said, dragging out the thick stack of paper that one of the *Project Next* producers had handed her after the semi-final show. "Right, we're meant to be meeting someone from Catch-22 here in the arrivals hall. I wonder who they'll send."

"Judging by your adorable accents, I believe that would be me," a voice from behind them said.

Lucy turned towards the voice and found a handsome stranger grinning at her. He just *looked* LA, she thought, if LA had been transformed into a cute guy just a few years older than her. He had spiky, sandy-coloured hair, which fitted perfectly with his elegantly rumpled linen shirt, dark jeans and deck shoes that were just worn in enough to believe he'd been in them on an actual boat once or twice. He was brandishing a professionally printed sign that read *Catch-22 welcomes CRUSH.*

A tall, bearded man with a camera stood a couple of metres behind him, capturing the meeting.

"That's us!" Harper stuck out her hand. "I'm Harper McKenzie, lead singer."

"Ash Chester, manager's assistant," Ash said, quite obviously playing to the camera.

Lucy thought she must be imagining it, but his dramatically blue eyes seemed be laser-focused... on her.

"Welcome to the city of angels, Crush," he continued, eyes still lingering on Lucy. "If you'll follow me, I'll escort you ladies to your chariot. Today, your wish is my command."

"I think I'd like to be carried around on a divan with male models to feed me grapes – can you make that happen?" Harper said as she threaded her arm through his, effortlessly ignoring the camera that trailed behind them as they wove through the heaving arrivals hall.

"Naturally," Ash replied.

"What about you?" he asked Lucy, leaning in to help haul her ancient acid-pink suitcase. "Shall I find some grapes to feed you?"

Lucy giggled, trying not to look at the camera as she said, "Nah. I'm pretty good at feeding myself. Kind of mastered it when I was an toddler."

"My, my, how non-rock diva of you." He shook his head in mock dismay. Then he pitched his voice down to a whisper too low for the camera to pick up and added, "Any time you feel like forgetting, let me know."

Then he turned to help the others retrieve their bags, and Lucy wondered if she'd imagined it. Had he really just ignored Harper's attempts to flirt in favour of chatting her up? That was ridiculous. No sane boy would pick Lucy Gosling over Harper McKenzie, particularly not a glamorous Hollywood-type like Ash.

Iza giggled helplessly as Ash staggered theatrically under the weight of her sensible black suitcase. The other girls were texting or chattering brightly on their mobiles.

Talking to their families, Lucy thought.

Suddenly, she wanted to cry all over again.

But she couldn't leave her mobile switched off all summer. She'd have to deal with her family eventually and now was just as good a time as any. Lucy pulled her elderly Nokia from her rucksack and powered it up. The screen whirled and whirled, searching for service amongst the unfamiliar signals.

"C'mon, Lucy!" Robyn shouted.

Lucy looked up to find that the whole group was spilling out of the sliding glass doors of the terminal, leaving Lucy behind.

Lucy sighed and tucked her mobile into the pocket of her jacket. "Coming."

She broke into a trot that ended abruptly as she collided with a rugged, bald man in a baseball cap and sunglasses.

"Bugger," she muttered. "I mean, I'm so sorry."

"Hey, Bruce," Ash said, dodging back to her side. "How's it going?"

"Not too shabby, Chester," the man rumbled. "Not too shabby. Your girl here is in a hurry – must be excited to see you."

"Of course she is," Ash said, pulling Lucy against him.

Lucy stared at the stranger. He looked so familiar… Bruce… Nah. It couldn't be.

"Say hi to your dad for me," the man said as he moved on towards a waiting limo.

"Come on," Ash said, dragging her along towards the sleek black limousine that the other girls were already piling into, leaving the cameraman behind.

"OMG," Harper stage-whispered when Lucy slid into the seat beside her. "Was that who I think it was?"

"I'm not sure… he looked familiar but he couldn't be—"

"Yes, he could be," Ash said. "He's one of my dad's clients. I interned on set while they were shooting *Intrigue* last year too."

"Our first celebrity!" Toni crowed.

Lucy couldn't help but join in the overjoyed shrieking that followed. It was official. They were in Hollywood!

The shrieks settled into lively chatter, but it didn't take long for the unbelievably intense traffic to lull them each into their own separate worlds.

Lucy didn't have any more excuses. It was time to check her phone.

She stared down at the envelope icon that pulsed on the screen. She had a text message. And it was from her dad. With shaking fingers, she clicked the OPEN button.

Pls let us know you've arrived safely.

It wasn't exactly warm and fuzzy, but at least they cared enough to want to know she hadn't died in a fiery plane crash.

She tapped in –

Just landed. Love you. Pls don't be angry.

– and hit SEND.

Lucy stared down at the dim, cracked screen and waited for the buzz that would mean her dad had texted back. And waited. And waited.

How long can this drive possibly be? she wondered. It felt like it'd been hours already.

She clicked the mobile's screen back on and saw that only five minutes had passed. How was that possible? It was as though the longer she stared at the little screen, the longer each minute got. She couldn't just sit there, waiting for her parents to reply. It would drive her mad. She needed to distract herself.

Lucy deliberately tucked the phone into her pocket and looked up at her friends. Toni and Iza were completely zonked out. Robyn was scribbling in her notebook with such ferocity that Lucy didn't want to interrupt. Harper was staring out the window.

"I grew up here, you know?" Harper said quietly. "It's kind of weird to be back."

"I'd forgotten," Lucy said, turning to follow Harper's gaze out of the tinted window as the limousine slipped out of the gnarled traffic and accelerated down an exit onto a palm-tree-lined street. "Does it look the same?"

"Sort of. Like, I remember this street, but I remember it being a lot bigger. And it feels strange to see cars on the right side of the road, which is totally weird since seeing cars on the left back in London still freaks me out sometimes. But now that I'm back here, the right side doesn't look normal any more either!" Harper laughed. "I'm not making any sense, am I?"

"Obviously not," Lucy kidded. "Cars clearly belong on the left. Any sane person knows that."

"Guess I'm insane then," Harper giggled.

"We're here, aren't we?" Lucy said. "I think that's proof enough we're all mad."

The girls fell quiet again as the odd assortment of grubby shops, expensive cars and tropical greenery that crowded the wide street blended into bigger and more expensive buildings with even flashier cars parked in front of them and grander, lusher plants lining the pavements.

Lucy strained to get a better view of the gorgeous wedding dresses, elaborate cakes and fancy beauty salons that called out from understated display windows. Eccentric and beautiful men and women strolled between the nail bars and boutiques wearing everything from full business suits to beach cover-ups that barely hid their bikinis, to faded, ancient sweatshirts and leggings. Strangely, no matter how ragged the outfit, every woman Lucy saw seemed to be toting an oversized – and obviously pricey – designer bag.

"Look, Lucy!" Harper said. "There's The Ivy."

"Oh wow! I can't believe that's it. It looks so much bigger in magazines."

"Look at all the paparazzi," Harper said. "Hey, they'll be papping us soon!"

"Who do you think—" Lucy cut her own question off with a squeal. "Omigod. Seriously? It that really him?"

"Of course it is!" Harper said, smirking at the look of awe on Lucy's face. "We're in Los Angeles. There's an *OK Magazine* moment waiting to happen on every street corner. I'm surprised you recognised him though – he's got so fat lately I wouldn't have known it was him."

"He has not got fat!" Lucy protested. "And besides, I read he's beefing up for a new role, so you can hardly—"

But then the limo turned up a steep hill onto a wide,

curving street that quite literally took Lucy's breath away. The plain green signs that stood at each intersection they passed seemed so familiar that Lucy could hardly believe they existed outside of a movie screen.

"Sunset Boulevard?" Lucy whispered, unable to squeeze more than that out of her awestruck vocal cords. "We're actually on Sunset Boulevard? We just took a left turn and we're on honest-to-God Sunset Boulevard, just as though that happens every day?"

Harper giggled. "It *does* happen every day when you live in LA, silly. Look! The Beverly Hills Hotel! Isn't it pretty? And there's the House of Blues!"

Lucy let the brilliant billboards and neon lights of the Sunset Strip dazzle her eyes as Harper narrated their trip through the heart of Hollywood. Then they turned left and started uphill again. Less than a block from the crazed mish-mash of neon lights, expensive cars and enormous film posters that was Sunset, the street faded into a twisting two-lane road that wound past huge trees and private roads that Lucy was sure led to fabulous mansions where movie stars hid from the prying eyes of the world.

The driver slowed and turned up one of the narrow side streets. Wonderland Avenue. *Only in Los Angeles*, Lucy thought, *could a place called Wonderland Avenue really exist.* But the name fitted the house at the end of the driveway where the limo pulled to a stop.

It looked like some science-fiction princess's castle more than it did a house. Enormous and angular, the building seemed to have more windows than walls. The glass rippled as it reflected the maze of sparkling water that ran between the slate pavement tiles of the courtyard.

A red SUV stood in the driveway beside a black BMW roadster, and a camera crew was already waiting by the front door.

"Wake up, gang," Harper said, prodding Toni with her foot. "We're here!"

"Is this really ours?" Lucy asked, quickly checking her mobile one last time. Nothing. She fought back the sting of tears. If Mum and Dad didn't want to reply to her, there was nothing she could do about it just now. No use crying over it.

"Yes, it is! This is 8242 Wonderland Avenue. One of the four *Project Next* houses for the finalists," Ash said, speaking slowly and clearly for the camera's benefit, "and your home, for the next two months."

"Isn't it gorgeous?" Robyn asked.

"It's almost enough to make up for it being full of hidden cameras," Iza said.

"I can show you how to avoid the cameras in the house," Ash said quietly with his back to the camera crew. "You'll be able to get up to plenty of trouble with nobody the wiser."

Lucy looked up in awe at the soft yellow and dark green hills that rose around the narrow cul-de-sac.

"Laurel Canyon," Lucy breathed, taking in the sharp, tangy scent of the eucalyptus trees and the vague hint of salt water on the air. "I actually live in Laurel Canyon."

"What's the big deal about Laurel Canyon?" Toni asked, watching the cameramen film Iza and Harper, who had taken off their shoes to splash in the water maze. "I mean other than the fact that it's intensely gorgeous."

"This place is, like, built of rock and roll history. Everyone has lived here. Jim Morrison. Long Road. The Byrds. Joni Mitchell."

"And now, Crush!" Toni crowed. "YEE-HA!" She charged at Iza, twirling her about in joy. "Crush is here, LA! Watch out!"

Lucy couldn't help but grin. They were in bloody Laurel Canyon. In bloody Hollywood. In bloody California. Nothing could make this less than amazing. Not even her parents.

"I'm glad you like it."

A slim man in obviously expensive jeans and a soft black T-shirt that somehow managed to look hand-tailored stepped out of the house. His spiky blonde hair and deliberate stubble framed a smooth face that could easily have belonged to a university student, but the way Ash scurried to the blonde man's side as he crossed the courtyard told Lucy that this was the boss Ash had mentioned. Their new manager.

"I had to fight for it, but no band of mine was going to live in a house with fake Greco-Roman pillars in their front yard." He shot them a grin so full of mischief that, for a moment, he looked even younger. "I'm Jason

Darrow. Your new manager. You got lucky, girls. I'm the best Catch-22 has to offer."

"Even if you do say so yourself," Toni snarked.

"That's right. I do. And so does Sir Peter Hanswell. He personally selected me for Crush and I can already tell this is going to be a good fit." Jason Darrow winked at Toni. "I like smart-asses. And I love great musicians. With a little help from my team, I think you girls can be both. I have no doubt that Crush is going to be just as huge as my first client." He stretched out a dramatic pause before adding, "You all have heard of a little group called Electric, haven't you?"

"I *love* Electric!" Lucy exclaimed. "Sorry! I didn't mean to interrupt. I just... You're Electric's manager? That's brilliant. They're brilliant. I—"

She clamped a hand over her mouth, having just realised how mental she must sound. "I'll just stop talking now, shall I?"

Jason chuckled. "I discovered Electric when I was still an assistant and I helped them become what they are today. I'm glad you're a fan. Crush is going to be just as big as they are, if not bigger. But getting there is going to mean a lot of hard work. Get some rest tonight. You're going to need it."

Lucy had intended to do exactly as Jason said after he left them to settle in. Somehow, though, instead of watching a film in the cinema-sized screening room in the basement and making themselves milkshakes from their fully stocked ice cream and smoothie bar, she'd ended up agreeing to go to a house party that Harper swore had been Ash's suggestion for a 'mellow first night in LA'.

"I dunno," Iza whispered to Lucy in the third row seat of the red SUV, which turned out to be the transport *Project Next* was providing them for the summer. "Mr Darrow said we ought to stay in. Are you sure this isn't going to get us into trouble?"

"Relax, Iz," Harper called from the front passenger seat. "Your mum's five thousand miles away. She doesn't know you're out after curfew."

"It'll be fine," Lucy added quietly. "We won't stay long."

"Yes, we will!" Toni crowed. "You grannies will just have to get used to having a little fun."

Rafe Jackson was bored. Sometimes he thought he'd spent more of his life being bored than he had doing anything else. His earliest memory was of standing on a red carpet, surrounded by sweeping skirts, sequins and black-tuxedoed legs and being stupefied with boredom.

He relaxed into the grungy, oversized sofa in the porch at the back of his fraternity house. Rafe took another hit off the big glass bong and passed it to his girlfriend, Skye Owen, who tried to pass it on to Jack Logan without taking a hit.

"Come'on, sexy," Rafe wheedled. "Let's get high and go watch the stars. It'll be romantic." *And maybe I'll get a little action tonight*, he added silently to himself.

Skye was almost never in the mood if she wasn't at least a little off her face. Getting his girl high to have his way with her probably made him a crap boyfriend, but he'd just spent the last forty-five minutes listening to her chat Jack up about some remake of a 1970s television programme that her dad was producing and she thought Jack's dad should star in. She owed him.

"It's good herb, babe," Rafe added. "You'll love it."

Skye rolled her eyes. "Okay, fine." Then she shot him the wicked look that had made it so easy to fall for her in the first place. A look he hadn't seen in a while. "Shotgun, please."

Maybe this was going to be his night after all.

Rafe drew a lungful of smoke and leaned in to kiss Skye, letting the intoxicating stuff flow between them as her mouth opened under his. No matter how dreadfully boring Skye was when she was in mini Hollywood-mogul mode, she was blisteringly hot when she wanted to be. Rafe usually went for blondes, but there was something about Skye's rich mahogany hair and ivory skin. There was no denying her when she got that particular look in her big violet eyes.

"Oh please. Toni will destroy you at beer pong. I guarantee it."

The sparkling female voice floated in from the living room, penetrating the pleasant fog of smoke and Skye that he'd managed to wrap his brain in.

"In fact," the voice continued, "let's make this interesting. Whoever loses, loses their shirt."

It couldn't be.

"I'm serious. Are you too chicken for a little strip beer pong?"

But it was.

He'd know that voice anywhere. A voice he thought he'd left behind. Far behind.

He pulled away from Skye and struggled out of the ancient sofa's depths.

"Don't move. I'll be right back."

Then he let the familiar cascade of crystal laughter that seemed to fill the house draw him in.

There she was. Looking like a fairy princess who had just wandered into a troll's den. Milky skin and effortless blonde hair making the short black skirt and ribbed vest she wore totally irrelevant. She would have been beautiful dressed in a sack.

It was her. It was Harper McKenzie.

"So you just throw the ping pong ball into the cup?" Lucy asked. This game seemed simple enough, and the cheerful Asian boy who was teaching her the rules was gorgeous.

"You got it, your ladyship," he said with a playful bow. He thought her accent was hilarious. She only hoped he thought it was a bit sexy too.

"Okay, peasant," she declared, playing along. "Let's have a try then!"

It was shaping up to be a perfect first night in Los Angeles, after all. She'd been suspicious when Ash had pulled up to a fraternity house that just happened to be at USC, but the boys there all really did seem to know Ash well, and they were actually great fun. Lucy was having a blast learning beer pong from her adorable new friend and Toni had dragged Robyn off to play late-night volleyball in the backyard. And Lord knew where Iza was, but hopefully she was having a good time. Lucy was glad she'd come.

Then Rafe Jackson walked in.

Lucy dropped her ping pong ball. "Sorry," she said to her instructor. "I'll be back in a sec. I need to speak with my mate for a moment."

Without waiting for a response, she grabbed Harper and dragged her down the hall, past the queue and into the loo before the girls who had been waiting had time to object.

"You swore to me! You swore this had nothing to do with Rafe."

"I wasn't lying!" Harper said.

"Oh sure. We just happen to end up at a party in what is clearly Rafe Jackson's fraternity house on our very first night in Los Angeles and you want me to believe you weren't looking for him? That you haven't been planning this all year? I know you, Harper McKenzie," Lucy snapped.

Harper looked like she was about to argue, but then

she sighed and slumped onto the edge of the bath. "Yeah, I guess you do. I'm sorry, Lucy."

Lucy felt something shrivel up and die inside her. All of the suspicions she'd ignored for so long, that she'd allowed Harper to talk her out of because she was pleased they were friends again – they'd all been right.

Even worse, her mum had been right.

"I cannot believe you've done this to me. Again! My parents aren't speaking to me, Harper. I'm going to lose any chance of getting into Oxford. I needed to study all summer to have any hope for decent A-level results next year. And all for what? For you to have a band so that you could worm your way into *Project Next* and back into Rafe's life?"

A horrible thought darted across Lucy's mind. "Did you fix this with Rafe's dad? Did you pay the judges off? Is that how we got here?"

"Lucy, no!" Harper actually looked offended. "We got here because we're amazing. How can you not see that? I might have had the idea because I wanted Rafe back, but Crush has become something way bigger than I ever *dreamed.* We're brilliant, Luce. The band is amazing. And so is having you back." She drew in a shuddering breath. "And maybe, just maybe, I can find a way to get Rafe back as well."

She looked up at Lucy with pleading eyes that brimmed with tears. "I love him, Luce. I can't stop. Believe me, I've tried. That's where our songs came from, you know.

I couldn't stop thinking about him so my therapist suggested I try writing poetry about it to get him out of my system. But it didn't work. I still love him. I can't help it."

Lucy shook her head. "You should have told me. You shouldn't have played it like you really wanted to be friends again."

"But I do!" Harper exclaimed. "I didn't realise how much until we started hanging out this year. I'm sorry I didn't tell you about Rafe. I just... I knew you'd react this way and I didn't want Rafe to come between us. I know I don't deserve it but... I missed us being friends too much, Lucy. I couldn't pass up the chance."

The ghost of Dad's words echoed in Lucy's brain. *I'm not going to let you follow Harper McKenzie off a cliff.*

Was he right? Had she followed Harper off a cliff for the second time in her life? If so, she was already mid-air, legs pinwheeling over the vast canyon of disaster she'd only just noticed was below her.

She had two choices. She could keep running, hoping she'd sprout wings and soar, or she could crash to the rocks below, call her parents and stagger home.

It wasn't much of a dilemma.

"You're right. You don't deserve it," Lucy said, finally. "But I deserve to have my best friend back. And Crush deserve the chance to win this thing. I just hope you remember that we're way more important than some bloke who's done nothing but let you down."

Harper threw her arms around Lucy in a sudden

bear hug. "You're the best, Luce. Thanks for understanding." Then she yanked the door open and hurried back up the hallway.

Lucy watched her go and hoped, with everything she had, that this wasn't a huge mistake.

Iza was lost. Well, as lost as you could be inside a packed fraternity house. She'd got separated from the others whilst looking for the loo and by the time she'd retraced her steps to where she'd left them, they were gone.

She'd searched the entire ground floor of the house and found no one who looked familiar. She'd been on the brink of panic when someone had suggested that she check the rec room in the basement.

That's where she'd found the piano.

She hadn't meant to play. It just happened. It was always that way. Pianos were like magnets, drawing her fingers to the keys like the needle on a compass finding north.

She found herself slipping into Gershwin, her absolute favourite. She let the notes uncoil the tension in her shoulders and wash away the unwieldy blocks of anxiety that were crammed into her brain. When she could play like this, with no agenda, no audience, no need to do anything but enjoy the notes, she felt invincible.

As Iza rolled out the final phrase, she heard clapping behind her. She whirled to find a tall, broad-shouldered boy with closely cut blonde hair standing in the doorway.

"Oh, sorry, I..." Iza jumped from the piano bench as though it were suddenly on fire. "I didn't mean..."

"Don't apologise," said the boy. 'Short Story', right? Gershwin? The violin part is just amazing. It's my favourite thing to play in the whole world."

"You play the violin?" Iza blurted, surprised. He looked more like an athlete than a classical musician.

"I know, I know," the boy said with a grin. "A frat boy who likes classical music. We're a rare breed. But I come by it honestly – my dad's a conductor, so I've spent most of my life surrounded by the stuff."

He stuck out his hand. "Luke Thomson."

Iza just stared at him. He was chatting her up. Voluntarily. Which meant she should say something. She needed to say something. Anything. Now. She knew how to talk. Didn't she?

Come on, Iza. It's your very own name. Just two words. You can do it.

"Izabella Mazurczak," she managed.

See, that wasn't so hard.

Feeling bolder now that words had successfully made their way out of her larynx, she added, "But my friends call me Iza," as she reached out to shake his calloused, long-fingered hand.

He smiled. "Does that mean I get to call you Iza?"

"Um, sure." She hoped she wasn't blushing.

"So, Iza," he said, collapsing into one of the garden chairs that were the room's only other furniture and gesturing for her to join him. "How did you end up in my rec room, playing one of my favourite pieces, during a house party?"

"I, um, I came with some friends," she said, perching in another of the rickety chairs. "I was looking for them, but then I stumbled on this and... I didn't mean to play that long, actually. I just can't seem to help myself."

She winced. Now she sounded like some deranged piano addict. If there was such a thing as a deranged piano addict, which there obviously wasn't. But Luke was nodding, as though he actually understood what she meant.

"I'm the same way with the violin," he said. "I missed an exam once because I found some sheet music for a Chopin nocturne I hadn't played in a while when I was packing up for class. I decided to take a couple minutes to play and, like, relax before the test and stuff. Two hours later I realised I was still playing and I'd missed it."

"It's mesmerising, isn't it?" Iza said. "Almost like time stops."

"Exactly." Luke nodded vigorously. "It's like the music puts me under a spell or something. I can't believe... How come I've never seen you at one of these parties before?" He sparked a mischievous grin. "Please tell me you're not here visiting one of my frat brothers."

She giggled. She'd never been flirted with before, but this was a lot like she'd always imagined it'd be. Better, actually. "No, my friends and I were invited by a guy who used to live here... I think he graduated two years ago. Ash Chester? He's our manager's assistant. We started a band this year and tried out for *Project Next* – you know, the reality show?"

He nodded. "And you won the UK round? I mean, you must have if you're here. You don't sound like you're from LA. Not that that's a bad thing or anything – I like your accent. A lot. I mean... Ack! Shut up, Luke!" He smacked himself in the forehead. "Sorry. I babble around pretty girls sometimes."

He thought she was pretty? This time Iza could definitely feel herself blushing.

"Um, yeah, we won. Or at least, we're one of the UK finalists. We're here all summer for the show." She couldn't seem to restrain the stupid grin on her face. "I'm completely nerve-wracked, of course, but I am excited as well. I've never been to America before. I hope we'll get a chance to sightsee, though I've no idea how much time we'll have really, what with performing and recording and what not."

"What do you want to see most?" he asked.

"That's easy," she said. "The Walt Disney Concert Hall. They say it's got the best acoustics in the world. I would die to play there, but I'm sure they won't have a band like Crush in, so I'll have to settle for one of the guided tours."

"Actually," Luke said, almost shyly, "I play with the LA Philharmonic sometimes. I'm way too young for them normally, but I was filling in last summer while Dad was guest-conducting and they invited me back full-time this year."

"You must be good," Iza said, impressed.

He shrugged. "I guess. I just love to play. Anyway, I've got rehearsals for the new season all month at the Hall... If you ever wanted a tour, I could... I mean I'd be happy to—"

Then Toni's head popped through the door.

"There you are!" she said. "Come on, we're drawing up beer pong teams. We need you."

Iza jumped up, shyness slipping over her like a suffocating cloud. She really wanted to say, "Sorry, I'm busy, Toni," but what came out was, "Okay, coming, Toni."

Iza half ran for the door. She'd totally blown it, the first time a boy had ever asked her out on a real date and she'd behaved as though she wasn't even interested. Like she was trying to get away when she wanted nothing more than to stay there and talk to him for hours. Iza just wasn't cut out to deal with boys.

Just outside the door she stopped. In the last six months she'd joined a rock band, been on the telly and travelled five thousand miles to a terrifying city on the other side of the world, all on her own. She wasn't cut out for any of that either. But she'd done it.

Before she could talk herself out of it, Iza whirled back into the room where Luke was slumped in the garden chair looking depressed.

"Give me your mobile," she demanded.

"What?"

"Your phone," she tried again. "Give it here."

He laughed a little as he fished an iPhone from his pocket and handed it over. With shaking hands she dialled her own mobile number and hit CALL.

As her mobile began to ring, she tossed his iPhone back to him.

"That's my number, so you can text and tell me when you're taking me on my tour," she called over her shoulder as she dashed back towards the door.

Skye Owen couldn't decide exactly how she was going to murder Harper McKenzie, but it had to be done. Behead her with one of the alien battleaxes that Dad had let her keep after she'd been his assistant last summer on *Mars Must Die 3*, maybe? Or push her off the top of the US Bank Tower? Maybe Skye could steal a bucket of acid from the chemistry lab and replace Harper's shampoo with it, make all of her hair fall out and her face melt. That would be nice. Maybe once Harper was all oozy, Rafe would take his eyes off of her for three seconds.

She could still throw a fit and force Rafe to take her home, she guessed. She'd been building up to exactly that when Harper had mentioned that her stupid band was a *Project Next* finalist. Sir Peter's favourite *Project Next* finalist, no less. Which now meant that, as much as Skye wished Harper would come down with swine flu, she'd *have* to play nice.

No wonder Sir Peter had insisted that Skye and Rafe intern on *Project Next* this summer. He'd known that Rafe's friends from high school were likely to be on the show.

Skye wished she'd vetoed the idea, but at the time it had been a godsend. Hell, it still was. Anything was better than interning at her mother's office at the studio again. The last thing Skye wanted was another summer of people whispering and tiptoeing around her because she was the daughter of the President of Feature Film Production and calling her "the Dragon Lady's Mini-me" when they thought she couldn't hear them. Of course, hanging out with Rafe's dumb-blonde ex-girlfriend all summer might not be much better.

"I should have known Dad was up to something," Rafe was telling Harper. "He told me Crush were his favourite, and that he thought they'd be mine too. Arsehole. I'm sure he's planning to surprise me with you at some point. I'm glad you found me first."

He meant it too, judging by the stupid grin on his face. Skye sighed on the inside, though she kept her smile planted firmly in place. He was such an idiot, sometimes. Okay, most of the time.

If Skye was going to be stuck with Harper McKenzie in her life, she figured she'd better take control of this situation – and fast. "I have a great idea!" She beamed, suddenly glad she'd gone through her acting classes phase two summers ago. "Why don't you all come to Malibu tomorrow? My mother's got the most amazing house up there and she never goes because she's always working. So it's all mine. We'll barbecue, swim... What do you say?"

"I dunno," said the tiny girl with the enormous shock of dark curls. Was her name Lucy? Skye thought it was. She looked even less happy to see Harper and Rafe grinning at each other like idiots than Skye was. "We're in the studio tomorrow and—"

"We've got a session with our stylist after that. We couldn't possibly make it all the way out to Malibu tomorrow," Harper cut in.

The curly haired girl looked relieved, but then Harper continued, "How about this weekend? I'm dying to see Malibu again."

"Great!" Skye lied, through her teeth. "I can't wait."

Three hours later, Lucy curled into the pile of snowy white pillows that festooned her bed in Crush House. She knew there was some manner of duvet or quilt on the immense, squashy thing, but she was too tired and fogged with drink to be sure she knew which end was the proper one to put her head on, much less how to undo the elaborate arrangement of pillows, blankets and sheets enough to get under the covers. But there was a soft blanket artfully draped over the spotted navy-blue and hot-pink chair that stood at the foot of the bed. Lucy lunged for it and managed to hook a finger through one of its cabled edges, dragging it back over her incredibly inebriated body.

She would regret not taking off her make-up when she woke up in... She looked at the glowing face of the sleek alarm clock that rested on the bedside table. Three hours. She had to wake up in three hours.

Lucy rolled onto her back and stared up at the blank whiteness of her ceiling. She'd had no idea what she was signing herself up for. Not really. How could she, with Harper keeping that one, very important Rafe-Jackson-shaped detail tucked away and out of sight? Would Lucy have still come to Los Angeles if she had known?

She sat up and looked out of the floor-to-ceiling glass panels that lined her room. The lights of LA sparkled quietly below her, but the distance and the glass couldn't disguise the pulsing beat of the place. She felt so alive here. How could she even consider the prospect of giving it all up? In her whole life, nothing had felt so right. Ever. So what if Harper was here for Rafe? She was here to be a drummer. It didn't matter why Harper McKenzie had convinced Lucy to come. Lucy was exactly where she belonged.

And with that, she collapsed into the nest of pillows and closed her eyes.

4. IF I WAS PRETTY, WOULD YOU LOVE ME?

Lucy's head felt like it was full of broken glass. She'd never been so hungover. Ever.

And she wasn't the only one. Robyn and Harper were moving as though they might shatter at any second and Toni was positively green. Even Iza groaned every time she moved her head too fast. They were in a bad way and they were also late for their first recording session.

The recording studio was gorgeous. A big white room lit by wide, high windows that filled the place with brilliant natural light. A sturdy man with short curly hair, that was more salt than pepper, and dark chocolate skin was bent over the mixing board in the booth, a chunky set of headphones clamped over his ears.

Lucy stared through the glass. Was that really... No, they couldn't be that lucky.

"Hey, Ash," she asked quietly as he pushed past her towards the booth. "That's not Alexander Holister, is it?"

"YES, IT IS," boomed a deep voice over the PA system. "And you are LATE!"

Ash turned to walk backwards towards the booth, mouthing, *Be careful, he can read lips*, before he slipped inside.

Lucy ducked across the room to Harper, who was trying to comb out her hair and wincing every time the brush touched her skull.

"Alexander Holister is producing our album!" Lucy breathed, hangover forgotten.

"So?" Harper pressed a hand to her head. "Not so loud, Luce, I'm dying."

"He's only the most important producer, like, ever. He's got more Grammys than anyone. He's a legend. He—"

"I'm glad at least one of you knows what you're getting into."

Lucy spun to see Alexander Holister standing in the doorway of the booth.

"But apparently my reputation isn't enough to inspire you to be on time."

"We are s-so sorry, sir," Lucy stammered. "We're, um, having trouble with jet lag this morning. It won't happen again."

He studied them coldly, clearly not buying the jet lag excuse.

"Young ladies, you have been offered an opportunity that thousands of your peers would kill and die for. But for some reason, you choose to show up for it late and clearly not ready to work. You are wasting my precious time and your talent, though looking at you this morning, I have my doubts if you have that much to waste."

He looked from Harper, who was leaning weakly against the stool behind her mike, to Toni, who looked as though the bass guitar she was half-heartedly tuning was too heavy for her bowed shoulders. "And, apparently, you are also wasting your brain cells. Lord, save me from little girls who think they're rock and roll."

He's going to reject us, Lucy thought. *The very best rock producer on the planet is going to refuse to produce our album all because we had to go to that stupid party so that Harper could find Rafe.*

He shook his head and continued. "Pete swears you girls have real potential, so you have one hour. Get it together. And never show up in my studio anything less than ready to work your butts off again. Do you get me?"

"Yes, sir," Robyn said.

"Sorry, Mr Holister," Toni added. Then a queasy look came over her face and she fled.

Alexander sighed and turned back into the booth.

"McDonald's," Robyn pronounced. "That's what we need. There's one just up the street. Who's in?"

"Me," Iza said. "I need a cola to settle my stomach."

"Ditto," Harper sighed. "And a large helping of grease."

"I'll stay here, thanks," Lucy said.

After the others cleared off, Lucy settled behind the drums and ran a few rolls, just tapping them out to give her head the chance to steady itself on her shoulders. She liked the feel of the kit – not really a surprise since it was better than anything she'd ever played on.

"Not bad."

Lucy jumped half out of her skin. She'd been so focused she hadn't noticed that Alexander Holister was standing right in front of her.

"Loosen it up some and you might be able to get more speed on the hi-hat at the end of the chorus there," he said. "That was 'I'll Cross the World', right?"

"How could you tell from the booth? I wasn't even really playing," Lucy blurted. Then she remembered who she was talking to. "Sorry, that was a rude question. I didn't mean to sound like I didn't believe—" She cut herself off mid-babble when she realised he was struggling not to laugh. "I mean, yes, that was 'I'll Cross the World'."

"Questions are always allowed, young lady," he said. "It's the not asking that's rude." He stared contemplatively at the drum kit and then added, "You might try starting the run on the snare, then rolling it up to the toms."

"Yes, I will. Thank you," said Lucy.

"You don't want to try it now?" She thought she saw a flash of laughter in his black-brown eyes. "Or are you so good that you can rework a beat in your head?"

"No, I mean... Of course... I..." *Shut up, Lucy*, she thought. *Just play the drums.*

She ran the sequence as he suggested and, of course, it was better.

"I like it," she said after the second pass. "Of course. But..."

"Spit it out, kid."

"But what if I double up on the thirteen at the end?"

He looked at her, head cocked, considering. "Maybe. Try it."

She did the run again. It felt amazing – right in a way it hadn't been before.

"Good instincts," he said, nodding. Then he turned and walked back towards the booth.

She sighed. She had a million more questions to ask, but she couldn't expect him to hang around chatting to her all day. He definitely had better things to do. But still, he had said not asking questions was rude. She didn't want to be rude.

"Mr Holister? There's this moment on 'Emotional Bloodbath' that desperately needs a different cross-beat and I haven't been able to sort out what to do, I..."

She trailed off as the door to the booth closed behind him. Of course. He didn't want to talk beats with a 'little girl who thought she was rock and roll'.

Maybe she'd just go meet Robyn and Iza at McDonald's.

Then warm blues guitar poured out of the speakers around her. A sleek drumbeat ran under the melody, twisting and snaking through the notes like a living thing. It was beautiful.

A sharp rapping sound broke through the music. It was Mr Holister, knocking on the glass between the booth and the studio. He waved, clearly indicating she should join him. She scrambled out from behind the kit and hurried to the door before he could change his mind.

When she stepped inside, he was already sliding another record out of its sleeve.

"You know the Dirty Dozen Brass Band, right? Think about the beats on 'Voodoo'. 'Emotional Bloodbath' needs something like that... with a little bit of an extra uptick."

"I, um... Dirty Dozen Brass Band?" Lucy asked.

"You don't know the Dirty Dozen?" Mr Holister looked heartbroken for her, as if she'd just told him she was a starving orphan.

"No, I'm sorry, Mr Holister," she said.

"We'll have to do something about that," he snapped, dropping the needle on the record. "And don't call me Mr Holister. My name is Alexander."

"Okay... Alexander," she said. "And I'm Lucy."

"I know. Short for Lucille," he said with a smirk. "I, for one, came prepared today."

Lucy's feet were hardly touching the ground when Crush left the studio, hours later. Whilst the others had been recovering from their hangovers, she'd spent nearly three-quarters of an hour listening to classic vinyl with

Alexander. Then, when the rest of the band had finally been ready, they'd had a session that even he had admitted "wasn't half bad for a first try". Perhaps best of all, as they'd been packing up to go, Alexander had pulled her aside once more.

"You've got homework to do," he'd said. Then he'd piled several books on drum theory and jazz, as well as a fully loaded iPod, into her arms.

"I'll talk to Jason about scheduling some extra sessions with you. There aren't many youngsters who are worth my time, Lucille, but if you're willing do the work, I think you might just be. Don't prove me wrong."

She'd never been so excited about doing homework in her whole life.

Lucy listened to the fascinating mix of classic rock, blues, jazz and tribal drumming Alexander had crammed into the tiny iPod as Ash wove the SUV through traffic. She couldn't even bring herself to switch it off as she and her bandmates dutifully followed Ash into what looked like a grubby mechanic's shop. Well, if the mechanics in question had a taste for hot pink, that was.

The sign above the door spelled out *Garage* in a pink, neon scrawl, which made much more sense after they stepped inside the cavernous space. Instead of cars and oil cans, beauticians' chairs lined the walls and manicure stations were scattered across the concrete floor. The place had been converted into a beauty salon. *Only in LA*, thought Lucy.

"Makeovers!" Harper crowed.

"They'd better not shave my head or anything," Toni said. She pointed at one of the cameramen, who Lucy had nearly forgotten were tailing them. "You got that on record? No head-shaving."

"If I want you to shave your head," a sharp voice called from somewhere behind Lucy, "you will shave it. And you will thank me. Britney did."

A tiny woman strode dramatically into the centre of the room.

"I am Debra Zeeee!" she proclaimed. "And I am your stylist."

She was hardly taller than Lucy's five feet and so thin that Lucy thought she could see the ligaments moving under her shockingly pale skin.

The melodramatic little woman swept around to face them, playing to the camera.

"Alexander Holister may be in charge of your music, but I command your image. And believe me, in this business, your look is more important than your sound. I am not just your stylist – I am your fairy godmother. You bring me pumpkins and I give you Bentleys. You bring me rags, I give you ruby slippers. You bring me mice," she waved a hand at Lucy, "and I give you princesses. Now, my ducklings, prepare to become *swans*!"

Lucy had been petrified that Debra Z would actually shave Toni's head, or try to put that awful chemical stuff on her own hair to straighten it or something, but their makeovers actually went quite well. Debra Z came off a bit more like the Wicked Witch of the West than a fairy godmother, but Lucy had to admit that she knew her craft. Lucy hadn't expected to enjoy being dolled up like some kind of music video diva, but her perfectly tousled, carefully highlighted curls and her blunt, dark-green manicure suited her. Lucy still looked like herself, just a vastly prettier, vastly more interesting version of herself. Even the thick blue streak that ran through the very bottom layer of her hair was perfect.

"Rebellious," Debra Z had said, "but without the need to show it off. Like any good drummer."

She'd done just as well with the others. Iza's shining pixie cut perfectly highlighted her big eyes and fantastic cheekbones and Toni's thick fringe gave her just the right touch of sophistication. Harper's blonde had been lightened to a platinum that made her blue eyes even brighter and her perfect skin glow, while Robyn's rich red hair had been razor cut around her face into a long, shaggy bob that looked so perfectly undone that you'd never guess how carefully styled it was.

"Now, my darlings," Debra Z proclaimed. "It's time for a surprise. Ash, please take the girls to my studio. I will meet you there."

"More?" Iza whispered excitedly to Lucy as they filed out of the salon, their camera team trailing behind them. "After all this? What else can there be?"

"Plastic surgery?" Lucy wondered, only half-joking.

Debra Z's studio took up the entire fifteenth floor of a Beverly Hills high rise that looked down on Rodeo Drive. When they arrived, they found rack after rack of brand new clothes lined up and waiting – complete wardrobes for each of them, courtesy of Debra Z and *Project Next*.

The girls dug through their racks as Debra wandered between them, tweaking their outfit choices, or in Lucy's case, completely vetoing each attempt and making her start again... and again and again and again. Debra seemed to think Lucy's hopeless lack of fashion sense was charming, but unfortunately so did Ash and the cameramen. They stayed glued to Lucy and her fashion nightmare until Harper finally rescued her by dragging the camera team off to film the other girls learning to create a proper smoky eye from one of the make-up artists instead.

Lucy studied the skinny jeans, hot-pink vest and oversized men's tuxedo shirt she'd assembled. This outfit just might score her a nod of approval from Debra, she reckoned. She hoped. Then she noticed Robyn standing in front of her own rack, looking as though she was on the verge of tears.

"Robs?" Lucy said, crossing to her. "What's wrong? Don't you like your new gear?"

"No," Robyn said. Then she cleared her throat, fighting back tears. "I mean yes, it's all lovely... apart from the fact that most of it won't fit."

"What? That doesn't make sense at all." Lucy leaned

in to check the labels. Sure enough, most of them were a US size two or four. Robyn was at least a US ten.

"Perhaps it's a mix-up?" Lucy asked hopefully, though a look at the funky blend of hippy and hipster that lined the racks told her it wasn't. These clothes were perfect for Robyn, they were just three sizes too small.

"No, they're for me. This is just her way of telling me I'm a horrid, enormous cow who must lose weight before they can even be bothered to dress me. There are a few things that fit, but not enough for a whole summer. Not if we're going to be playing shows and going to events and all that."

Tears were running down Robyn's face now, turning her splotchy.

Lucy shook her head. "We'll speak to her. They've no right to wind you up like this. You're gorgeous just as you are, Robyn. We'll just tell her to find you the proper sizes."

"We can't do that!" Robyn moaned. "Imagine going on camera and announcing I'm too fat for my new wardrobe. I'll die of shame."

"Is something wrong, Robyn, dear?" Debra Z called across the studio.

She was deliberately making a scene, Lucy realised, her heart in her throat. Robyn was going to be humiliated.

"Is there a problem?" Debra continued loudly, when Robyn didn't reply.

The nearest cameraman swung around at the word problem, zeroing in on Lucy and Robyn.

"Um, sort of," Lucy said, trying to stay between Robyn and the cameras. "We'd really rather talk to you privately, Debra, if you don't mind."

"Of course, sweetie. I was actually just looking for Robyn. There's someone I want her to meet," Debra Z simpered. "Come along up to my office, darling," she said, dragging Robyn forwards into the camera shot with her tiny, steel cable arms. "Lucy, my dear, you stay here with the other girls. We'll be back in a tick."

Lucy tried to follow Debra, but the lead make-up artist, Paulina, turned out to be something of an octopus and manhandled Lucy into a make-up chair before she could escape.

It didn't really matter, Lucy told herself. Robyn would manage. It wasn't as though Lucy would be much help anyway. She wasn't like Harper. She hadn't even had the guts to stand up to Debra for her own sake; why did she think she could help Robyn? Robyn would be just fine on her own, once she was off camera. Wouldn't she?

Robyn dutifully followed Debra Z to her sleek, ultra-modern office. A pale boy about her age with hair so blonde it was nearly white was sprawled on the sleek grey sofa, playing some sort of game on his iPhone.

"Tomas, darling," Debra Z called. "This is the lovely young lady I wanted you to meet."

Tomas's mobile mooed as he finished his game. He took his time closing the program then locking the screen before languidly transferring his attention to Robyn.

His grey eyes were nearly as pale as his skin and hair. Dressed in white linen and soft, flesh-toned leather boat shoes, he was unsettlingly monochromatic.

There was something quite creepy about him, but Robyn couldn't decide if that was due to his eerie appearance or the look in his pale eyes. He was studying her so closely, she could almost feel his gaze, like light fingers running over her skin.

She stuck out her hand. "Robyn Miller. Nice to meet you. Your name is Tomas, right? I..."

Her greeting trailed off as Tomas took her hand and, instead of shaking it, raised it to his lips to kiss. Her stomach did a hard flip. Her brain couldn't decide if it was turned on or terrified. Who was this boy?

In a light Swedish accent that flowed like warm milk he said, "Tomas Angerman. It's awesome to meet you, Robyn."

"Robyn, darling," Debra Z continued, "Tomas here is a friend of my daughter's from Beverly Hills High. He's about your age, actually, but he's simply my favourite person to introduce to clients who need a little help... pharmaceutically speaking. So discreet. And he has the very best diet pills in town. His mother brings them home from business trips in Korea, doesn't she, dear?"

Diet pills? Of course. Robyn had almost forgotten why she was there.

Debra Z must have noticed Robyn's falling face because she threw an arm around her and gave her a squeeze.

"No, no. Don't take it that way, dear. You're gorgeous. I'm simply helping you attain your full potential. Isn't she lovely, Tomas?"

"Beautiful." He almost purred the word. "That hair. That skin. You're quite right, Debra, a little CZ92 and she'll be irresistible."

Debra Z pulled a roll of cash from a desk drawer and began to count out bills. "CZ92 is the most amazing stuff, Robyn. You'll see. Of course they're not available here, only in Asia, which is why we get them from Tomas. You'll figure out how much she needs?"

Tomas nodded, and with a flurry of air kisses, Debra was gone.

"I meant it, you know," the pale boy said, smiling at her.

For a moment, Robyn seriously considered doing a runner. Was she really going to take dodgy diet pills from Asia?

"You're going to be something extraordinary," he continued, scooping up the cash Debra had left behind. Then he pulled a bottle of pills from his coat pocket and held it out to her. "Especially after you're done with these."

Robyn looked at the bottle for a long time. Debra Z thought they were safe, obviously, or she wouldn't suggest them. She didn't want Debra to think she wasn't willing to do what it took to make Crush a success.

"You do want to be extraordinary, don't you?" Tomas asked gently, clearly sensing her hesitation. "You can't be afraid to be your best self, Robyn."

He was right. She'd never been able to lose weight on her own, and she didn't want everyone to think of her as the sad, chubby girl that held the band back. She needed help, and if they were going to win *Project Next*, she needed it now. Before she could think better of it, Robyn reached out and took the bottle.

"How many do I take at a time?"

"One pill, four times daily," he said, reaching out to massage her shoulder. "You'll see, they're perfectly safe and they work. It's just like magic."

It was too good to be true, Robyn was sure, but it was also too good a chance to pass up.

"No time like the present," she said. She shook a pill into her hand and gulped it down.

"See," Tomas said, reaching up to tuck a strand of hair behind her ear. "That wasn't hard at all."

Jason Darrow stepped through the brushed steel doors of the lift in Debra Z's Beverly Hills high rise and jabbed the button marked *Fifteen* in cursive letters. He was reaching out to press the Door Close button when Ash burst into the lobby.

"Wait!" his assistant called. Jason's finger hovered over the button for just a moment before relenting and pressing the Door Open button instead. He couldn't avoid being alone with his assistant forever. He knew Ash would take the opportunity to ask for a promotion. He'd been assuming that he was about to make junior manager very loudly to anyone who would listen, so of course it had got back to Jason. Discretion was high on the list of things Ash still needed to practise before he would be ready to stop answering phones and buying coffee.

"Sorry!" his over-styled assistant gasped, slipping into the lift beside him. He brandished a large paper bag brimming with tubs of frozen yogurt. "I went to get snacks for the girls, but Debra Z said pastries have too many carbs, so I had to run out to Pinkberry instead."

"Great," Jason said, pulling out his iPhone. Maybe if he looked busy, Ash would take the hint and not start a conversation that was only going to end in humiliation.

No such luck.

"I'm glad I caught you, actually," Ash said, too casually. "There's something I've been meaning to ask you about."

Jason sighed, just a little too loudly.

"It's not a big thing," Ash assured him. "I just would love to be more involved with Crush, that's all. Like, I could set some gigs for them and stuff. I mean I've been with you eleven months, and it wouldn't have to be an official promotion or anything. I just feel like I've learned so much—"

"Everything you need to know to nurture a band?" Jason snorted. "In eleven months? Unlikely."

"What?" Ash said, clearly jaw-dropped. "I mean... you... I thought I was doing a good job."

The kid looked both shocked and hurt at the idea that he wasn't ready to build an international hit band after less than a year of answering Jason's phone. Jason sighed. He should have known better than to hire a Hollywood dynasty brat. Not that he could really have said no when Sir Peter asked him to mentor a friend's son.

"Look," Jason said. "Do you know how long I was Sir Peter's assistant before I got promoted?"

"No," Ash said.

"Well, you should," Jason said. "First of all, a good manager does his homework on anyone he deals with. Always. And second of all, I was his assistant for three years. I only got promoted because I discovered Electric in a rest-stop dive bar on the way to Las Vegas. You want to get promoted? You've got to show me why you deserve it. You want to do that by getting more involved in Crush, then great – but that doesn't mean you're not still going to be the guy picking up the Pinkberry order. You read me?"

The doors slid open onto a massive room that looked, at the moment, like a teenage girl's wardrobe on steroids. Clothes, make-up and shoes that looked more like they belonged in an art installation than on someone's feet were everywhere.

"Jason—" Ash began.

"Hey, boys," a bright, feminine voice cut in. "Check it out!"

Jason turned to find Toni walking towards them. Or at least, he thought it was Toni. She was almost unrecognisable as the pretty but overly made-up teenage girl he'd met the day before. A heavy, blunt-cut fringe and just the right hint of make-up had transformed her into an unspeakably gorgeous young woman.

"Not bad, huh?" she said, eyes dancing.

"Toni," Ash said, "Jason and I were just—"

"Bringing Crush some frozen yogurt," Jason said. "Now, I left a bunch of hungover teenage girls here a couple hours ago, and they seem to have been replaced by supermodels. You have any ideas what happened to my band?"

Toni giggled, tossing her long hair over her shoulder into an exaggerated swimsuit model pose. "What can I say? Debra Z does good work."

"I'll say," Jason said, shaking his head. Maybe he'd underestimated Toni. They'd have to make sure the episode producers paid special attention to her. She was going to be a star.

"I still need to talk to you," Ash objected.

"No," Jason said, firmly. He didn't mind a little ambition, but Ash had to know when enough was enough. "You don't. You need to deliver these yogurts before they melt."

He could tell Toni was clocking the barbed exchange. Covering, he turned a bright smile on her. "So, Toni, what do you think of all of this? Do you feel like Cinderella yet?"

She broke into a blinding, unrehearsed grin. "It's brilliant!"

Jesus, she was pretty.

"This isn't even my best outfit," she added with a saucy smirk, daring him to play along.

Shake it off, Jason, he warned himself. *She's only seventeen, even if Debra Z can doll her up to look twenty-five.*

But he didn't seem to be in the mood to listen to his own good advice.

"Hmmm." He shook his head, trying to contain the echo of her infectious smile that was tugging at his lips. "I think you're wrong. You couldn't possibly get prettier."

"That's what you think!" she said, and darted away back into the racks.

"She's gorgeous," Ash said with the same over-emphasised casualness that he'd attempted to ask for his promotion. "Isn't she?"

"I'll say." Jason reached for one of the tubs of Pinkberry that Ash had dumped on a side table.

"Almost as pretty as your wife is," Ash continued.

Jason dipped a spoon into the frozen yogurt and ate, keeping a firm grip on his poker face.

"Why don't you make sure the girls get their yogurt, Ash?" he said coolly. Then he turned to follow Toni towards the cameras. He was clearly going to have to cut his assistant down to size, but this situation was just as much his fault as it was Ash's. What was wrong with him? He was flirting like an idiot teenager, with an idiot teenager, right in front of the person who talked to his wife more than he did some days. He was clearly losing his mind.

Across the studio, Lucy finished applying blusher for the third time and stared at the results in the mirror. She looked more like a little girl playing with her mum's make-up than a pop star.

"Almost there!" Paulina the make-up artist wheezed through her smoker's cough. "But do you see how Izabella has highlighted the cheekbones? You don't quite have the angle right. Can you show her how you did it, Izabella?"

"Huh?" Iza looked up from her mobile, which she'd been staring at for the last ten minutes. "Sorry. What am I showing her?"

"Your blusher. Why don't you just do mine, so I can see how it's done?" Lucy asked. Paulina nodded and fluttered over to Robyn, who was chattering at hyperspeed as she attempted to apply liquid eyeliner. She seemed happy, thought Lucy. Her conversation with Debra must have gone well.

"Sorry," Iza said, taking the big make-up brush from Lucy. "I got distracted."

"I saw." Lucy grinned. "Important text, hmm?"

"Remember that guy from last night? Luke?"

"He texted already?" Lucy said as Iza swirled the brush across Lucy's cheekbones. "That's great!"

"I know! But I don't know what to write back," Iza moaned.

"Ladies of Crush!" They spun to find Jason standing behind them with the camera crew. "I see that Debra Z has worked her usual magic. You all look like superstars."

Toni curtsied, making Jason chuckle and give her knee-high boots, miniskirt and tartan bustier an approving once-over. Toni shot him a twinkling smile back.

Lucy stared in amazement. They couldn't be... No, Jason had to be almost thirty, even if he didn't look it. Toni must just be flirting on autopilot, as she did with every guy.

"I've also listened to your morning session," he continued, "and I had an interesting conversation with your producer."

Robyn groaned noisily. Then she clamped a hand over her mouth and giggled when she realised she'd done it out loud. Lucy shot her a covert glance. It wasn't like Robyn to be so nutty on camera. Had Debra Z given her a drink up there? Or three?

"Exactly, Robyn," Jason said. "We can't have a repeat performance of that. Alexander is a genius and we're lucky to have him, but he's not a patient man. I don't mind the partying – I'll even insist on it as we develop your publicity – but no matter what you've done the night before, you need to show up at the studio ready to work. "Also, remember you're all underage, so no getting caught buying drinks in any clubs and ending up with your mug shots on TMZ," Jason continued. "If you want to go out, make sure you have a legal adult with you – like Ash.

In fact, he'll be going out with you tonight. You've got a table for four booked at The Ivy – and that was hard to get ladies, so enjoy it – and after that, Ash has the password to Basement. There will be photographers at both doors, so look your best."

"Reservations for four?" asked Harper. "If Ash is coming along, wouldn't there be six of us?"

Jason nodded. "There would be, but Lucy isn't going."

Oh no, Lucy thought. Her parents had somehow managed to get her kicked off the show. They were about to walk in and drag her off in a dramatic on-camera confrontation. She just knew it. She'd known all along this was too good to be true.

But then Jason shot her a brilliant grin and said, "Alexander was impressed with you, Lucy. So much so that he has suggested we take you with us to the Long Road benefit tonight at the Nokia. It's Sir Peter's annual fundraiser for throat cancer. It's a really big deal for Sir Peter and we'll be with him in his personal box. You can, of course, pick a friend to accompany you."

Lucy couldn't believe it. She turned to look at the other girls.

Me! Toni mouthed. *Please!*

"Toni? Will you come with us?" Lucy asked.

"Sure, I guess," Toni said, doing a bad job of faking casual.

"Excellent," Jason said.

Was Lucy imagining the fact that he looked pleased

with her choice as well? She had to be. Jason Darrow had better things to do than flirt with some seventeen year old. Didn't he?

"Let's get a move on, ladies. We've got a big night ahead of us."

5. EMOTIONAL BLOODBATH

Harper couldn't believe that it was already Saturday. She had thought the wait to see Rafe again would be unbearable, but the week had flown by.

Alexander might be a relentless tyrant whose favourite word was 'again', but he knew what he was doing. He kept a sharp eye on them all. Harper and Iza couldn't miss a note without him noticing and he'd taught Robyn and Toni the fingering for flamenco-style guitar, which sounded incredible on 'Delicate'. But Lucy was the one who had really transformed since they'd begun working with Alexander. At first Harper had resented the hours that Lucy spent studying technique and practising, both with Alexander and alone at the house. But after a while she had realised that Lucy was happier now than she had ever seen her. Even if Harper wished Lucy was around more to hang out, it was worth it to see her best friend blossom.

And Crush... Crush were outstanding. They'd started out good, but every day with Alexander made them better. That made it easier to get up on the evil side of seven o'clock in the morning to work, despite the late-night whirlwind of parties and clubs and restaurants that often stretched past one or two a.m.

Between rehearsing, clubbing, making sure Crush were 'caught' by all the right paparazzi teams, and their daily sessions with Debra Z, there hadn't been time to even think about Rafe. Harper loved the fact that they had their own personal stylist to critique their outfits for the evening each day and restyle them if necessary. Not that Harper ever needed restyling, of course. She was always Debra's favourite, a fact that she enjoyed almost as much as she enjoyed watching Debra force Toni to wash her face and reapply her make-up every day.

It was mean of Harper to be secretly happy that Debra had made it her mission to embarrass Toni. She knew it was. Toni was her friend now, after all. But Harper couldn't help it if she had a competitive streak. Besides, somebody needed to teach Toni that less was the new more when it came to eye-shadow. It was for her own good.

Lucy was a walking fashion emergency, of course. She always had been. But with Harper's help, even she was starting to improve – and it was paying off in more ways than one. Ash clearly had a huge crush on Lucy. He was gorgeous, obviously, and a lot of fun, even if he wasn't the brightest spark Harper had ever met. But brains were not as much of a requirement in a summer fling as a six-pack was, and Ash had a very nice one of those. With Harper's help, Lucy could wrap Ash around her little finger if she wanted to. It could be fun, Harper thought, making a boy fall at Lucy's feet.

Thank God Lucy seemed to have forgiven her for lying about Rafe. She hadn't exactly said, "I forgive you, Harper," or anything, but at least she was still wearing her BFF charm. The matching charms dangling from each of their wrists made Harper happier than she would ever admit to anyone, especially Lucy.

Harper threw a glance into the rear-view mirror and smiled to see Lucy and Robyn with their noses practically pressed up against the window as Ash powered the SUV up the Pacific Coast Highway. She couldn't blame them for staring. She'd seen Californian sunsets many times before, but the streaks of red, pink and gold that flared across the sky as the sun dipped into the vivid navy blue of the water still took her breath away.

This summer was going to be good for Lucy. Harper had known it would be, even if Lucy's uptight parents didn't think so.

She could still remember the total hatred in Mrs Gosling's eyes when she'd seen Harper for the first time after that stupid car crash. Harper had just wanted to see Lucy, to know she was okay, but instead, Mr Gosling had led her out into the hospital car park and coldly explained that Harper was no longer welcome in their home or anywhere near their children.

Harper had cried for hours that night. Not just because of Lucy; the Gosling house had been her second home – the one place Harper knew she could always find dinner and company when her parents were out of town or at work until all hours. One stupid mistake had ruined it all. The long nights at home, alone in her empty house, had almost been more than finally dating Rafe was worth. Almost.

She wouldn't have to worry about being home alone this summer. That was one of the best parts about life in LA: coming home from exclusive restaurants and awesome clubs and being sure that a late-night swim with the girls was waiting.

The new tradition had started on their second night in LA, when Harper and Robyn and Iza had come back from Basement to find Toni and Lucy splashing around in the heated infinity pool under the dim Los Angeles stars. They'd all jumped in, Robyn still in her clothes, and just chilled out together for almost an hour before heading to bed.

They'd done the same thing the next night, and the next. It made everything that happened in the day better, somehow. Funnier. Easier. Less intimidating. Knowing it would soon be a just a story to share with the girls.

The SUV turned away from the water then, winding its way up a narrow, twisted road into the yellow hills.

Fifteen minutes of steep inclines and hairpin turns later, Ash pulled up to a set of enormous stone gates and rolled his window down to reach for the buzzer.

"Wow," Iza said. "Is this all for the one house?"

"Nah." Ash shook his head. "It's a gated community. Just a fancy suburb really."

The gate swung open and they rolled down a narrow access road lined with mailboxes and long driveways, many of which plunged steeply downwards, making it impossible to see the houses they led to from the road.

Ash picked one of the blind turns and eased around it, cautiously following the big bronze arrow that directed cars to enter the oblong driveway on the right.

As the house came into view, Harper burst out laughing. Not only was the house ginormous, it had been designed to look like a log cabin. "OMG, it's like someone put *Little House on the Prairie* on steroids."

"Only in LA," Ash said as he parked the SUV.

Harper stepped down from the car and drew in a deep breath. It was at least five degrees cooler here than it had been at Crush House, and the tangy sea breeze was delicious.

"Watch out!" A pair of unfamiliar hands clamped around her waist and yanked her backwards as a white open-topped jeep ploughed through the space where she'd just been.

"Every time," muttered a soft baritone voice near her ear.

Harper clutched her pounding heart and turned to look up at her rescuer – a tall boy with warm caramel skin and a flop of black hair that stuck to his sweaty forehead. He wore thick leather gloves and she could see a pair of gardening shears discarded on the driveway behind him.

"Thank you so much," Harper breathed, her hands shaking a little as she smoothed her hair. "You saved my life."

The handsome boy nodded distractedly. "*De nada, señorita.*"

Then he shot a deadly glare over her shoulder and called out, "You're going to kill someone someday, *cabrón*, coming the wrong way down the driveway like that."

She followed his gaze to see Rafe getting out of the jeep.

"Go trim a hedge, Cesar," Rafe snapped, striding towards them, eyes flashing. "I don't need driving advice from the help. Come on, Harp." Then he grabbed her hand and pulled her away from the gardener and into the house.

Two hours later, Cesar Delgado retreated into the cool dark of the garage with his ancient laptop and his lunch. He'd avoided working in the pool area for as long as he could, hoping that Skye and her guests would get tired of swimming and go inside so he wouldn't have to watch them while he worked. But of course they hadn't. Instead he'd had to watch Rafe shamelessly flirt with the British

Barbie doll whom Skye seemed determined to pretend was her new best friend. Cesar wasn't sorry to see Rafe putting his slimy moves on someone who wasn't Skye, but he hated the humiliation he'd seen flash in Skye's eyes when she thought no one was looking.

Cesar was glad to escape into his writing for a while. Having Rafe in the house always made him want to write gory murder scenes full of unrealistically creative violence, which was just what Skye thought his newest screenplay needed. The serial killer genre wasn't his thing, but if Skye thought it would help him sell a screenplay and become a real writer faster, then he'd do it. Especially if Rafe Jackson kept showing up to provide the inspiration.

The garage was soothing. Comfortable. Uncomplicated. He'd eaten all of his lunches in there when he first started working for the Owen family. He'd been too intimidated by Skye's mother, Jennifer, with her overstretched face and the bluetooth earpiece that might actually have been surgically implanted in her ear, to take a break anywhere he thought he might run into the family.

But then Skye had stumbled on him eating his sandwich in the cave-like dimness one day. She'd been looking for a vintage Gucci bag that she thought might have been tucked into one of her mother's carefully sealed storage boxes, but she'd lost interest in it when she saw Cesar. The next thing he knew, he was sitting at the kitchen table across from Skye as the chef scooped fresh salad and seared tuna onto his plate.

They'd become friends. Then, out of the blue one day, Skye had leaned over and kissed him. From that moment on, they'd been more than friends. They'd been in love.

They'd also been a secret. Skye had dated other boys, but Cesar knew that was just to keep her mother from becoming suspicious. He'd been fine with it. After all, if Jennifer ever found out about them, he'd probably lose his job. But Rafe Jackson was different to the others.

Skye swore she didn't care about Rafe, that she only saw him to appease her mother, who'd set them up in the first place. But no matter what she said, Cesar knew something had changed.

She was out there right now, hanging all over Rafe. She'd be with him all day every day now that they were interning together for his father's company and that ridiculous reality show. *Just another excuse to go out and party,* Cesar thought. *Another excuse to never be home. Another excuse to never have time to see me.*

Before Rafe, they'd gone out sometimes – always in neighbourhoods where she wouldn't be recognised, but that hadn't been a big deal. He'd thought she loved going salsa dancing and hanging around at his Auntie Lourdes's, helping his family make dinner. But then Rafe had come along, and quietly, in almost invisible steps, she'd started to slip away from him.

"Cesar?" Skye called into the dim of the garage. "I know you're back here."

Part of him wanted to just walk away. Let her do the

suffering for once. But he couldn't do that. He loved her too much.

"I'm here, *querida*." He stood and turned to face her.

Skye crossed the garage and laid her head on his chest, over his heart. He wrapped his arms around her and dragged her closer, resting his head on her hair, feeling her lighter, faster heartbeat pull his into sync.

"I'm sorry, baby," she said. "I know you don't like it when he's here."

"So why do you bring him here? And his plastic friends?"

"They're not plastic, they're nice girls," Skye said. "Don't judge them just because they're on a reality show."

"Even the blonde? What's her name – Harper?" he asked. He saw the flash of embarrassment in Skye's eyes and regretted his words immediately, but it was too late. They were out now.

"Rafe wants to hang out with her," Skye said, an edge sharpening in her voice. "Being a crazy jealous bitch isn't going to help the situation."

"Why do you even care?" Cesar asked, feeling the anger bubble up again. "Let him have his blonde and we can be together. For real."

A long quiet. Each passing second made his heart heavier.

"C, you know I can't do that." Skye sounded on the verge of tears when she finally spoke. "Mom would—"

"I know she wouldn't approve," Cesar snapped. "She doesn't think I'm good enough for her precious girl."

"She doesn't think you're good enough for her friends," Skye said. "She doesn't care what happens to me, you know that."

He held her away from him, forcing her to look him in the eye. "You don't think I'm good enough either, do you?"

Skye shook herself free and glared up at him. "Of course I think you're good enough, Cesar. I love you. What kind of person do you think I am?"

"I know who you are, Skye," he said, "but I'm not sure you do. You're too brave to be hiding your life from the world, just so your mother can have the trophy daughter she wants."

"You don't understand, babe. There is so much pressure on me right now. Mom just goes on and on about how I'm going to be producing movies before I'm thirty. And Dad is off shooting in Tunisia or something. He's not here to back me up. I can't just announce that..."

"You're in love with the gardener," he finished for her.

The tears started to slide down her cheeks.

"I love you so much. Please, C, don't doubt that. We just have to do this until we can sell one of your screenplays. Then you'll be the next big thing and she'll be thrilled that we're dating because that will mean she can convince you to reboot *Attack of the Killer Tomatoes* for her. God, I can already see it. She'll act like us being together was her idea in the first place. But it has to be this way, just for a little while longer. You understand that, don't you?"

Cesar wanted to keep arguing with her, to tell her she was better than this, better than her mother. But he couldn't stand to see her cry.

He reached out and drew her close again, kissing away her tears. She caught his mouth with hers and, for a long time, his mind emptied of everything but her.

Lucy was relieved to step into the cool dimness of the house. It was a beautiful day but the white-hot sun was relentless, even through the oversized vintage sunglasses Debra Z had picked out for her. She needed some cold water, more sunblock and her iPod, in that order.

Who was she kidding? It wasn't only the sun she needed to escape from. It was Harper and Rafe, who were flirting so enthusiastically that she'd thought they might start snogging in the pool at any moment, right in front of Rafe's girlfriend.

Was Rafe really falling for Harper again? That was the last thing any of them needed. With any luck, he was just flirting with her for sport.

Lucy felt like a horrible friend for wishing such a thing. She knew it would break Harper's heart. But perhaps that was for the best. Dangerous things happened when Rafe Jackson was around. He'd already almost killed Harper once that day with his dangerous driving, and the disastrous car accident on Lucy's fifteenth birthday party had been his fault as well. Rafe had been the one who had dared the already drunk Harper to do two shots of coconut rum and drive around the block.

Who knew what might happen if they started dating again?

Lucy suddenly realised that she was completely lost. The Owens' enormous imitation log cabin had two wings, and she was evidently in the wrong one. The open doors on either side of her revealed sprawling bedrooms, an office and even a huge gym... but not the kitchen or the guest suite where Skye had told them to leave their things.

Lucy was retracing her steps when she heard the sound of someone retching. She hesitated, unsure what to do. If someone was ill and needed help, she hated to just walk away. But, "Excuse me, I know you've no idea who I am, but I've just been listening to you vomit and wondered if you needed a hand," wasn't exactly a great introductory line.

The noise stopped. Time to do a runner before whoever it was came out.

But it was too late. The door was already opening.

Lucy's apology died on her lips as a pale and jittery Robyn stepped out of the loo.

"Hey, lady," Robyn said, just a little too fast. "What are you doing here?"

"I was looking for the kitchen and my bag, but I got a bit lost," Lucy said. "Are you okay? It sounded like—"

"Oh, yeah, that was nothing. Must have had some bad clams at dinner last night," Robyn said brightly. "I think the kitchen's that way." She pointed down the hall. "See you outside?"

And with that, she was gone. Galloping off like a little kid who'd had too much sugar.

Robyn had been like that all week. Maybe it was all the extra coffee she was drinking, or all the food she wasn't eating. Robyn hadn't eaten much of anything that week, now that Lucy thought about it, and she certainly hadn't had any clams at dinner the night before. She'd ordered a green salad and spent most of the evening pushing lettuce around her plate.

Lucy had been relieved to see Robyn stuffing herself with the barbecue at lunch, but now she'd clearly gone and thrown it all up again. And lied about being sick to boot. And Lucy was the only one who knew it.

If only she knew what to do about it.

Finally, Lucy found the guest suite. Their bags lay on the bed in a jumble – bits and pieces spilled across the spotless white duvet cover in their owners' hurry to get to the pool.

Lucy grabbed Alexander's iPod from her bag. Her new mobile wasn't there, which meant it was one of the three that were sprawled amongst their rubble. A *Project Next* sponsor had given all of the contestants brand new iPhones, which was awesome, but they were all identical, which was clearly going to be a problem.

She shouldn't check her mobile, anyway, Lucy told herself. It wasn't as though there was likely to be a text from Mum or Dad. Her brother John thought they'd forgive her eventually, but said at the moment they were still steaming mad.

Lucy wished eventually would hurry up and arrive. She was dying to talk to Dad all about the new stuff she was learning and to tell Emily about the movie stars she'd seen. And now she desperately wanted to ask Mum what to do about Robyn.

Perhaps Mum had called. Perhaps John was wrong. She'd just check, Lucy thought. It wouldn't hurt.

Lucy grabbed for the first of the identical iPhones. When the screen came to life she could see Iza's bright pink wallpaper. She put it back in Iza's bag and picked up another.

This one had a text message waiting. From Jason.

Sounds beautiful. Send me a picture.

Lucy stared down at the mobile. It was Toni's. She could see that from the photo of Bella that Toni used as her wallpaper. Why was Jason asking Toni for pictures? That was the sort of thing John and his girlfriend liked to do when they were apart – not the sort of chat you'd expect between a musician and her manager.

No, no, Lucy thought, dismissing the very idea. Toni got on well with grown-ups. That was all. And Lucy was being an awful snoop, reading other people's texts. They were going to have to get charms or stickers or something for these mobiles. It wouldn't be good to have everyone grabbing the wrong one all the time.

Lucy put the mobile in Toni's bright red shoulder bag and reached for the third – her own.

No replies to her texts. No missed calls.

With a sigh she tucked it back into her studded white bag and headed in the direction she hoped would lead to the kitchen.

She was standing in front of the sink guzzling water when she heard a soft moan from the open door into the garage.

Was everyone in this house ill? Lucy tiptoed to the door. Just to make sure someone wasn't lying on the floor bleeding, she told herself. Not to snoop.

What she saw left her jaw lying on the pink marble kitchen floor.

Skye Owen stood in the middle of the garage, wrapped in the strong arms of the gardener who'd saved Harper from being knocked down by Rafe in the driveway. Their lips were locked with the kind of passion you just couldn't fake.

Lucy slipped back into the kitchen and half ran through the maze of a house, not stopping until she found the family room that opened outside. Toni and Iza were splashing in the pool and Harper was standing on the diving board, belting out 'Natural Woman' while Robyn giggled and strummed along on her guitar.

They looked so happy.

Then again, *they* hadn't stumbled onto every deep,

dark secret in a five mile radius today. Lucy didn't want to know any of the things that were jostling around in her head now, unravelling visions of potential disasters in their wake. But she did.

"You're the drummer," she said to herself. "It's your job to keep them on beat. To hold it all together."

But how the bloody hell was she supposed to do that?

6. LIGHT IN THE DARK

She was trying to focus, Lucy thought grumpily. She was. But the tangle of beat-marks that danced across the page just refused to make sense today. They were taunting her, picking at her brain like tiny little fingers. With claws.

Christ, she wasn't even hungover. What was wrong with her?

Secrets, Lucy thought. *It's all the secrets destroying my brain.* She didn't want to know any of the things she'd learned that Saturday at Skye's. But you couldn't un-know something, no matter how hard you tried.

All Lucy wanted to do was call her mum. Not that she thought she'd really tell Mum all of the crazy things she suspected her bandmates were up to. Mum would go completely mental if she knew.

Mum and Dad would chat to her about the flower beds and how Emily was learning to do double pirouettes and was destroying the kitchen in the process. And somehow, if they stayed on the line long enough, Mum would guess that something was wrong. They'd harass her about it for a while, and then they'd reel off every cliché piece of advice ever known to man and Lucy would be thoroughly annoyed by the time she got off the phone.

And she'd feel better.

"Lucille!" Alexander's voice barked over the intercom from the booth. "Where are you today, and when do you plan to join the rest of us here on planet Earth?"

"Um, sorry, Alexander," she said, suddenly terrified that she was about to start blubbing. She scrubbed at her eyes to clear them. "I just... I can't seem to get this beat."

"You had it yesterday," he pointed out.

Robyn caught Lucy's eye from where she stood between three low-slung mics set to catch her guitar solo and mouthed, *You okay?*

Lucy nodded – unconvincingly, apparently, because Robyn mouthed back, *What's wrong?*

Lucy shook her head vigorously and looked straight ahead. Robyn's sympathy would do her in if she let it.

"Let's try it again," Alexander boomed. "With a little less day-tripping, shall we?"

Lucy nodded, still avoiding Robyn's concerned gaze. She just wanted to get through this song. That was all. Then they'd be done for the day.

"One, two, three, four," she counted off.

They made it thirty seconds into 'Sucker Punch' before Alexander cut them. Lucy knew it was her fault. The others had been dead on, Toni's deeper bass guitar flowing smoothly under Robyn's picked-out melody as Iza pounded out a percussive piano line to punctuate the first few verses of the song. Lucy had blown the beat. Again.

"You girls can go," Alexander said, stepping out of the booth. "Lucille can stay."

Lucy sagged. Now she was in for it.

She didn't look up as the others gathered their things and cleared off.

Someone squeezed her shoulder as they passed. *Robyn*, she thought, catching a glint of the yellow nail varnish Robyn had discovered last week on Melrose and fallen head over heels in love with. Trust Robyn to be the one who saw she was sad. She always did.

Robyn's sensitivity to every little thing could be quite annoying. You constantly had to reassure her that you weren't upset or she hadn't offended the waiter or that a passerby didn't think she was odd. But Robyn always knew when someone was sad or upset or had PMT and needed an extra coffee and muffin. Lucy tried to smile up at her as she left, but she knew she was doing a crap job of it.

Just like she was of everything else.

"Okay, Lucille," Alexander said, settling on a stool beside the drum kit once the others had fled. "What's going on?"

She wanted to blurt it all out, right then. Harper and Rafe. Robyn lying about having food poisoning.

Toni and Jason. But what would Alexander do? What could he do? A lot of things that might bloody well ruin all their chances, that's what he could do.

"Don't hold out on me, miss," Alexander snapped. "I am neither blind nor deaf. You could hit that beat backwards and forwards and upside down in a hurricane, but you can't get it to come out of your sticks to save your own life today. Something's eating you and it's getting in the way of my record, so it's time to spill."

She had to tell him something. She should tell him everything. Or maybe she shouldn't. What if she was wrong. What if—

"It's my family," she blurted. She was a bit surprised, actually, when the words popped free of her mouth. She'd honestly thought she was covering for her real concerns, but once she'd said it out loud, she realised it *was* her family that was bothering her, as much as it was anything else.

She'd been fine, at first, being at odds with them, but now as the days went by and LA and Crush and all the rest became more demanding and the girls all had their own concerns... She was just lonely, Lucy realised abruptly. So bloody lonely.

She didn't know she was crying until Alexander reached out to pat her shoulder, his expression much the same as if he'd stumbled across a stick of dynamite primed to explode. Lucy tried to stop crying, but now that the tears were flowing, they didn't want to stop.

Alexander fumbled for a box of tissues stashed on one of the side tables beside the sofa at the back of the room, then stamped back to her and thrust a wad of them into her hand.

"What's wrong with your family?" he asked. Then he awkwardly added, "Dear?"

She almost smiled, despite herself. Poor Alexander. Comforting crying teenage girls was *not* in his skill set. She blew her nose on the tissues rather violently.

"I'm sorry, I didn't mean to blub," Lucy said, trying to gather herself. "I'm fine, really."

"Young lady," Alexander said. "You will learn, someday, that most problems are bigger inside your head than they are when you take them out and look at them in the light of day. I think it's time this one saw daylight, don't you?"

She gulped back more tears and nodded.

"So..." he prodded.

"They don't approve, you see," she blurted. "My parents, I mean. I didn't tell them about *Project Next* when we tried out because they wanted me to focus on my studies and were never going to let me join a new band, much less try out for the show. I meant to tell them eventually. I did. But then my little sister destroyed the answerphone and before I knew it we were about to fly to Los Angeles and they'd seen me on the telly and they didn't know I was on the show and it was just a disaster. Now they're not speaking to me, and John

– that's my brother – says they're still livid and I think they'll never forgive me and I just want to talk to them. I just want them to irritate me with too many questions and tell me all about rebuilding the gutters and the like until I die of boredom, you know? I've no idea why but... I want that. And I'll never have it again."

Alexander sat quietly for a long time.

"I know the feeling well, unfortunately," he said finally.

"They just don't understand," Lucy said. "They don't understand why it matters. Why music is so important. They never have."

"Have you explained it to them?" Alexander asked.

"I tried," Lucy said. "Well, I meant to. But I'm not sure it's ever been as much a case of explaining as making a lot of stuttering sounds and waving my hands, then running off to LA and sulking for days."

Without a word, Alexander stood and crossed to the booth. When he came back, he was carrying a notepad and a pen.

"You can't expect them to understand if you don't at least try to explain it to them. They might never get it. And if you tell them and they still don't feel you, that's their problem, not yours. But you do have to try."

"How do I do that?" Lucy asked. "They won't call me back or return my texts."

"Then write it down, Lucille," Alexander said, handing her the pad and pen. "Write them a letter and make it as long or short as it needs to be to tell them how you really feel about your music. Then tell them that they will have two seats at the Las Vegas final, if they want them. All they have to do is call me."

"But Jason said family wouldn't be invited," Lucy said.

"They will be if I say they are," Alexander said. "Now write, Lucille. We've got beats to run through and I want this out of your system!"

Then he strode away, as though he didn't want anyone to catch him taking care of a teenage girl instead of glowering at a band from his booth.

When he was gone, Lucy stared down at the pad.

How was she meant to explain why she loved music? There *was* no explaining it. The feeling that the heartbeat of the universe was pulsing in her fingers, just waiting to drive outwards, into the air, through her drums. The throbbing snap that you could feel all the way up your arms while you played. And the feeling you got, if you were really doing it properly, that it wasn't you playing at all, that you could look down on yourself and see this awesome, impossible dance of sticks and arms and cymbals and think, *Christ, nobody can do that*, and then realise that *you*, in fact, were actually doing that.

But how was she meant to describe it to her parents?

Alexander's voice rang in her ears once more.

Write it down, Lucille. Write it down.

Lucy picked up the pen and started to write.

7. DELICATE

The sign on the door read **CRUSH** in bold, capital letters.

Jason hadn't been messing about when he said that his bands played only the best venues. *Who'd have thought it?* Lucy smiled as Paulina fussed over the last bits of Lucy's make-up. Crush were about to play the Hollywood Bowl. She'd only seen pictures of it in magazines and in films, and now she was about to play on the stage.

The previous two weeks had been a mad dash of rehearsals, practice and, of course, parties. Lucy would happily have focused on nothing but her drum kit 24/7, but getting dolled up and running about Los Angeles to get papped was part of the deal, she supposed. She could scarcely believe they'd been in America nearly a month, but it was true. She could only hope they'd learned enough from Alexander to do him proud on stage tonight. Crush were just the opening act, obviously, but that didn't matter.

Lucy couldn't even allow herself to think of the band

Crush were opening for. Just being here was enough to leave her alternating between clammy nausea and fizzing excitement. If she considered the fact that they were playing at the Hollywood Bowl as the opening act for Electric she was afraid she might actually faint.

Electric. They were going to play on the same stage as *Electric.* She was, at this very moment, breathing the same air as Trent Eisner. It just wasn't possible.

"Huddle up, ladies!" Jason strode into their dressing room.

"You are about to do something that a band only gets to do once in a lifetime, and I want you to enjoy every last second of it," he declared. "You will never have another first gig, and I guarantee you, no matter how many sold-out stadium shows we play, or how many platinum records are on your wall, you will never match the feeling you're going to have tonight when you walk out onto that stage. There is no greater high, so savour this moment, girls. This is the first breath of the beast that Crush is going to grow up to be. Don't miss it worrying about your hair, or whether or not you blew a chord or dropped a line. Tell those nerves they can kiss your collective asses and have fun out there. You've earned this, and you're about to show the world exactly how much!"

Jason was right, Lucy thought, this wasn't the time to worry about Robyn's issues. Or the fact that Rafe had insisted that Harper went with him in the equipment van on the way to the show, whilst Skye rode with the hair and make-up team. Or to wonder why Iza had been sobbing in the bathroom yesterday. None of that was Lucy's problem – not tonight. Tonight was just Lucy and her drums. That's all that mattered.

Toni squeezed into the first wing of the Bowl's enormous stage beside Jason and peered out at the rows of people that stretched up and up into the dying light of the summer evening. It was almost time to go on.

"It's quite full, isn't it?" Toni asked. She couldn't believe it was possible to be this nervous. "I was expecting people to still be coming in during the set. Opening act and all that."

"They want to see you girls as much as they want to see Electric," Jason said, shooting her a quick grin. "There's a lot of curiosity out there about *Project Next* – especially after the first special aired last week. Perfect timing for your first big show, if I do say so myself."

"Well, bragging about yourself is one of your best skills," Toni smart-alecked.

"No, bragging about you is my best skill. The fact that I make myself look like a genius in the process just proves that I'm good at what I do." He matched her smile. "You ready for this?"

"Yes." Toni didn't hesitate. She'd been ready for this her whole life. Nerves be damned. She was going to rock the Hollywood Bowl's world. "I'm ready."

But she wasn't ready for the spark of pure electricity that shot up her arm and straight into her heart when Jason reached down and squeezed her hand. The look on his face as he stared down at their intertwined fingers, then back up at her face, told her he'd felt it too. He looked a bit like he'd been hit by a bus.

A muttered curse from behind them snapped the moment like a twig. Jason dropped her hand as though it had suddenly caught fire and took a big step to the left.

"Good. You'll be fantastic, Toni," he said, sounding distant and managerial all of the sudden. Toni shot a covert look over her shoulder. Bloody hell. One of the cameramen was there, aiming his lens their way.

Jason strode past the camera into the backstage prep area and called to the others, "You're on, ladies. Let's go kill this thing, shall we?"

"YEAH!" Lucy crowed. "Come on, rock star." She grabbed Toni's hand and pulled her onto the stage.

Toni glanced back at Jason, a confusion of thoughts and emotions and hormones stumbling through her brain, but then she plunged into the blinding bubble of light and sound that was centre stage and, just like that, everything else fell away. She pulled the shoulder strap of her bass over her head and found the glowing slice of tape that marked her place stage left, down a bit from Lucy's drum kit. Robyn bounced in behind Toni and Lucy, gripping her guitar, and zipped to her own mark, splitting left of stage with Toni as Iza slipped quietly to her seat at the white baby grand that dominated stage right.

This was it! Crush's very first gig was about to start.

Toni shot the crowd a saucy grin as Harper strode casually to the front of the stage.

"Hello, Hollywood Bowl!" she said, easing into the mic. "It's lovely to meet you. Our name is Crush!"

She let the applause die down for a moment, then leaned in again and said, "Believe me, the pleasure is all ours... but if you're good, I promise we'll share."

"One. Two. One, two, three, four!" Lucy called from the back, punctuating each number with a crack of her drumsticks.

That was Toni's cue. She slammed into the first chord of 'Revenge is Fun' and let the music run free.

The roar of the crowd made Lucy feel like every cell in her body was carbonated, caffeinated and completely on fire. She was practically floating after the other girls down the back corridors of the Bowl on the way to their dressing room.

Lucy had thought it would be no big deal – after all, they'd already played the *Project Next* UK semi-final, which had housed a live audience almost as big as this one, as well as countless eyes watching on the telly. But it hadn't been like this.

She could have sworn that all 17,396 people in the packed amphitheatre had been on their feet, singing along with 'I'll Cross the World'. As the final chorus had blasted through the bowl, she'd felt as though she was about to break apart into a million happy little pieces.

They had just played the freaking Hollywood Bowl. No... not just played – they had just ruled the Hollywood Bowl.

"Whatever's putting that smile on your face, I could use a hit," said a midnight-blue sort of voice.

She looked up to find a willowy guy with a tangle of dark curls and rich brown eyes grinning at her. He looked quite familiar. Who was he? One of the technicians from Alexander's studio, perhaps? Or a *Project Next* crewman?

Whoever he was, he was downright dreamy, and at that moment she felt like she could flirt with bloody Ryan Gosling if he happened to be wandering about backstage at the Hollywood Bowl.

"Can you play the drums?" she asked, tossing her curls in her best Harper imitation.

The guy shook his head. "Nope."

"Then I can't help you," she fired back with a cheeky smile, enjoying herself too much to listen to the tiny voice in the back of her brain that kept insisting that this wasn't just some random roadie.

"Would the guitar do?" he asked, still grinning like an idiot.

She opened her mouth to say something clever about teaching him a few things on her drum kit when a middle-aged man in a *Friday the 13th* T-shirt and cargo shorts hurried past. "Trent! Need you on stage in two."

Wait. This adorable, cocky guy's name was Trent? And he was needed on stage... where Electric was about to take over for Crush as the main act of the show?

Realisation crept over her face in a hot, red blush. How could she have missed it? She'd seen his face a hundred times. Possibly a thousand. Stared at it. Studied it. Dreamed about it. But it looked different now. Still attractive, but plainer, somehow. Ordinary. Younger as well. She'd never thought of him as nearly her own age, but he was.

Yet there was no denying it. She hadn't recognised the guy with the beautiful brown eyes because he was a studio tech or *Project Next* crew; she'd recognised him from the poster on her bloody bedroom wall. And the wallpaper on her laptop. And...

"Trent? You're Trent Eisner?" she blurted. "As in, Electric Trent Eisner?"

He nodded, clearly amused by the fact that her jaw was pretty obviously lying on the floor.

"As in, number one in the UK for ten weeks running, Trent Eisner? Best New Artists Grammy and MTV Music Award winner for Best Album *and* Best Video too, Trent Eisner?"

She wanted to stop babbling, but her mouth just kept spilling words like an open tap. "*NME*'s Artist to Watch, Trent Eisner? Headlining this show, Trent Eisner?"

Stop. Freaking. Talking. Lucy.

"Trent! Ninety seconds!" hollered the stage manager.

"Gotta fly," he rumbled, still grinning wickedly at her. He unfolded from his slouch and loped down the hall.

She was still struggling to form a non-lame-moronic-fan-girl comeback when he called over his shoulder, "What? You're not gonna come cheer us on? You're breakin' my heart, Drummer Girl."

Lucy could feel a totally ridiculous grin forming on her face as she moved to follow him, but she didn't care. She was really here. In the actual Hollywood Bowl. About to go and watch Electric play from the wings because Trent Eisner – possibly the hottest guy on the face of the planet – wanted her there. It was the best night of her life.

And it was just the beginning.

The after-party at Blvd3 was in full swing when Iza took another little sip of champagne. She was beginning to like the stuff, though the taste was still quite odd to her. But then again, it was better than beer. Or tequila. God, she hated tequila.

"Lemon-drop shots next. What do you say?" Robyn shouted over the blasting music. She grabbed Iza's hand and twirled her about, chanting, "Lemon drop, lemon drop, I want a lemon drop."

Iza giggled helplessly, trying to steady them both before they fell. Robyn was hilarious, but she was also completely plastered. In fact, neither of them really needed another shot. But now Robyn was swinging her around in a mock Irish jig and Iza just couldn't bring herself to be the one who pointed out they should go home and get some rest. She never could.

"Where's Harper?" Iza called over the music. "And Toni and Lucy? They've been gone for ages."

"Harper is right here," said Harper, pouting her way into their corner of the dance floor, by the VIP tables. "And she brought friends."

Iza wasn't surprised to see Rafe Jackson and Skye Owen approaching just a few steps behind Harper. That particular pout of Harper's almost always meant that Skye was nearby. But Rafe and Skye weren't alone.

Iza's heart slammed out a sonic-boom-level thud.

"Aren't you going to say hello, Iz?" Harper smirked. "I was going to introduce you to Rafe's fraternity brother, Luke, but I hear you two have already met."

Iza wasn't sure she remembered how to say hello. She wasn't sure she remembered how to speak at all. She hadn't replied to the handsome violin player's texts and now Luke was here, staring at her with his gorgeous blue eyes full of questions and she'd been struck mute. Maybe she'd never talk again. Maybe she was going to be a piano-playing mute from now on. Maybe—

"I'll get the next round. I've got my brother's ID," Luke said, breaking the insanely awkward pause. "What do you girls want?"

"Lemon drops, please," Robyn said. "Thanks, Luke."

"You're welcome..." Luke looked confused. "Wait... how did you know my name? I don't think we've met... have we?"

"Oh no," Robyn said, giggling. "But we *have* read your text messages, haven't we, Iz? And that's almost the same thing."

"Robs!" Harper said, elbowing their drunken bandmate.

"What? It's true," Robyn said. "It was a lovely text. *Last night was fun.* Deep, thoughtful stuff that."

Rafe burst out laughing. Skye rolled her eyes.

Iza was fairly sure she was going to die of pure, unadulterated embarrassment. It would be a relief, really. It was likely to be the fastest route out of there.

"Sorry, Luke," Harper snorted, choking back giggles. "Robyn loses all filter when hammered." She shoved Iza gently in Luke's direction. "Iza, why don't you go with Luke and help him carry everything. It's too much for one person to handle."

Iza was surprised she even managed to choke out, "Sure," before she found herself following Luke to the bar.

He queued up behind a trio of middle-aged guys who were trying to convince the girl at the other end of the bar to let them buy her a drink, which naturally was taking an age.

Come on, Iza, she thought. *Speak. Talk. Enunciate. Do SOMETHING.*

"I, um." *Must. Not. Hyperventilate,* Iza commanded herself. "I showed them your picture from the LA Phil website. They made me, after they saw your text."

"So they'd know who to make the restraining order out for?" Luke said, mildly. It sounded like a joke. Sort of.

But it also sort of sounded like his feelings were hurt.

The old guys left and Luke stepped up to the bar.

"Four lemon drops, a tequila and a Coke, please," Luke told the bartender.

They watched in silence as the bartender poured the Coke and Rafe's tequila then started to mix the bright yellow vodka shots.

Luke took a long drag of the Coke.

Iza tried to force her brain to form full sentences.

It wasn't working.

Finally, Luke blurted out, "I won't bother you. I promise. I thought... You gave me your number. I thought you wanted... but that's okay. It is. It doesn't have to be awkward."

Why hadn't she just texted him back? What was wrong with her? He was so wonderful and he liked her and she was letting him think she didn't like him back. She was being such a complete blithering idiot and ruining everything and she had to do something. She had to.

What Iza wanted to do was find a cupboard and lock herself in it. She wanted to burst into tears. She wanted to run all the way to the airport, get on a plane and go home. But instead she grabbed Rafe's shot of tequila and tipped it down her neck in one ugly gulp.

Tequila was awful.

Choking, she gasped out, "No, Luke. I did want to go out with you. I'm just... I'm a complete idiot. I was so nervy about what to say that I spent two days fiddling with my stupid text back to you and then... and then it had been so long it seemed like *anything* I replied with would be weird and... I... just chickened out. I'm so sorry. I've never been asked out before and you're so perfect and I just... I'm sorry. I understand if you don't want to go out with me any more."

"But I do," Luke said, quickly. He grabbed her hand, holding tight like he wanted to make sure she wouldn't get away. "Want to go out with you, I mean. Tomorrow. If you're free tomorrow, that is. My rehearsal is over at three. Can you meet me at the concert hall then?"

Iza still could feel the dizzy courage of the tequila running through her brain as she looked up into Luke's eyes and said, "Yes!"

The smoking patio of Blvd3 was nearly empty, thank goodness. So there'd only been a few curious stares when Lucy and Trent had settled into the corner with the best view.

"So I wake up, and I'm lying in the middle of a cornfield – naked," Trent snorted with laughter at his own story, "with my guitar still strapped around my neck, and my mother standing over me."

Lucy giggled. "No! Did she go absolutely mental?"

He matched her grin. "Nah, my parents thought a little psychedelic exploration was healthy. We lived on a commune after all. She just gave me a lecture about tripping without adult supervision."

"That's brilliant," Lucy said. "My dad would have murdered me. And then my mum would have sent me to convent school. They're the opposite of cool at all times."

"At least they care."

"Yeah, they care so much neither of them is speaking to me." Lucy looked out over the glittering web of city lights that spread below their perch. "They aren't keen on the music-as-a-career-path bit. They want me to get a degree. But without studying like a mad woman this summer, which I'm obviously not doing, Oxford is probably out of the question. I know I should care, but I'm not sure I do."

"And you shouldn't," Trent said. "Sometimes the music won't let you wait until after someone tells you you're officially grown up. You just gotta let it out. It's not a choice."

Lucy nodded, keeping her eyes glued on the city lights so she could be sure they wouldn't tear up. "Still, I wish they understood. They're a pain but I miss them, you know?"

Trent's big, calloused hand cupped her bare shoulder for a moment, and then slid down to rub her back.

"They'll come round," Trent said. "After all, I've just met you and I already know you're great. They've known you all your life. They won't let this come between you for long. Promise."

He was right, he barely knew her. And pretty much everything she knew about him came from *NME*, and *MTV*.

But somehow she felt like she'd known him forever.

At first she'd thought it was just the excitement of chatting to the actual, honest-to-God Trent Eisner – after all, he was literally the rock and roller of her dreams – but as the night had worn on, she'd decided it was more than that. Being with him felt like being on a rollercoaster and being curled up in the world's comfiest chair at the same time – Lucy had only ever felt that way before on stage, behind her drum kit with the beat pounding through her fingertips.

They were standing close together, leaning on the patio railing. His hand was still resting on her back, his rich brown eyes on hers.

Lucy had never made the first move with a boy before, much less attempted to kiss a rock and roll legend, but the kiss was right there, just waiting to exist. It seemed so obvious that kissing him was the proper thing to do at that moment that she didn't actually consider not going through with it. Not even once. She just went up on her tiptoes and pressed her lips gently to his.

Trent's hands slid up her back and into her hair, and then cupped her face for a long, perfect moment. But then, instead of pulling her closer, he took her by the shoulders and set her away from him.

Startled, Lucy looked up at him and found regret in his beautiful eyes.

Oh. He didn't want her. Of course he didn't want her. He probably had ten model girlfriends who were all ten thousand times prettier than some girl drummer from a stupid reality show competition band.

"I'm... I'm sorry, I didn't..." he said, cutting himself off.

It was too humiliating. She had to get away from him. Now.

She was almost through the door back into the club when she felt his hand on her arm.

"No, Lucy, please. Let me explain," he said.

He looked as awkward as she felt.

Good. He deserved it.

"I'm sorry. I don't want you to be embarrassed. You weren't wrong to think... I definitely wanted to kiss you too," he said.

Then why had he pushed her away?

As though he could read her mind, Trent continued, "I think you're awesome, Lucy. But..."

There it was. The 'But'.

But, you're too young. But, I have a girlfriend. But... "I'm on tour. If we start something now, I'll want it to be real, and so will you. But I'll almost never be around and there'll be a thousand girls throwing themselves at me every night and you don't know me well enough to trust me the way you'd have to."

He slid his hand down her arm to squeeze her fingers. "I don't want you to be just another tour girlfriend that finally gets sick of wondering if whatever *TMZ* said about me last night was true. You deserve better."

Lucy wanted to brush it off, to pretend he was

overreacting to a little kiss, but she couldn't find the words to make the lie real. It was too obvious, she thought, that she wanted more from him than he had ever considered wanting from her. She found that she couldn't even force herself to run off, which she desperately wanted to do. Her feet were glued to the floor, like a deer in the headlights of an approaching car.

Finally, very, very slowly, he leaned towards her and planted a feather-light kiss on her forehead.

"You have no idea how sorry I am to say it, Lucy Gosling, but I already like you too much to let you get hurt. And if we did this..."

He shook his head.

"I'll see you back in there, right?"

When she didn't respond, he stepped around her and walked back into the club.

Robyn stared at the toilet cubicle. This was a terrible plan. A monumentally terrible plan, in fact.

She really should just go back and convince Lucy and Harper to dance like maniacs with her for another hour. That would take care of the basket of chips and onion rings she'd guzzled after the set. Not to mention the three glasses of champagne and the sugary lemon-drop shots.

She couldn't believe she'd been such a glutton, not after all the work she'd done. Robyn had dropped another size in the last few days and she was determined to make it to an American size four by the end of the month. She couldn't destroy her work now by eating all that crap and not doing anything about it.

She *needed* to do something about it.

She had to.

Right?

No. Not right, she thought, mentally smacking herself. The throwing up wasn't good at all. She was terrified of ending up like those wretched, skeletal girls with their hair and teeth falling out everywhere, madly yammering about how pretty they felt for some sad BBC documentary.

But just thinking of all the grease and fat and carbs floating around inside of her made Robyn heave. It would be so easy to get rid of it all.

No. She wasn't going to do it. End of.

Distracting herself, Robyn reached into her bag for her lipgloss. Her fingers brushed the little bottle of pills that lay at the bottom of her lime-green snakeskin clutch. Maybe she'd just take an extra dose to take care of the nosh session. Yes, that was a better idea.

She fished out two pills and downed them. That was better. Robyn always felt better when she took her pills. She looked into the amber depths of the plastic bottle. It was nearly empty. She'd have to see Tomas about a refill – and soon. She couldn't be without her pills.

She'd been positive there would be some kind of weird side effects to the little pink tablets, but there'd been absolutely no problems. In fact, she felt bloody amazing. It was as though she'd never truly been completely awake before she'd begun taking the pills. She hadn't even known what it was like to be as awake and alert as she was now. The world was brighter. Crisper. Fresher. Her eyes open wider. Her body super-charged.

It had got even better after she'd tried taking them two at a time. The other girls were always knackered, but Robyn was breezing through the early mornings and late nights. In fact, she used the time they spent napping in the afternoons to swim laps in the pool.

Robyn dabbed on her gloss and studied herself in the mirror. She barely recognised the gorgeous, thin girl she saw there. This was the kind of girl who made the cover of glossy mags and played on world tours. This was the kind of girl who she'd always dreamed of being. She wasn't about to lose this new Robyn now. The pills should do the trick, but just to be safe...

She turned back towards the toilet cubicle and nearly jumped a mile when Lucy stepped out of it.

"Christ, Luce," Robyn exclaimed, clutching her pounding heart. "You nearly gave me a heart attack, you know?"

"I've been clanging about back there trying to use the loo without contracting typhoid for at least five minutes," Lucy said, dragging the back of her hand across her eyes like a tired kid. "I would have thought you'd have heard me, but you were quite intent on whatever you were doing out here, I suppose."

Robyn turned back to the mirror and poked at her hair, trying not to look guilty.

"Intent? I don't know what you mean, lady," Robyn said, unpinning one strand of her hair and twisting it back again into the messy French-twist that Debra Z had taught her to do. "I'm not intent on anything. Just standing here, catching loo-based diseases, same as you."

Lucy didn't even crack a smile, she just busied herself washing her hands. Robyn could almost see the black thundercloud hovering over her. Something was clearly wrong. She should ask Lucy about it, but could she really concentrate properly on Lucy's problems with a queasy stomach full of junk?

Robyn looked up at the cubicle behind them in the mirror. All she needed was another few minutes alone, then she could be a sympathetic ear to Lucy.

"Robs?" Lucy said. "What are these?"

Robyn's eyes widened in horror as she looked back to Lucy. She was holding up Robyn's bottle of pills, which she'd apparently left by the sink.

Stupid, stupid, stupid. How could she have been so stupid?

"Um, nothing," Robyn said. "They aren't mine, actually."

"They're not?" Lucy asked, sceptically. "But you took one, when I was in the loo. I heard you."

Robyn didn't want to lie to Lucy about the pills. She shouldn't have to, anyway. They weren't illegal or anything. Why should she hide something that was helping her so much?

She'd wanted to talk to Lucy about it from the start.

Lucy had become one of Robyn's best mates since they'd joined Crush. She wasn't like most of the other girls in their class. You never had to worry whether Lucy was judging you, or at least, Robyn had never used to worry. Ever since Lucy had caught her throwing up after Skye's barbecue that first week, things had been off between them. Robyn felt as though the drummer was watching her all the time now, waiting for her to screw up again.

But would telling Lucy about the pills make things better? Or worse?

"You can tell me, Robs," Lucy added. "I won't say anything to the others. I swear. I'm just worried about you, that's all."

"Fine," Robyn said, her stomach feeling like it would twist up so tightly that it might actually explode. "They're diet, um, supplements that Debra Z asked me to take. That's all."

"Diet supplements? Like vitamins?" Lucy said, not looking quite convinced.

"Not exactly," Robyn said. Before Lucy could ask more questions, she quickly added, "Tomas says they're totally safe. I haven't had any weird side effects or anything and I have so much energy now. I feel amazing! He gets them from his mum when she goes to Asia for work. She's a consultant, Asian markets and that. Anyway, they should totally be approved here, but the diet industry probably doesn't want them to be because then they'd lose their monopoly. Why are you looking at me like that, Lucy?"

"Do you know how fast you're talking?" Lucy said softly.

"I'm-not-talking-fast-you're-talking-slow."

"You kind of are."

Robyn felt a hot stab of bitterness. She had known Lucy wouldn't understand, hadn't she? And here Lucy was, proving she was just like all the others. A skinny, judgemental bitch.

"Just because you're too tiny to need help doesn't mean you get to judge me, Lucy Gosling," Robyn said, fighting tears. "I *knew* you'd all judge me. I knew it!"

A tear slipped out, then another. Robyn let them come. She'd been so afraid the other girls would be this way, that Lucy would be this way – and she'd been right. She couldn't stand it.

"Robyn, no! Please don't cry. I didn't mean to... I mean, I guess I did mean to say something. I honestly don't want to be judgemental but..."

"But you are," Robyn said. "You think I'm crazy, or too lazy to lose weight on my own. You have no idea how hard—"

"Oh no, Robyn, that's not true!" Lucy looked like she might cry now as well. "I'm just worried about you. I want you to be healthy, that's it. I swear. You're my friend, Robs. I want you to be happy. That's why I have to say—"

Relief coursed through Robyn. Of course Lucy wasn't judging her. Lucy never judged. Sweet Lucy. She was just being overprotective.

"Right," Robyn said, so relieved she didn't even notice she was cutting Lucy off. "Right. And I am. I honestly am being totally healthy, Luce. I'm swimming every day and eating healthily and—"

"But, Robs... the pills..."

"Don't worry about those. I'm fine. And I swear I won't become a bulimic or anything gross like that. That thing at Skye's... it was a one-time thing. I promise."

Lucy blew out a big breath and reached out to squeeze Robyn's shoulder. "Oh, thank goodness. I was so worried, Robyn... I didn't know what to do! Just promise me you'll be careful with the pills. We need you in tip-top form and that stuff can be—"

"I promise!" Robyn said. "Now, if you want me to stay healthy, you'd better come help me dance off those chips we had for dinner."

"We'll see," Lucy said, her face falling again. "Not really in a dancing mood."

"What happened?" Robyn asked, mentally kicking herself for completely forgetting that Lucy had been upset about something when she came in. "I'm so sorry, Luce. I knew you were down and I meant to ask, but then I got all wrapped up in my silly business. I'm a crap friend."

"No, you're not," Lucy said. "And nothing's wrong. Not really. I just lost my head a little, that's all. Decided I was something special."

"You are *so* special!" Robyn protested. "Who said you

aren't and how do you want me to beat them up?"

Lucy snorted a laugh. "Oh no, you can't beat him up. It was my fault, anyway."

"Him?"

"I completely threw myself at Trent Eisner, and of course he wasn't interested." Lucy shook her head. "I'm mainly just humiliated. What was I thinking?"

"That you're a kick-ass, ultra-gorgeous, up-and-coming rock star and he'd be a fool to pass you by," Robyn declared firmly. "Say it with me now. I am a rock star."

Lucy smiled and shook her head.

"Come on!" Robyn demanded. "I. Am. A. Rock. Star."

"Fine!" Lucy said, giggling. "I am a rock star. Happy now?"

"No!" Robyn declared. "I will only be happy when you go out and dance with me like the hot chick you are, so that Trent Eisner can see exactly what he's missing."

"Okay, deal." Lucy reached out and grabbed Robyn's hand. "Come on."

Robyn took a few steps towards the door. She knew she should just go with Lucy, but... She glanced back at the toilet cubicle. It would be so easy. Then she wouldn't feel so nauseous and she'd be able to properly focus on cheering Lucy up. Just as soon as she got rid of those chips.

"Hey, lady, I need to pee," Robyn said, dropping Lucy's hand, "but I'll be on the dance floor in two minutes and I expect to see you partying like a mad woman when I get there."

"Partying like a mad woman," Lucy said, already looking cheerier. "You got it." Then she ducked out of the Ladies.

As soon as the door was closed, Robyn stepped into the cubicle and lifted the lid of the toilet. Just once more wouldn't be the same as breaking her promise to Lucy. Twice didn't make it a habit after all. It was the exception really. Just once more would be fine.

Just once more.

Toni was buzzing and not just from the alcohol. She was buzzing from touch alone. Drunk on the gentle grazes of Jason's fingers against her bare arms, the warm press of his palm against the small of her back as they'd swayed together in the dark. Thought was no longer part of the equation.

She wasn't sure who had brought up the idea of dancing first. They'd been talking, that was all. And drinking. He'd bought her a rum and Coke to go with his scotch and the bartender had kept the rounds coming. Somehow, they'd ended up here.

It was a mistake. Being like this with him. She knew that.

Her flirtation with Jason had been just for laughs at the start. She hadn't meant it to be more than that. But apart from the flirting, she enjoyed simply talking to him. He adored jazz as much as Toni did and he loved her stories about touring with her granddad when she was small. It had been so nice to have someone to talk to who wasn't a seventeen-year-old girl that she'd found herself seeking him out more and more frequently. Toni liked her bandmates, but five girls together all the time was enough to drive a person mad. Somewhere in between rehearsals and random texts and laughing at each other's embarrassing anecdotes, she and Jason had become proper friends.

And now, here in the sweating lightning storm that was the centre of the dance floor, he was something else entirely.

The music was slow now, the primal beat like a pumping heart thudding around them, echoing the blood that sang in Toni's veins as her eyes locked with his.

"Toni," Jason said, his voice a hoarse whisper under the pulse of the music. "You should go back to the girls. Now."

She knew what he meant. He wanted her to leave before something happened between them.

Part of her wanted to go. To do the smart thing and find Harper and Lucy and drink enough to forget any of this had ever happened. But that part of her wasn't strong enough to stop her speaking.

"I don't want to."

He grabbed her hand and squeezed it hard. He looked down at her so intensely that, for a breathless moment, Toni thought he was going to kiss her right there in front of the world.

Then he turned and strode off the dance floor, pulling her behind him. Moments later, they were alone in a dark, close hallway that smelled of cigarettes and sour drink.

Jason pulled her into the darkest corner. "This is a horrible idea," he breathed.

"I know," Toni replied. "But—"

And then he was kissing her.

Toni sank into the kiss and let herself drown. It was like time had just given up and gone on holiday, leaving the two of them wrapped up in each other, the only citizens of a blind, silent world of sensation.

She had no idea how long they lingered there before the sharp *tick-tack, tick-tack* of high heels on the linoleum floor shattered their sanctuary. Jason pushed her away, sending her stumbling against the wall just as Harper came round the corner.

Harper shot Toni a penetrating, ice-blue look. Toni replied to the silent question with a shrug. Harper had grown on Toni over the last six months. They were almost friends. But she was still the last person on planet Earth who needed to know that Toni had just shared the most amazing kiss of her life with their manager.

"What do you need, Harper?" Jason asked, his voice still a bit hoarse. He cleared his throat and tried again. "Everyone okay out there?"

"Ye-ah," Harper replied slowly, clearly still trying to compute exactly what was happening in the dark back halls of Blvd3. "Everyone's great. I was just looking for

Toni, since we hadn't seen her for a while. Iza was worried that she had got herself kidnapped or something."

"Well, here I am, right?" Toni said, trying to hide the fact that she couldn't quite catch her breath. "Quite un-kidnapped. We were just discussing a, um... new..."

"Publicity campaign," Jason jumped in as she floundered for an excuse. "I wanted you girls to take one of the endorsement deals we've been offered, and Toni was arguing against it so loudly I was afraid the whole place would hear. So we found a, er, quieter place to talk."

"Right," Harper drawled, casting a dubious gaze from Toni to Jason. "I'll just let the two of you get back to talking business in an out of the way corner conveniently far away from our friendly neighbourhood paps."

Cheeky witch, Toni thought. She knew. Or she suspected, which might be worse.

"Right, well," Toni said, trying not to sound worried. "You'd better head back. Wouldn't want Iza to think you'd been kidnapped as well."

"Sure," Harper drawled. "You two have fun with your... publicity talk." And with a toss of blonde hair, she was gone.

When the *tick-tack* of Harper's heels had faded into silence, Toni looked up at Jason. She could feel the pull of him, making it impossible for her to look away. She really ought to go after Harper and make sure that she didn't suspect anything, or at least make sure she was sworn to secrecy. But instead Toni reached out and took Jason's hand, guiding it back to her waist. She couldn't resist, couldn't force her brain to think of anything else.

"Now," she whispered. "Where were we?"

8. DREAM + NIGHTMARE

Iza wondered, as she'd done several times in the past couple of weeks, whether LA was meant to look as though it had been constructed by time travellers. Only in this place could buildings that looked straight out of the ancient black and white films her mother loved share the same block with structures that could have been built in ancient Greece and glass towers that might as well have been dropped in by invading aliens from the future. She'd even seen more than one house built to look like a miniature castle.

But standing outside it, Iza thought the Disney Concert Hall was perhaps the strangest and the best of the lot. It somehow looked old and space-age at the same time, like an armoured giant from the future, rising from its resting place beneath the city. Iza could hardly believe that her very first date *ever* was going to be in this hypnotically beautiful building. She could hardly believe she had a date in the first place.

For a moment she wished Luke had picked somewhere that would involve more disgusting-but-helpful tequila, but she shook the thought away. A private tour of a world-famous concert hall from a cute boy was miles better than anything places with tequila shots could offer. If Iza could play a full house at the Hollywood Bowl and not faint on stage (which had been a very real possibility after a few minutes under the burning hot spotlights), she could certainly do this. And then Headmistress Littleton could bloody well kiss her arse.

"Iza."

The sound of her own name startled Iza out of her musings so abruptly that she let out a shriek of surprise.

Oh hell. What was wrong with her? It was only Luke, and here she was screaming like a daft nine year old who'd sneaked into a zombie film. And, as if emitting noises so high-pitched that only dogs could hear them wasn't unattractive enough, she was positive she was now the colour of ripe tomatoes. Perfect. Absolutely the best way to start a first date. Hands down. Perhaps she could manage to sink into the cement below her feet and disappear too.

"Hello to you too," Luke said.

He was trying really hard not to laugh. Less than thirty seconds into their date and he was laughing at her! What was she thinking, coming here? She was Izabella Mazurczak. She didn't go on dates.

Iza considered just legging it, but then a flash of Headmistress Littleton's condescending smile played across the back of her brain. Iza wasn't going anywhere. This date was going to go well, no matter how many colours she turned in the process.

"Um, sorry," Iza said, regaining her grip on the English language. "You startled me."

"Sorry about that," Luke said. "You were communing with the building; I shouldn't have interrupted."

"I wasn't communing, I... Well, yeah, actually, I suppose that's actually a good word for it. It's so beautiful. I've never seen anything like it."

"I love it too. When I'm here for rehearsals, I come outside to eat my lunch, just to look at it. It's almost, like, alive."

"Absolutely," Iza said, amazed. He always knew exactly what she meant, no matter how mental she was being. It was as if they shared a brain, even though they hardly knew each other at all. "Pictures just don't do it justice."

"You haven't seen anything yet!" Luke held out his hand. "Ready?"

Iza reached out and took his hand, letting his long, calloused fingers twine through hers. Yes, she was ready. She was ready for anything.

Luke was right, too. The inside of the hall was even more astounding than the outside. The glowing wood of the stage, the sweeping curves of the ceiling, the jagged beauty of the pipe organ – which Luke said was designed to look like fallen logs.

"I kind of grew up here; my dad was directing the Phil when I was in grade school. I used to do my homework right in this very spot," Luke said a few minutes later. He pulled Iza down to sit beside him in a snug corner of one of the boxes that spread above the stage like wings.

"How did you ever manage to focus on studying with a view like this?" Iza asked.

"I'm probably the only kid in the universe whose parents threatened him with *not* being allowed to practise the violin in order to get him to do his homework," Luke mused. "When I got an A, I was allowed to play on stage in the off-hours."

"You got to play up there?" Iza breathed. "I mean, before now? When you were little? That must have been just... beyond brilliant."

"It was," Luke agreed, grinning. "Wanna try it?"

"No," she exclaimed. "You're not serious. I can actually go down there? I can play the piano on the stage of the Walt Disney Concert Hall?"

"Why not?" he said, his grin growing even wider. "I'll race ya."

"Hey!" she called as he took off across the wing. "I've no clue where I'm going! That's cheating!"

"Then you'd better run faster!" he called over his shoulder.

Iza was glad she'd chosen a pair of soft gold ballet flats to wear today as she pounded up the aisle of the main floor. She was hot on Luke's heels, though she suspected he was deliberately letting her catch up.

He made a grab for her as she ducked past him up the aisle.

"Too slow!" she crowed, darting up the stairs to the stage and half sliding the last few metres to the piano.

She started to play without even thinking, still laughing so hard she could barely see the keys. Her fingers picked out something familiar. Gershwin. The same song she'd played the night she'd met Luke.

The first few notes quietened the giggles that fizzed in her throat. With a single key stroke, you could fill the entire hall with sound. Even the quietest brushes of her fingers produced tones that swelled to fill the space – delicate, effervescent bubbles of sound that burst from her fingers and sparkled around her like crystal.

Suddenly part of her was terribly sad. She loved Crush, but they would never play here. There would never be a moment when she'd hear notes tumble from her fingers and ring around her like this whilst on stage with Crush. But she'd never have had the nerve to play on any kind of stage in front of other people without the girls, much less had the chance to play at the Disney Concert Hall. She couldn't regret being in the band – ever.

Iza didn't realise that Luke had come to sit beside her on the piano bench until she let the last riff roll free, swimming up into the golden wood of the ceiling.

"That was..."

"Incredible," he said softly.

"Yes, it's incredible," Iza said in the same half whisper. It seemed wrong to waste the perfect sonic harmony of the place with words. "This place... it's just incredible."

"No," Luke said, laying one of his big hands over her slender ones. "You're incredible."

Their eyes met, and the quiet that filled the room around them was the most beautiful melody Iza had ever heard.

And then Luke leaned down and pressed his lips to hers.

Robyn thought it was really quite weird that her leg was twitching.

If she hadn't looked down and seen it, jumping rhythmically against the brown vinyl seat of her booth in the 101 Diner, she'd never have known it wasn't sitting still. It was as though her body had consumed *way* too much sugar and forgotten to tell her brain.

She *had* consumed too much sugar, actually – two milkshakes and a green salad without dressing for dinner. It was a wonder she hadn't vibrated right through the damn bench.

She looked up at the clock again. Where the bloody hell was Tomas? They were meant to meet here at half past nine and now it was almost half past ten. In another ten minutes she was leaving. She'd have gone long ago if she wasn't out of pills.

Robyn needed her pills. Desperately. They really helped her to not feel hungry, but even with watching the little she ate, and getting rid of what she shouldn't have eaten, she still was a size away from her goal and the final show was only five weeks away.

Twenty to eleven now. In another five she was definitely leaving. She didn't care about the pills. She really didn't. Tomas Angerman could—

"Robyn, baby, you look wonderful!" Tomas said, dropping into one of the retro seats on the other side of the gold-flecked formica table. "CZ92 really does do wonders, yeah?"

"Yeah," Robyn snapped back. "It does wonders, which is why I've been waiting for more than an hour to get more of it. Where have you been?"

Tomas rolled his eyes. "Being so uptight isn't good for your skin, you know."

He thought she was uptight? Was she uptight? She was. She was worse than uptight, she realised – she was being a right stroppy cow. He was being so sweet and the first thing out of her mouth had been to yell at him for not being punctual.

"I'm sorry, Tomas," Robyn said. "I swear I didn't mean to be such a bitch about it. I just need my pills, you know?"

"I know, beauty," he said, "and I am late; I'm sorry. I got stuck with another client across town."

"No, no," Robyn said. "It's all right. I'm just glad you could meet me on such short notice."

"Anything for you, Robs," Tomas said, smiling at her warmly. "You know that. I would have set up a meet earlier, but I didn't expect you to be running low so soon."

"I've been doubling the dose a bit," Robyn admitted, blushing. "I just... They work so well and I wanted to keep on losing weight despite all the dinners and shows and events and things... the Sprinkles cupcake truck has been at the last FOUR parties we went to, you know and—"

"You needed something stronger," Tomas finished for her. "That's perfectly understandable. I admire your dedication."

"Thanks," she said. She just knew that her face was turning the colour of her hair but she couldn't help it. He must think she was a complete idiot, blushing like she'd never been given a compliment before.

"It's too bad Debra won't pay for anything more aggressive," he said, casually picking up a menu and opening the plastic-covered tri-fold. "I've got something that would do wonders, but DZ thought it was too risky for you."

"There's something better?" Robyn said. "Can I try it? I don't care what Debra thinks. I can handle it."

"Oh I know you can," Tomas said, lazily eyeing the dessert section of the menu, "but DZ just won't hear of it."

"Do we have to tell her?" Robyn asked, breathless.

If Tomas had something better than CZ92, she wanted it and she wanted it now.

"You'd want to go behind her back?" Tomas asked, shooting her a considered look over his menu. "Are you sure?"

"I mean, I don't *want* to. I just... I don't want to let her hold me back, do I?" Robyn said tentatively.

She couldn't tell what he was thinking. Did he want her to challenge Debra's wishes? Or would he think her too eager? She was being too eager. She really was. What kind of person was this excited about super-strength diet pills?

But then a broad smile spread across his face. Robyn let out her held breath. He didn't think she was bonkers after all.

"I should have known you were hardcore," Tomas said.

"I'm up for anything, as long as it works," Robyn said, straightening up a bit at the thought that Tomas Angerman thought she, Robyn Miller, was hardcore.

Tomas's face fell. "Wait, I've just thought of something. If Debra isn't going to know about this, she can't pay for it."

"Are they expensive?" Robyn asked, praying the answer would be no though she knew it would be yes.

"Sadly," Tomas said. "You get what you pay for. Cliché but true."

"Oh," Robyn sagged in disappointment. "I suppose I'll just take some CZ92 then."

"Such a shame," Tomas said, reaching out to squeeze her hand again. "I'd love to see what the good stuff could do for you, but I suppose we'll have to stick with the CZ92. Unless..."

"Unless?" Robyn breathed, quite literally on the edge of her seat.

"I might have a way we could finance you getting some of my best product, and without Debra or my suppliers being any the wiser."

"What is it?" Robyn asked eagerly. "I'll do anything, well, almost anything. Not *anything*, anything, obviously. I'm not going to do anything illegal or—"

"Don't worry," Tomas said soothingly. "You don't have to do anything shady at all. Just get me on the list for the parties and events you girls do. I'll handle the rest."

"But how will that help finance the new pills?" Robyn asked.

"I'll sell a ton at those events. I can charge all the drunk rich people double. My suppliers only care about being paid, they don't care where the money comes from," Tomas said. "They'll have the cash they want, that's all that matters."

"Really?" Robyn asked, barely hearing anything outside of the fact her pills would be paid for. "It's that easy?"

"It is," Tomas said, fishing a blue plastic pill bottle out of his pocket. "In fact, you can take these right now if you promise you'll help me out later."

"Of course I will!" Robyn said, reaching for the bottle.

"You're amazing, Tomas. Thank you so, so much!"

"Anything for you, darling," he said. "Go ahead."

He pushed her water glass closer to her as she fished one of the square yellow pills from the bottle. It looked powerful, Robyn thought, even just sitting in her palm. She lapped the pill up and swallowed it greedily.

"That's my girl," Tomas said. "That's my girl."

All Lucy ever seemed to be able to do at Skye Owen's house was get lost. She would freely admit that if she'd just stay put and enjoy herself, she wouldn't end up in these situations. Doing that was impossible, though, when Rafe and Harper were determined to win the grossest-couple-who-aren't-actually-a-couple-and-are-also-right-in-front-of-his-actual-girlfriend award.

It wouldn't be so bad if the other girls were there, but Iza was on her date with Luke and Robyn was off on some mysterious errand. Toni had come along, but she was so oddly distant today that she couldn't even properly be considered company.

Lucy had practically bashed Robyn over the head with hints that she'd rather go with her than go back to Skye's, but Robyn seemed to have missed them all. Either that or she was doing something she didn't want Lucy to know about.

Stop being such a mother hen, Lucy, she told herself, *and focus on working out where in the world you are*. She'd made it back to the guest suite easily enough this time, so she had her iPod, restocked by Alexander that morning, and her mobile. Now all she needed to do was find a quiet spot to hole up and wallow.

Her iPhone buzzed insistently. John was sending her pictures he'd taken at Emily's ballet performance. It was the closest Lucy had come to actually being part of the family in weeks. She was dying to look at the next picture but she had to work out where she was first.

God knows what she'd stumble upon today. After last time, she wouldn't be surprised to find that Skye's mum had the lost treasure of the Incas stashed in one of her cupboards.

Finally, Lucy turned a familiar corner and found herself in the family room. She didn't bother turning on lights, she just plopped down on the couch, plugged in her ear buds and opened her latest text from John – a picture of Emily wearing her ballet shoes like elephant ears and pulling a silly face for the camera. The text said,

We miss you, sis.

Lucy swiped at a tear. She was such a brat, Emily. If Lucy were home, Emily wouldn't give her a moment's peace. But she wasn't at home, and apparently she was actually crazy enough to miss being nagged, told on and generally followed about like she was under surveillance.

Lucy wiped her face again. She wasn't going to get caught crying. Not here. Switching to a happier track on her iPod, she stared out at the starlit hills beyond the dreadful faux-log fence that Mrs Owen had installed around the garden.

It's worth it, she reminded herself. *Even if Mum and Dad never speak to you again, Crush is worth it.*

But was it really?

She'd learned so much, already. No one could deny that. She'd spent part of every afternoon for the last few weeks in special studies with Alexander. They'd worked on her drums – the drum lines on all of the tracks were so vastly better it was hard to believe she'd ever played them any differently – but most of the time they talked about musical history or went to visit musicians he knew and listened to them play. Alexander was even teaching her to play the piano, because he thought it was a basic skill every musician should have.

Lucy hated to admit it, but she'd learned a lot from Debra Z as well. It had been positively humiliating at first, but after two weeks of flailing about, she'd acquired the ability to construct outfits that Debra almost approved of. Lucy couldn't really see the difference between the outfits Debra liked and the ones she didn't, but she could feel the difference when she wore them – a little extra dose of electricity simmered through her, sparking off the people she met and highlighting every step she took.

She felt like a different person now. A better one. But the band...

They'd been so brilliant last night. They'd had the entire Hollywood Bowl on its feet. But this morning's rehearsal had been a disaster. Robyn had been so jittery she'd barely made it through a song. Iza had been daydreaming as much as she'd been playing. Harper and Toni had spent the entire morning shooting vicious glares at each other, especially after Ash had told them Jason wouldn't be stopping by the studio that day. For a while, Lucy had been afraid they'd come to blows.

It was just a bad day, she reassured herself. They'd had bad days before. They'd have them again. But Crush would be brilliant again tomorrow. They had to be. Growing and changing and being an awesome drummer with a sense of fashion was great, but it wasn't worth it without her friends.

If only Alexander wasn't leaving. He was going to be gone for five weeks touring with his own band. She would miss him dreadfully, but he'd done his job. They had laid down a fantastic EP, all recorded and ready to go if Crush won *Project Next*. He was a producer, after all – it wasn't up to him to see to it that their gigs went well or that Lucy kept up her musical studies. That was *their* job, and she was sure Crush could handle it as long as they stuck together. Maybe that was why this day was setting Lucy's teeth on edge. Today, for the first time in a long time, Crush didn't feel like they *were* in it together at all.

So why did she have such a dreadfully bad feeling about it?

Light abruptly flooded the room.

Lucy looked up to find the gardener she wished she

hadn't seen kissing Skye the last time they'd visited, standing in the doorway and clutching a beaten-up laptop.

"I'm so sorry," he said, blushing. "I thought all the guests were out on the patio. I would never have come in otherwise."

"No, no, please. No worries. I am meant to be out there but I needed to check a text from my brother and... I should head back, though, so I'll be out of your way."

"Oh, you're not in my way. Skye lets me work back here sometimes when I'm done outside. But I don't want to—"

"What are you working on?" Lucy said. "I mean on the laptop. Not the garden, obviously. Though the garden *is* beautiful," she added, hoping she didn't sound totally mental.

"You don't have to ask," he replied, setting the old laptop on the coffee table.

"I know. And you don't have to tell me, if you don't want to. I'm just curious, that's all," Lucy added, trying not to sound as awkward as she felt. "Besides, if you tell me about it, I won't have to go back out there for a few more minutes."

He laughed. "Okay... Lucy, right?"

"Oh, right, sorry, I'm so rude! Yes, I'm Lucy. Lucy Gosling."

"Cesar Delgado," he said, extending a hand to shake. "And you're talking to me like a normal person. You're not rude."

"People don't normally talk to you?" Lucy asked, shocked. "Really?"

Cesar shook his head. "And the fact that it surprises you makes me like you even more, Lucy Gosling."

"Thank you... I suppose," Lucy said. "Does that mean you're going to answer my question properly now?"

He flipped open the laptop. "It's a screenplay. I know, I know, I'm a walking Hollywood cliché. But I can't help it. I love to write. I can't stop, even when I'm working in the yard or whatever. When I've got a new idea, my brain is always in the story."

"I know the feeling," Lucy said. "I get that way when I'm working on a new beat. What is it about? Your screenplay, I mean."

"I have a couple of things I'm working on," Cesar said, "but this one is about my family. The story of how they came here from El Salvador. My older brother almost died. So did my father. It's called *Crossing Over.*"

"Wow," Lucy replied. "That's incredible. How far along are you?"

"It's done, actually," he replied. "I'm just making some changes that Skye suggested. She's done a ton to help me, you know," he added, almost defensively.

"That's cool," Lucy said, hiding her surprise that stuck-up Skye would spend hours reading her gardener's screenplays. Even if she was sleeping with him. "I'd love to read your work sometime. When it's done, I mean. It sounds fascinating."

"It is." Skye's voice cut through the room like a sliver of ice. "Which is why we're keeping it under wraps, right, C?"

Cesar shot Lucy an apologetic look.

"It's nothing to get intense about, Skye. Lucy can read it when I'm finished. It's fine."

Skye was intense all right, and at that moment she looked like she intensely wanted to slaughter Lucy.

"Er, great," Lucy said. "You know, I think I need to get back to the girls. They're probably looking for me. Lovely to meet you, Cesar."

Then she fled.

Lucy made it as far as the living room. She was just a few steps from the door to the patio when she heard a voice call out.

"Lucy!"

Damn. Skye had followed her.

Lucy turned back to face Skye, who still looked murderous. What was this girl's issue, anyway? Was she really worried that Lucy was going to steal her gardener's film idea?

"Hi, Skye," Lucy said, trying to sound casual. "What's up?"

Skye deliberately stalked into Lucy's personal space.

"Stay away from Cesar," she hissed.

"What?" Lucy said, baffled.

"You heard me," Skye said. "Cesar is not on the market, so go find some other guy to hit on."

"Hit on? Lucy said, reeling at the sudden turn of the conversation.

"You can have a zillion other guys, Lucy, but not that one."

"Fine," Lucy said, holding her hands up in a placatory way.

Skye was being such a cow that Lucy was tempted not to be reassuring, but she looked so miserable at the idea that Cesar might be interested in another girl that Lucy couldn't help but feel sorry for her.

"I wasn't trying to flirt with Cesar; I just happened to be in there checking my texts when he came in with his laptop. I asked him what he was working on because I was actually curious about it, not because I was trying to flirt."

Lucy could almost see Skye's muscles unwinding from attack mode. "Really? You really just wanted to read it? Just... because?"

"It sounded interesting and he seems nice. Why is that such a surprise?"

"I... I'm sorry." Skye dragged a hand through her hair, suddenly looking like just another insecure teenage girl, rather than her haughty Hollywood Princess self. "I just... Sorry."

Skye turned to walk back up the hallway.

She really loves him, Lucy thought. As impossible as it seemed, Skye Owen hadn't just been snogging her gardener for a cheap thrill. She was in love.

"Skye?"

"Yeah?" Skye said, turning back.

"If you love Cesar that much, why are you still with Rafe?"

Skye just stared at Lucy for a long beat.

"Is it that obvious?" Skye asked finally.

"No," Lucy said, "but you don't seem like the type to go ballistic over another girl talking to a guy you're only messing around with."

"You saw us?"

"I didn't mean to," Lucy said quickly, "and I haven't said anything to anyone. But really, if you've got a sweet, smart and – let's be honest, hot – guy like Cesar, what on Earth do you want with Rafe?"

"You wouldn't understand," Skye said, still wary. "Just please don't tell Harper. You know she'll rat me out."

"Would that be so bad? Cesar... I mean, I only talked to him for a few minutes, but compared to Rafe... I just don't get it," Lucy said.

"You don't need to get it," Skye snapped, her hard shell of Skye Owen-ness falling abruptly back into place. "It's none of your business, Lucy. Just stay out of it."

Then Skye stormed off, leaving Lucy alone in the living room.

Outside she could hear Toni and Harper arguing loudly while Rafe sang something off-key, banging away on the strings of Toni's guitar without even bothering to try to form notes.

The pocket of her jeans buzzed. Lucy fished out her iPhone and checked the text. It was from Robyn.

> **Totally out of it and no money for cab. Can someone give me a lift?**

It's just a bad day, Lucy tried to remind herself. *That's all.* Tomorrow would be a better one. It had to be.

9. NO ONE TO SAVE ME

The acoustics at The Echo were so bad that Lucy could hardly hear Harper over the clatter of her own drums and the misaligned screech of Toni's amp. The cave-like room was only half full and most of the crowd were milling about at the bar in the corner rather than watching the stage. Not that Lucy blamed them. Tonight's set had been awful. Just like the set before it and the set before that.

Lucy crashed her sticks down into her last roll, letting the beat drop out as Toni sang the final line of 'Soft' with Harper. They were out of tune. Great.

Applause smattered and then died as the murmur of bored voices rose to overtake it.

Harper stomped off stage, followed by Toni, Iza and Robyn, who stumbled going down the uneven steps and nearly fell on her face.

Lucy stayed at the drums for a moment, listening to her own heart breaking.

Everything had been so fantastic before the Hollywood Bowl, but since then Crush had got worse and worse with every passing gig.

Lucy felt more alone than ever. It was like her bandmates had been abducted and secretly replaced by malfunctioning robots. Lucy wouldn't be at all surprised if one of them simply crumbled into a pile of smoking mechanical parts on one of these disastrous nights.

She finally got up and followed the other girls.

"We're doomed," Harper moaned. She slunk over to one of the grim duct-taped chairs in the backstage nook that had been labelled their dressing room, then wrinkled her nose and retreated before her white mini touched the greasy vinyl seat.

"Not only are we stuck playing The Echo for the fourth time in two weeks, the show's producers aren't even bothering to film our gigs any more and the freaking audience isn't even listening!' Harper continued. 'And I can't blame them! We SUCKED. You were totally off, Robs, and don't even get me started on how many intros you missed, Toni. Seriously, how can you not remember the melody line to 'I'll Cross the World'? How many times have we played that song?"

Lucy couldn't tell whether her headache was due to Harper's shouting or due to an extreme case of déjà vu. She knew where this was heading – the same place they always ended up after a show these days. A fight.

"It might help if you could stay in tune," Toni snarled.

"I wasn't the one out of tune, you crazy—"

Harper's jibe was cut off by Robyn diving for the nearest bin and vomiting violently.

"Robs, are you okay?" Lucy said, kneeling to hold Robyn's hair away from her face and trying not to gag at sound of retching.

"The screech of our instruments clashing obviously made her sick," Harper snapped.

Toni looked from Robyn back to Harper and her eyes narrowed. "You insensitive bi—"

"Oi!" Lucy hollered, cutting them off before they did each other actual damage. "Robyn is ill and we're still in the venue. Stop behaving like children and help me with her, will you? Iza, put your bloody mobile away and get Robyn something cold to drink. Luke will understand if you wait more than thirty seconds to reply to a text."

Iza paled, as though it was the first time she'd noticed Robyn vomiting right in front of her. Lucy shook her head as the pianist scurried off. She was glad Iza was happy, but she was so wrapped up in her new boy that she'd been useless in the past few weeks. And Lucy could have done with Iza's help - keeping Harper and Toni's inexplicable feud from going nuclear had been a full-time job. And that was on top of Robyn completely losing the plot.

"If Jason were here," Harper noted, ice trailing through her words, "we would have a real dressing room and a production assistant to help us. Wait. No. That's not true. If Jason were on the case, WE WOULDN'T BE HERE AT ALL BECAUSE WE'D HAVE A REAL GIG!"

"He isn't here, so there's no point in screaming about it, is there?" Toni snapped back.

"Oh, there's a point. Whose fault do you think it is that all of a sudden our manager's dumb-ass assistant is booking all of our gigs and we've fallen so far off the radar that they've taken one of our camera crews and given it to Dead Kitten Mambo?"

"Given that I am the only one interested in booking gigs for you ladies these days, you might want to be nicer to me," Ash said dryly as he pushed through the door from the venue into the backstage area. He helped Lucy hoist Robyn into a chair. "Jason promoted me to coordinator, remember?"

"Right," Robyn said, shaking her head like a wet puppy. "Be nice to Ash, Harper. He's a lovely boy and he's doing his best to help us. It's not his fault he isn't that bright."

"Are you okay, Robyn?" Ash asked, ignoring her slurred chatter.

"I'm fine," Robyn said, waving off his concern. "A few too many cocktails, that's all."

"Good," Ash said, his tone flat. "I'll get started loading up the equipment."

He turned on his heel and left.

Great, thought Lucy. Now they'd alienated Ash as well. Just want they needed.

Iza returned with a bottle of water, a wet bar towel

folded into a compress and a mini bag of pretzels.

"Sorry," she said breathlessly. "I had to beg for something that even resembled food."

"You've got to stop this, Robs," Harper said, taking the compress and applying it to the back of Robyn's neck. "We can't have you nearly collapsing all the time on stage. It's not good for the band."

"It's not good for *you* either," Lucy said, shooting Harper a look.

"Well, yes, that too," Harper agreed. "I know you think you need to lose weight, or whatever, but you also have to eat. You know that."

"I'm fine!" Robyn said, her voice already clearer after a handful of the pretzels. She took the compress from Harper and nudged her away. "I'm fine. You guys worry too much."

"Well, excuse me for trying to help," Harper snapped. "Whatever. Don't we have another party to get to? At Darkroom? I'm going to find Rafe and Skye and we'll meet you there."

"Oh sure, you just run off with Rafe. Leave us to load up all on our own. Again," Toni said. "That's fine, Harper. We don't need you anyway."

"Hey, it's not my fault we're here at this dive. *You* know whose fault that is," Harper threw back at her.

What the bloody hell was she on about? Lucy knew that Harper somehow blamed Toni for Jason's inattentiveness of the last few weeks. Without him, Crush had gone from the *Project Next* favourite, making waves at the Hollywood Bowl, to last place on the internet polls, playing the same crummy gigs. Something had happened, and they clearly knew what, but Lucy hadn't been able to get an explanation out of Harper or Toni.

"Why do you keep putting it all on Toni?" Iza asked, her voice quivering. "It's not Toni's fault that Jason's abandoned us."

More to the point, Lucy thought, *why isn't Toni denying it?*

"*She* knows why," Harper snapped.

"Shut it, all right?" Toni hurled back. "And you stay out of it, Iza. You can just go back to texting your boring boyfriend and pretending you care about the band."

"I do care..." Iza's voice broke. She scrubbed tears from her eyes. "I do care," she whispered again, though Lucy could barely hear her over Harper.

"See, now you've made Iza cry, you witch. I wish I'd never let you join my band. You've ruined *everything*!"

Toni was practically trembling with rage. "What do you care about the band being ruined? You've got what you wanted, haven't you? You've wormed your way back into Rafe Jackson's life. Why don't you go cry to him? A touch of sympathy might be just what you need to finish stealing him from right under his girlfriend's nose."

"Oh don't worry," Skye Owen's sharp voice cut in. "She won't be stealing anyone."

Lucy's stomach dropped like a stone. Skye and Rafe

were standing right behind them all, and they'd clearly heard every unfortunate word of Toni's vicious little speech. Skye was practically glowing with rage.

"I can't *believe* you just said that!" Harper shrieked at Toni. "I can't believe... after what *you've* done... How do you have the *nerve*?"

"It's the truth, isn't it?" Toni snapped back, without a hint of apology.

"What's the truth?" Skye snapped. "That Harper is trying to seduce Rafe and doesn't care that she's doing it right in front of me because she's an evil slut? Did you think I hadn't noticed?"

"Babe," Rafe said, looking a little panicked in the face of his furious girlfriend. "That's not true at all. Harper and I are just friends, you know that."

Lucy could feel Harper tense beside her at the words 'just friends'.

Please, Harper, Lucy prayed silently. *Please don't say anything foolish right now. Please.*

"You know what?" Skye said to Rafe, voice still snapping with anger. "We're going home. I've had enough of your *friends* tonight."

"Don't you want to go to the party, babe?" Rafe wheedled. "I think we should go. We'll all feel better after a nice round of shots."

"No," Skye said firmly. "We won't because we are going home. Now."

Then she turned and marched away.

Rafe shot Harper an agonised look. "I'm sorry, Harp. I gotta go. I... I'll call you."

Then he turned and dashed after Skye.

When they were gone, Harper rounded on Toni, eyes flashing and looking like she was about to punch Toni in the face.

Lucy reached for Harper's arm. "Harper, come on. Let's pack up. We can talk about this when we get home."

"No, we'll talk about it right now," Harper said.

Toni snapped. "Finally. It's about time that we stopped pretending you weren't using us to get Rafe back."

"Oh?" Harper hissed. "Is it? Then maybe it's also time to stop pretending that you haven't ruined our chances completely by hooking up with our *married* manager."

Toni's face went white so quickly and completely that Lucy was afraid the bass player would faint.

So that was it, thought Lucy. That was the missing piece that made it all make sense. Jason's disappearance. Toni and Harper's arguing. All of it.

"You... and Jason?" Iza said, staring at Toni. "You actually..."

"Yes, actually," Harper snapped. "I interrupted them at Blvd3 after the Hollywood Bowl. Our last decent gig, if you'll remember."

"You didn't see—" Toni tried to say, but Harper cut her off.

"I didn't have to see. It was obvious. And it should have been obvious to the rest of you. Why else would

Jason drop us just when we were really taking off?"

"The hard work was done," Iza said. "That's what Ash said. Ash said Jason always passes easy stuff off to him. Always."

"Ash wishes," Harper said, shaking her head in disgust.

"I..." Toni was crying now, fat, awful tears running black streaks of mascara down her cheeks. "I didn't know..."

"You didn't know he was married?" Harper snarled. "You ruined our chances because you're too much of a moron to use Google, or pay attention to anyone but yourself. He called his wife three times a night when he was out with us. You really are the blindest, deaf—"

Before Harper could finish, Toni turned and fled.

Lucy was going to be sick. She'd known something was wrong. She'd seen the texts, noticed the flirting... but she hadn't thought it was anything serious. And now... now it was too late.

"So what are we going to do?" Robyn asked quietly. She'd been so silent, sitting in the low, cracked chair with her bottle of water and her bag of pretzels that Lucy had almost forgotten she was there. "We can't just give up because Toni snogged the wrong bloke."

"What can we do?" Iza said, near tears. "Without Jason..."

"We've still got Harper," Robyn said. "Harper got us to Los Angeles, she'll get us to Las Vegas as well. Right, Harp?"

Lucy turned to Harper, desperately hoping to see the familiar, diabolical light of a plan being hatched behind her best friend's eyes. But Harper looked as lost as Lucy felt.

"Right," Harper said, with enough assurance that Lucy thought the others might believe it. "Of course I will. I always think of something, don't I?"

"And thinking is best accomplished whilst relaxing," Robyn said, grabbing Iza's hand and hauling herself to her feet. "Which means we need to find a nice drink and a loud dance floor, in that order. We'll all feel better after a good, happy night."

"I don't know," Iza said. "Maybe we should find Toni. She was really upset."

"No," Harper said, straightening up. "Robyn's right. Toni needs to sulk and we need to have a good time and forget about this craptastic gig. Right, Robs?"

"Right!" Robyn declared, hooking her arm through Harper's. "Let's do it!"

Lucy trailed the others out to the SUV, her brain racing. Robyn and Iza might be fooled by Harper's bravado, but Lucy knew better. This time, Harper McKenzie didn't have a plan. She hadn't got a clue how to save Crush.

If something was going to be done, Lucy would have to do it herself.

Robyn hesitated just inside the heavy double doors of Darkroom. She hoped she could talk the bouncer into letting Tomas through, but what if she couldn't? She didn't want to have go to Harper for help. She was sure Harper was beginning to suspect that Tomas wasn't just showing up at all the Crush shows and parties lately to cheer Robyn on.

Not that Tomas was Harper's biggest concern at the moment. Robyn couldn't believe that Toni had actually been seeing Jason. No wonder their manager had been making like the Invisible Man lately. Robyn had been terrified that the others wouldn't go for the idea of relaxing at Darkroom after Toni and Harper's blow-up. But it was a good plan for them all to relax, even if it had just been an excuse to get her there in time to meet Tomas. They needed some fun after these weeks of disaster. Maybe now that everything was out in the open, life in Crush House would settle down again and things would go back to normal. She really hoped so.

Perhaps she should just text Tomas and make some excuse for why she couldn't get him in. Then she could focus on helping Harper brainstorm ways to dig them out of last place on *Project Next*. It would be nice to have a night with just the girls for once. Robyn had missed that since they'd come to LA. When they'd still been just *Project Next* hopefuls back home, a lot of nights had been spent that way. Just the five of them, chilling out together, planning their destiny.

The big double doors swung open and Tomas strolled in.

"There you are, beautiful," he said in his liquid Swedish accent. "I was beginning to worry."

"I'm sorry, Tomas," Robyn said, straightening up and sucking in her stomach as she followed him to a dim corner of the club's entry hall. She didn't want him to see how bloated those pretzels had made her. "I was just going to speak to the bouncer."

"No worries," Tomas said smoothly. "It's handled. I had to slip him a hundred but that's cool. We'll put it on your tab."

Robyn swallowed back a protest. It seemed like her 'tab', as Tomas liked to call it, got bigger all the time.

"Don't look so glum," Tomas chided her, tickling her gently under the chin. "I'm not upset. We're going to have a fantastic time tonight."

He pulled the red canvas pouch he kept his drugs in from an inner pocket of his soft white jacket and set to sorting through it, pulling free little ziplock bags of pills.

Robyn's stomach flopped hard against her ribs. The sight of the little red bag out in public always made her edgy, particularly when Tomas was officially a guest of Crush.

"Just be careful," Robyn said, trying not to sound too much like a nervous schoolgirl. "Security is pretty tight. If you get caught... and you're a guest of Crush..."

"It's cool, babe," Tomas said. "I'm like a ninja; no one will even know I'm here. And if they stop me, I'll just tell them I'm here with the band. They won't bother me."

"But if they search you..."

"They won't," he said. He pressed a quick kiss to her mouth and dropped a bright green pill into her hand. "We've been doing this for weeks, Robs, and everything has been fine, hasn't it? Now go, have another round and drop this in it. It'll help you relax and get ready to tear up that dance floor with me."

Then he was gone.

Robyn stared at the pill. She shouldn't take it. After all, she'd no idea what it was. But if she didn't, Tomas would think she was turning uptight on him. She didn't want that.

Besides, he wouldn't give her anything bad. The little pink pills had worked well and the square yellow ones had worked like rocket fuel. The weight was just falling away. She'd be at her goal in a week, tops. When the final came around, she'd be exactly the person she'd always dreamed she'd be when she walked on stage. And it was all thanks to Tomas.

She would take it, she decided, closing her fingers over the pill. Then Tomas would see what a rock star she really was.

Harper let the pounding music fill her brain and clear her mind. Maybe then she'd be able to find a way out of this mess.

"Harper!"

Harper decided to ignore Robyn and keep dancing.

She needed to think. So far she had no clue how she was going to save Crush – and she *was* going to save Crush. Somehow. She had to. If she didn't, she'd have officially ruined Lucy's life for nothing and Lucy would never forgive her. As it was, Lucy had barely spoken to Harper since the big fight at The Echo, and she'd disappeared as soon as they'd arrived at Darkroom.

She'd make it up to Lucy. All she had to do was come up with a way to send Crush from last place to first place in the three weeks they had left. She could do that, if only she could just think.

But instead of spinning a crafty plot to rescue the band from the bottom of the *Project Next* barrel, her brain kept drifting back to Rafe. He'd texted her a few minutes before.

So, you're into stolen goods now, hmm? :)

Clearly, he wasn't all that upset by the thought that she might be trying to steal him back from Skye. In fact, she thought he'd looked pleased when Toni had blurted it out in front of everyone. Of course, he'd also given in when Skye had thrown her little temper tantrum and insisted on him taking her home, but that text... that text said he was ready and waiting to be stolen.

But she didn't need to be thinking about Rafe right now. She didn't even *want* to be thinking about Rafe, which surprised her. She wanted to figure out how she was going to turn Crush's sinking ship around and win *Project Next.*

But then Harper realised with a start that she didn't have to save Crush. If Rafe was actually hers to steal, as he seemed to be, then she didn't really need Crush any more. She had what she'd come back to Los Angeles for.

But somehow, Crush had become more than just a means to an end. It was just as important to her as Rafe was. Maybe even more important. She'd started out to get Rafe back, but in the process she'd built a really awesome band. She'd done it all on her own. The others would never have started playing together if she hadn't begged, tricked and cajoled them into it. She'd done something kind of amazing, she thought, and not even realised it.

"Har-per!" Robyn called again. "Come dance with me."

Harper sighed. It wasn't as though she was having any luck thinking deep thoughts anyway. She might as well go and calm her drunken bandmate.

Harper turned to see Robyn dancing on one of the low tables beyond the velvet-roped VIP section that lined the far side of the black-tiled dance floor. Iza was watching her from their corner sofa, looking as though she couldn't decide whether to laugh or be super-nervous about the whole thing.

"Table dancing?" Harper asked, crossing to perch on the hard grey sofa beside Iza. "Seriously?"

"Yes!" Robyn said. "Definitely!"

She was going to bounce right through the table if she wasn't careful.

"Robs, come down here," Harper called. "You're going to fall otherwise."

"I think she looks beautiful," a gooey voice purred in Harper's ear.

Ugh. Tomas Angerman was here.

Harper was pretty sure Tomas was her least favourite person in the world. And that was saying something, considering that he shared a planet with Skye Owen.

"Tomas!" Robyn chirped, half diving off the table into his arms. Soon her tongue was halfway down his throat. Gross.

"We have an ice bucket," Harper said, trying to convey her total disapproval in her flat tone. "Don't make me use it."

"Give it up, Harper," Iza said. "They're not on the same planet we are at the moment."

"Are too," Robyn said, coming up for air. "I just needed a proper greeting. I missed him!"

"You walked in with him, like, twenty minutes ago," Harper said, rolling her eyes and reaching for the carafe of cranberry juice in the bottle service caddy. "You really are wasted."

"Wasted on luuuuuuuvvvv," Robyn wheezed, giggling as she collapsed onto the sofa beside Tomas.

Tucking Robyn against his side, Tomas pulled out a roll of cash bigger than Harper's fist and started counting.

"Wow," Iza said. "That's a ton of money."

Tomas simply smiled. "I did well tonight."

Robyn actually cooed.

"You made all that tonight?" Harper said, trying to ignore the saccharine fest. "How?"

"I provide certain substances that improve the party spirit," Tomas said, still counting.

"Excuse me?" Harper snapped, straightening up in her chair. "Are you trying to tell me you're a drug dealer?"

"I provide recreational enhancements," Tomas corrected.

"And you used Crush's name to get into this club to do it?" Harper added, glaring at Robyn. It wasn't doing any good. Robyn was too busy cuddling against Tomas to notice or care.

"Drugs?" Iza said, wide-eyed. "You made all that money tonight selling drugs?"

"No, I made it selling Pokemon cards." Tomas kept counting.

"Have you been dealing at all the parties Robyn's brought you to?" Harper demanded, dividing her best death stare between Robyn and Tomas. Tomas just grinned back and didn't answer. Robyn ducked her head and reached for her drink to avoid Harper's gaze.

"How can that be safe?" Iza asked. "Aren't you afraid to walk around with all that cash and, um, stuff?"

"Nah," Tomas said, separating the bills into several smaller piles. "I know how to protect myself."

"He's got a..." Robyn leaned forwards and stage-whispered, "... gun."

"What?" said Iza, her eyes wide.

"Robs," Tomas said, "you're not supposed to tell anyone about that."

"You're armed?" Harper said, incredulous.

"Only when I'm carrying this much cash or product," Tomas said, casually tucking his folds of cash into various pockets. "It's the practical thing to do."

He looked Harper in the eye. "Don't worry, I know what I'm doing. Robyn is totally safe with me."

"You think?" Harper asked.

If this guy thought he was going to use her friends like this, he had better be prepared for a surprise. Harper might not have a clue how to salvage her band, or get her best friend to speak to her again or make the boy she loved admit he loved her back, but she *could* do something about Tomas Angerman.

"Iz," Harper said, turning to smile brightly at Iza. "You wanna dance?"

"Yes!" Iza said, sounding super-relieved to get away from Tomas. She bounced to her feet and held a hand out to Harper.

"No," Harper said. "I've got something to discuss with Tomas first. But Robs will come with you now, and I'll be there in a minute."

"No, Robs bloody well *won't* go with her," Robyn protested. "Robs is happy where she is."

"Just go, Robyn," Harper said. "Tomas and I need to talk."

"Its fine," Tomas told Robyn, eyeing Harper curiously. "Go."

"Whatever," Robyn pouted. She rolled to her feet and grabbed Iza's hand, pulling her towards the dance floor.

"You have something to ask me?" Tomas said, after Robin and Iza were gone.

"Not ask," Harper said. "Tell. I have something to *tell* you."

"I'm listening."

"You'd better be, because if you're not, you're going to regret it."

Tomas took a pull of Robyn's abandoned drink. "Am I really?"

"You have no idea how much," Harper assured him. "You've had your fun with Robyn. You've made a few bucks. But that's over now."

Tomas burst out laughing. "No, I assure you, it's not. I intend to have a long, close friendship with Robyn. And with Crush."

"Then prepare to be disappointed," Harper shot back, "because if I see you around Robyn, or I catch you using Crush's name for anything ever again, I will destroy you."

"You think you can do that?" Tomas said with a condescending smile.

"Let me tell you a little story, Tomas. When my ex-boyfriend broke up with me last year because he was moving to LA for university, I considered getting over him. Then I decided that I didn't want to. So you know what I did? I formed a band, wrote a whole album's worth of songs, made a demo, became a *Project Next* finalist and soon, very soon, I'm going to win *Project Next* and I'm going to be the kind of rock star who can have any man she chooses. Including the ex-boyfriend. So, Tomas, don't underestimate what I can do to get what I want."

Tomas just raised a pale eyebrow.

Harper raised one right back.

Tomas burst out laughing.

"You've got a lot of self-esteem, don't you?" he said. "But it takes more than a little girl making threats to scare me."

"What about a reality television star shouting 'gun' in a packed club?" Harper asked. "I'm sure you don't want to have a conversation with security about the concealed weapon you're carrying. Or all that cash."

"You wouldn't," Tomas growled. "Crush would be all over the news for being with a drug dealer in a club. You don't want that."

"Crush would be all over the news for pointing out a dangerous, armed dealer in a club," Harper said firmly.

"I'll tell everyone Robyn's on drugs."

"I'll tell everyone you're lying. It'll be great press for Crush, actually. Just enough scandal to make us interesting. In fact, no time like the present..."

Harper turned and strolled over to the bar. When she got there, she waved down the bartender.

"Excuse me," she said, making herself sound flustered. "Excuse me!"

She twisted to point at Tomas, who was already stalking towards her. She grinned at him. This was too easy.

She turned back to the bartender, her voice quavering just enough to make the bartender think she was terrified. "That man, right over there, he's got a—"

Tomas grabbed her arm and pulled her back to face him, irritation glowing from every pore. "Fine, bitch," he hissed. "Have it your way. But you'll regret this."

"Hmm," Harper pretended to consider it. "Will I? Maybe we ought to call security and test that theory."

"Miss?" the bartender said. "Is something wrong?"

Tomas shifted his furious glare to the bartender's direction, but the bartender didn't back down.

"Is this guy bothering you?"

"No." Tomas spat the word out, like it tasted bad. "He isn't. He was just leaving."

He looked back at Harper again. "This isn't over, Harper."

"Yes," Harper said sunnily. "It is."

With that she turned and strode towards the dance floor, making for the flash of Robyn's red hair she could see through the crowd.

That had almost been fun. Shame that figuring out how to give Crush a chance at winning Project Next *won't be as easy as getting rid of our little Tomas problem,*

Harper thought. Crush had fallen apart, and Harper had no clue how to put them back together again.

Lucy stood on the pavement and looked up at the graceful bungalow. The house was old but well kept, surrounded by flowering trees and bordered with fragrant rosemary bushes that crowded around the front door and ran down either side of the flagstone path. It wasn't at all where she'd imagined Jason Darrow would live. The little house in the hills of Silver Lake was beautiful but distinctly cosy. Not at all like the futuristic steel and glass penthouse she'd assumed a Hollywood power player like Jason would call home. But then again, she hadn't believed that Jason would make a pass at a seventeen-year-old client either, until she'd seen the look on Toni's face. There was clearly a great deal they didn't know about Jason Darrow.

But that didn't change the fact that Crush needed him. Badly.

Lucy marched herself up the front path to the little bungalow and rang the doorbell before she had a chance to lose her nerve.

There was no response from the darkened house. Was no one home? No, it was nearly midnight and Jason's car was parked just in front of the house. He was here.

Lucy rang the doorbell again.

This time a light switched on inside. After a few moments, Jason opened the door. He was dressed in trackies and a jumper, but he clearly hadn't been asleep.

"It's the middle of the night, Lucy," he said. "What are you doing here?"

"We had a gig tonight," Lucy said, fighting the urge to apologise. "What are *you* doing here? Why weren't you at The Echo with us? Why haven't you been at a single show since the Hollywood Bowl?"

"Ash had you play The Echo?" he asked. "Again?"

"Yes," Lucy said. She took a deep breath. She couldn't believe she was doing this but someone had to. "We played The Echo. Again. And we blew it. Again. We're a disaster, Jason, and I think you know why."

Jason stepped through the door and closed it behind him. He walked past her and sat down on one of the steps that led up to the porch, gesturing for her to join him.

"Toni told you?" he asked finally.

"No," Lucy said. "Harper figured it out for herself. She and Toni have been at each other like cats and dogs for ages, and tonight it finally came out why. I should have guessed but I didn't think..." She couldn't believe she was saying this. She couldn't believe she'd ever have the nerve to speak to anyone this way, much less their manager. But what did she have to lose? "I didn't think you were that stupid."

Jason stared out at his front garden for a long time. Finally he shook his head. "I didn't think I was that stupid either. I don't know how it happened. It just... did. And then I got even more stupid. I couldn't face Toni so I told myself that Ash could handle you girls. He's been bugging me to promote him for a while. But... I knew he couldn't really handle it. I knew I was letting Crush fall apart. And I knew that Sir Peter wasn't going to miss the fact that it was my fault. He'll fire me and Leah – that's my wife – she'll find out why. I'll be ruined. I can see it coming but... I don't know what to do about it. It's too late."

Lucy tried to think of what to say to the older man. He sounded so forlorn. So helpless. This wasn't what she'd thought she'd find here, although now, sitting with Jason under the luminescent grey of the Los Angeles night sky, she wasn't sure what she'd really thought would happen. But she knew one thing. She couldn't just let him give up.

"I didn't tell my parents that I was joining Crush," Lucy said finally. "Did you know that? I started out hiding it from them, and then... and then we kept getting further and further along on *Project Next* and suddenly I was lying to them all the time. For months. And I didn't know how to tell them. So I did nothing, and the secret just got bigger and uglier. Then they found out on their own and it was awful. They may never speak to me again – all because I didn't do something about my mistake before it was too late. It's not too late for you. You can still do something about this. You can still help us salvage Crush. You're the best, right? You told us so yourself. So prove it. Be the best. Fix this."

Jason didn't respond. He just sat there. He didn't even seem to have heard her.

Finally, Lucy stood and walked back down the path towards the cab that waited for her in the road. She hoped he'd stop her, but he didn't.

Lucy slid into the cab and whispered the Wonderland Avenue address to the driver. It was the loudest she could speak without bursting into tears. She'd been a fool to think she had a hope of talking him into coming back. She wasn't Harper. She couldn't talk people into things. She was just Lucy Gosling. No one ever listened to Lucy Gosling. And now, Crush were doomed because of it.

INTERLUDE: DO OVER

"RISE AND SHINE, CRUSH!"

Jason's voice booming through Crush House startled Lucy so much that she actually fell out of bed. Or rather, off the sofa she'd crashed on after creeping into the house at three a.m. that morning. She'd planned to wait up for Harper so that they could try to sort out what to do next, but she must have fallen asleep.

Now Jason Darrow was standing in the middle of their living room, a camera crew at his back, shouting at the top of his considerable voice.

"OUT OF BED, NOW! WE'VE GOT WORK TO DO."

"What the f—" Harper cut herself off as she peered sleepily over the balcony that ran around the open second floor and saw the cameras. "What the hell, Jason? What are you doing here? It's like... Six o'clock in the morning."

"You girls have a gig in Studio City in five hours and, as I hear it, you need some practice before we get you back on stage," Jason shot back at her. "Get your butt down here, Harper. And the rest of you come with her."

Five minutes later, a very sleepy and very curious Crush were gathered on the living room sofas in front of Jason.

What was he up to? Lucy wondered. She shot a covert glance at Toni, who was sitting as far from Jason as possible, her face sickly pale.

"Now, ladies," Jason said. "I realise that it's been a terrible couple of weeks. I've been... distracted by some personal issues, and I've let you down."

He swallowed hard, and Lucy wondered if the others could see how nervous he really was. But then, just like that, the flash of emotion was gone.

"You have every right to get me fired," he continued, "but I'm hoping that you won't. I may have made a mess of things, but I'm still the best Catch-22 has to offer. And I think we all know Crush need a miracle. I can give you one, if you're willing to accept it."

He was looking at Toni now, hope and sorrow and fear in his eyes. "Will you let me give you your miracle?"

Lucy held her breath and waited for Toni to speak. Jason might have addressed the question to all of them, but everyone knew it was really Toni's to answer.

Finally, Toni nodded. Just once, but it was enough.

"All right then, you ladies better wake up *quick*, because your miracle isn't going to wait for you to have a nice, restful morning," Jason declared.

"A midday gig on a Wednesday doesn't sound like much of a miracle," Harper said.

"It does when it's *The Eva Show* and Eva St Marie herself is naming Crush the new face of Young Women International, which is only the most visible international woman's charity in the world."

"WHAT?!" Robyn cried. "We're going to be on *The Eva Show*? No way. No way. We're going to—"

"Going to blow every other *Project Next* competitor out of the water?" Jason said, smirking. "You bet you are. You girls are going to work harder than you even thought was possible in the next three weeks campaigning for YWI, and when you're done, the world is going to know just how amazing Crush are. Especially after the benefit."

"Benefit?" Lucy asked, letting the excitement that was starting to buzz in her belly grow.

"Oh, did I forget to mention that Crush is throwing the party of the year in three weeks' time, right here in Crush House?" Jason said with deliberate casualness. "You're going to raise a million dollars for YWI, and you're going to have the best damn headlining debut in history while you're at it. *That* is your miracle. You ready to help me make it happen?"

10. It's a miracle

Three weeks later, Robyn tried to look casually sexy as she waited for Tomas to hand his cherry red, classic 1972 Jag over to the valet.

She couldn't believe how fancy Jason's party planner had managed to do up Crush House for the YWI benefit. There was valet parking, a full bar by the pool and a juice bar in the kitchen. Not to mention food trucks from the three hottest restaurants in town parked in the driveway. It was fantastic.

When Jason had promised them a miracle, he'd meant it. The past three weeks had been a blur. Crush had played all over Southern California, and once in New York. They'd been on every talk show there was. They'd even made an advert for Young Women International with Eva St Marie herself.

While their music had improved, they still weren't as good as they'd once been. But that was hardly a surprise

– Harper and Toni still weren't speaking to each other in more than one-word sentences and Iza was always off with Luke when Crush weren't practising, gigging or at an appearance. They were just a band now, and they'd been more than that before. A lot more. If the internet polls on the *Project Next* website were to be believed, being 'just a band' might not be enough, no matter how many TV spots they'd had or how many times 'I'll Cross the World' played on *The Eva Show*. Crush had risen from last place to second, but second wasn't enough – unless a miracle happened, they weren't going to win.

But Robyn forgot all about Crush as Tomas strode across the porch and lifted her off her feet, swinging her around into a full-blown snog before finally putting her back on the ground.

"When did you get so hot, girl?" he demanded.

She felt a bit dizzy, and not just from being swung about. Tomas had kissed her before but tonight he was looking at her as though she were something edible and he was starving. He'd never looked at her quite in that way before. No one had ever looked at her in quite that way before.

Tomas had been totally MIA for weeks, ever since that night at Darkroom. Even so, Crush had been so busy she'd hardly missed him. In fact, it had been a bit of a relief to be out with the girls and not have to worry about Tomas tagging along. But Robyn had run out of pills. She supposed she didn't technically need them any more. She fit into her clothes now. That had been the goal, after all. But... Robyn just *wanted* her pills. She wasn't addicted or anything... they just made her feel better. Besides, Harper would hardly notice him tonight.

"It was easy with your help!" Robyn said, grabbing Tomas's hand and pulling him into the house. "We should run through the camera blind spots before things get really mad in here."

"You've got quite a crowd already," Tomas said, pulling her closer and wrapping his arm around her shoulders as they walked. "I'm impressed."

"This is just the beginning," Robyn crowed. "You should see the guest list. It's going to be epic."

"Good," he said. "My supplier wouldn't be pleased if this was a dud."

He sounds a bit worried, Robyn thought, surprised. *He never sounds worried.*

"What's wrong?" she asked.

"Oh, it's nothing. I just pulled in more product than I could pay for upfront on this one," Tomas said, a nervous edge to his voice. "It'll be totally worth it, but my supplier just called again on the way over, making menacing noises."

"What do you mean by menacing?" Robyn tried not to let the panic show in her voice. It was one thing to have Tomas quietly do a little business at the party, but what if his supplier turned up? She hadn't a clue where Tomas got his drugs, but she could guess that whoever he bought them from wasn't someone Crush wanted turning up at their house.

"No, no." Tomas put a finger under her chin, lifting her eyes to his. "Not to worry, my sweet little Robyn. He just likes to protect his investments. All I have to do is see to it that he gets paid, which should be easy thanks to Crush."

Lucy stood at the mirror that Paulina and the make-up team had set up in the den, now converted into a temporary green room. The others were buzzing about, getting ready, but Lucy couldn't quite seem to tap into their pre-show excitement. She shoved, fruitlessly, at the explosive ponytail that Debra Z had taught her to tie her curls into for shows. Why did Lucy's hair always insist on being just a bit lopsided?

"Lucille!"

It was Alexander. He was back! She couldn't decide if she was relieved or terrified.

"I turn my back on you for a few weeks and you girls decide you have the burning need to become mediocre?" Alexander bellowed as he crossed the den to her corner. "What happened, Lucille?"

Terrified. Definitely terrified.

"I..." Lucy tried to find a way to explain it that wasn't going to get Jason fired and ruin his life. He didn't deserve that, not after working so hard to fix things for them. Finally she gave up. "It's complicated. But I'm glad you're back."

Alexander shook his head. "Why didn't you call me when Jason decided to take his little vacation from sanity and turn you over to Ash?"

"I didn't even think of it, honestly," Lucy confessed. "I just assumed... I mean, your job with us is over. I wasn't sure you'd still..."

"Care?" Alexander snapped. "You weren't sure I'd care? Well, you've got another think coming, Lucille. I put a lot of time and effort into *you*, and I'm not going to let whatever little feud you girls are indulging in ruin it. You are too special to blow your career on teenage melodrama, young lady. What is it? Boys? Drugs? Booze? I've seen too many good musicians go down that way, Lucille. Don't disappoint me and become one of them."

"No, I'd never..." Lucy stuttered. "I mean, there are no drugs. I swear. We're okay, it's just... there's just..."

"Fine." Alexander held up a hand to cut her off. "You don't have to tell me, but you do have to do something about it. Every band has a leader, Lucille. You may sit at the back of the stage, but for Crush that leader is you, whether you know it or not. Harper thinks she's the boss, but that's not what I see when I watch you girls work. If you want to win *Project Next* then *you'd* better fix whatever it is that's broken, you hear me?"

Then he turned and stomped out of the den.

Lucy looked around her at her friends. Toni was standing at the window alone, brooding as usual. Robyn was bouncing at the mirror, messing with her hair and guzzling something clear from a water bottle, but Lucy was willing to bet it was vodka, not water. Harper was in the corner, chatting with Rafe and Skye, completely oblivious to the look of exhausted annoyance on Skye's face. And Iza was in the corner, talking to Luke and ignoring them all. Alexander was right. She had to do something about this. But what?

"Five minutes!" Ash called from the doorway. "We go live in five minutes!"

Whatever she was going to do, she needed to do it now.

"HEY!" Lucy said, as loudly as she dared with a house full of guests just outside the door. "Hey, Crush. Huddle up. NOW!"

"Lucy?" Robyn said, her green eyes puzzled. The others were staring at her as well.

She resisted the urge to dive under the nearest table and hide. Now that she finally had their attention, she had to use it. Alexander was right. Jason might have got them back into the spotlight, but it wouldn't do them any good unless they could be Crush again, rather than the pale imitation of themselves that they'd become.

"This show is either going to set us up to win in Vegas or completely ruin us," Lucy said, trying to keep her voice from shaking as hard as her hands were trembling. "And we're going to blow it if we go out there like this. Jason messed up but he's done his best to fix his mistake.

We haven't. We play and we're fine, but we're not great. And we *were* great. We were amazing.

"We can't keep blaming each other for the fact that we aren't any more, because we're all guilty. I've been stressed out and snippy, which isn't putting anyone in a better mood. Robyn, you have to eat more and drink less. Iza, we're all happy for you and Luke, but we need your head back in the band! Harper, I know that you're mad at Toni, but it's over. She did something stupid over a guy... who hasn't done that?"

Lucy looked pointedly at Harper who avoided Lucy's eyes, instead staring down at her killer metallic-gold heels. She knew exactly what Lucy was talking about.

"This isn't a game for me," Lucy said, "and it shouldn't be for any of you either. We can do this, if we do it together."

Lucy couldn't think of anything else to say so she stopped talking. For a long beat, there was nothing but silence. Lucy could almost hear her own heart sinking.

Then Harper reached out and took Toni's hand. Toni stared down at their linked fingers for a long time, and then she reached out with her free hand and twined her fingers through Robyn's. Lucy felt a hand slipping into her own and found that Iza had silently crossed the room to stand at her side. Iza held her other hand out to Robyn, and Harper reached out to take Lucy's free hand. The circle was complete and so, for the first time in a long time, were Crush.

"Sixty seconds, Crush," Ash called.

"Are we ready?" Harper asked.

"Yes," Toni said. "I think we are."

This is the real miracle, Lucy thought, looking at her friends as they clustered together at the door that would lead them out onto the stage Jason's crew had built for them at the centre of the house. The question was, would it be enough?

Lucy couldn't believe that so many people were crowded around the stage, which was a perfect circle, built in the middle of the open plan ground floor. There were even people hanging over the balcony that lined the upstairs landing. Lucy settled in behind her drum kit as Toni bounced around the edge of the stage, stirring up the audience. Was it Lucy's imagination or was there just a little bit more energy to Toni than there'd been yesterday? A little extra sauciness in the toss of her hair than there'd been in the last show? Or even ten minutes before?

Lucy thought that she'd hardly have to play; her heart was pounding so hard. Her heartbeat alone had to be loud enough to keep time for Crush. This was it. The TV final might still be days away, but *this* was the show that would make or break the band, and they all knew it.

Harper strode out into the centre of the stage, looking just as though she owned every single pair of eyes that was pointed her way. She always did. Harper loved nothing more than being dead centre of everything, in the heart of the spotlight.

So why wasn't she saying anything?

Harper always began their performances by chatting to the audience a bit. With just a quick flirt or two she could have the crowd eating out of the palm of her hand before Crush even struck their first chord. But when Harper had leaned into the microphone just now, she'd just stood there. Like she'd lost her voice.

Was the mic turned off? Lucy wondered. Was the benefit going to make headlines for technical difficulties rather than musical awesomeness? Or, even worse, had Harper ACTUALLY lost her voice in some kind of freak episode of instantaneous laryngitis? That was silly. It couldn't be... could it?

"Oi," Toni hissed through a frozen smile. "Harper! What's up?"

"I..." Harper started, but then spun abruptly away from the microphone and stalked back towards Lucy.

Lucy desperately hoped this was some kind of dramatic new opening routine, but something told her it wasn't. She'd never seen that stricken look on Harper's face before.

"What are you doing, Harper?" Lucy asked, starting a low rumble on the kick drums to cover their whispers.

"I can't remember the words," Harper replied.

"What?" Lucy said, struggling to keep her voice low. "Harper!"

"I know! I don't know what's wrong with me!" Harper whispered. She sounded on the verge of tears.

"Okay, okay, don't panic," Lucy said. "Nothing's wrong with you – you're just nervous."

"I don't get nervous," Harper snapped.

"No," Lucy agreed. "You don't."

"I'm so sorry, Luce," Harper whispered. "I know how much this means to you. I know how much you gave up to be here… and now I'm ruining it all."

How could this be happening, after everything they'd been through? Could it really just be over, just like that?

Every band has a leader, Lucille. You may sit at the back of the stage, but for Crush that leader is you.

Alexander was right. This wasn't over until Lucy said it was over. She could keep them on beat. She had to.

"You're right," Lucy said, squaring her shoulders and lifting her sticks. "We've all given a lot to be here and we're not giving up now. You are Harper McKenzie and you don't get nervous. You *own* this stage and now you're going to bloody well sing on it. Get back to your microphone. I'm going to beat you in and then we are going to rock. You got me?"

"I don't know, Lucy," Harper said.

"I think you do," Lucy shot back. Then she raised her drumsticks and snapped them down on the drums. She wasn't giving Harper a choice. It was now or never.

"ONE… TWO… ONE, TWO, THREE, FOUR!" Lucy shouted.

Harper turned back to her microphone, opened her mouth and sang.

As Harper blasted into the third chorus of 'I'll Cross the World', the entire audience sang along, filling the air so completely that Robyn could almost feel the tidal wave of sound picking her up and carrying her away with it.

"I'll smash it to bits if I have to," Harper sang. *"I'll burn it all down just to show you, you belong with me."*

The audience was singing along. Five hundred people singing a melody Robyn had made up, just messing about on her guitar one afternoon. Five hundred people singing a song that Crush had bled and sweated and cried over for months. Robyn felt... small and enormous and terrified and happier than it seemed possible to be, all at once. She felt... Invicible.

"I'll cross the world to be with you," Harper crooned. *"Oh yes, I'll cross the world to be with you."*

Robyn picked her way through the last few chords as Lucy smashed down the final beat, and then reached up to quiet her cymbal so that Harper's voice could float out over the crowd without anything else getting in its way.

Harper leaned into her mic and called, "We're Crush, and we love you just as much as you love us!"

The house actually shook with the applause. They'd played three encores already, and if it kept up like this they'd have to play another. Of course, they'd already played every song they'd written plus pretty much all of the covers they knew, so that could be a problem, but Robyn didn't care. She could keep playing all night if that's what the crowd wanted.

Robyn was so happy she thought she might burst. Just drift into the air like a soap bubble and float away. She barely felt Harper's hand on her arm, dragging her back through the kitchen door they'd chosen as their route off the stage.

They had done it. They'd starred in a show, in their very own home, and the audience hadn't just loved it – they'd wanted more. They were Crush again and they were better than ever.

Once they were off stage, Harper threw her arms around Robyn's neck in a bubbling bear hug.

"We did it!" Harper crowed.

"We absolutely did," Robyn agreed, still struggling to keep her head and her body together. "I can't believe it."

"Believe it."

It was Tomas's rich, chocolate voice. Robyn's stomach spun as he wrapped his arms around her waist from behind.

"You ladies are stars. Nobody can argue with that now," Tomas continued, leaning down to drop a kiss on Robyn's bare shoulder.

"Tomas," Harper said. "You're here."

"Yep," Robyn said. "I invited him. Is that an issue?"

Harper didn't drop her gaze from Tomas's face. "No, Robs. Tomas and I have just had a bit of a misunderstanding, I think." She turned her icy blue eyes on Tomas. "I'm surprised though, Tomas. I thought I was extremely clear."

"You were clear, Harper," Tomas said coolly, his arm

tightening around Robyn's waist, "but a beautiful woman invited me to a party. I accepted. How does that surprise you?"

"What are you two on about?" Robyn demanded.

"We're just discussing a little promise Harper made me when we met at Darkroom," Tomas said.

"A promise I'll keep," Harper said grimly.

"We'll see," Tomas replied.

"Yes, we will," Harper shot back. Then she flashed a sunny serial-killer smile. "I always keep my promises, right, Robs?"

Then she swept away into the crowd.

Robyn turned into Tomas's arms. "What was that about?" she asked. "Did something happen at Darkroom? I know you haven't been around much since then, but I didn't think... Is she going to cause trouble for you?"

Instead of answering, he leaned down and kissed her, hard, until the world dipped and spun.

"I've got a little treat for you," he said. "To keep you entertained while I'm finishing up my business."

"Treat?" she asked, still breathless from his kiss.

"You'll like it," Tomas said with a grin. "Promise."

He dropped a round white pill engraved with a smiley face into her palm.

"A hit of that and you'll be having so much fun you'll never want to stop," he promised. Then he kissed her deeply once more before fading into the crowd.

Robyn stared down at the little tablet. She shouldn't

take it. She knew that. This wasn't like taking Tomas's diet pills. This sort of pill was purely recreational.

She didn't need it, Robyn knew that too. She was high enough on pure excitement after the show to party until dawn. She briefly considered flushing it and lying to Tomas, saying she'd taken it and she loved it, but he'd know she hadn't. Then he'd remember that she was really just a chubby, inexperienced girl and probably ditch her for one of the hoards of Hollywood beauties that were everywhere in the Crush house tonight. Before she had a chance to think about it any longer, Robyn downed the pill and swallowed.

There, that wasn't bad at all. Tonight was going to be the most perfect night of her life. She just knew it. And she wanted to be perfect for it.

She looked down at the clingy purple vest she wore draped over a pair of black leggings and flat, sparkly sandals. She loved this outfit. It showed off every sleek contour of her fit new body, but right now that included the slight bulge that her indulgent dinner of cocktail shrimp and chopped veg with ranch sauce had left in her otherwise perfect stomach.

Robyn had promised herself she'd stop the throwing up once she'd made it to a size two. And she had. Mostly. She hadn't thrown up after a meal in nearly a week, which proved, really, that she had it under control. She didn't have to worry about it because she could obviously stop whenever she wanted. She'd even gained two pounds since she'd stopped, and that hadn't started her up again. She had it all totally under control, especially now that Thomas had brought her a fresh batch of diet pills. It was just for tonight. For Tomas. It was totally worth it.

Iza sat on the edge of the patio, feet dangling over the canyon, head on Luke's shoulder. The city sparkled below her. Luke's hand traced lazy circles on the small of her back.

"I can't believe we actually did it," Iza said. "We rocked *so hard*, didn't we? I can't believe we were that good. I honestly thought we were going to fall flat on our faces, but we didn't... Of course we're still running behind in the online polls. We probably won't—"

Then Luke was kissing her and the anxiety just floated away. It was always that way when he kissed her. Luke was the only person in the universe who knew how to find each of the frantically ticking anxiety bombs in her brain and switch them off all at once.

"You were amazing," he said, pulling back and grinning down at her. "Which means you can stop worrying about all the ways you might not have been amazing and just chill out for a second."

"All right then," Iza said, closing her eyes and leaning against his shoulder. "Officially chilling out now."

She felt more than heard the chuckle rumble through his chest. She loved that sound. She loved everything about this moment. She would be quite content to never move again.

"Iz," he said. "I've got bad news."

Her heart plummeted from the stratosphere right through to the bottom of the pool beside them. It had been too good to be true, she thought. The whole summer had been too good to be true and now—

"I'm not going to be able to go to Vegas with you guys," he said in a rush. "I'm so incredibly sorry. It's the same day as the John Williams retrospective at the Bowl and three other violins have already called in vacation days and I just didn't check the schedule in time to beat them to it. I'm the world's worst boyfriend, I know, but I just hope... Please don't be too mad."

Iza looked up at him, dazed. He wasn't breaking up with her. In fact, he was terribly nervous that she would hate him for not rearranging his entire schedule to be in Vegas with her. But that wasn't the part that had struck Iza completely mute with... Lord, she didn't even know what this feeling was. The part that was turning her deaf and dumb was the part where Luke Greenfield, the man of her dreams, had just called himself her boyfriend.

"You hate me," Luke said and dragged a hand through his shock of blonde hair. "And you have every right. This is your big night and I should be there for you."

Iza couldn't help it. She started to laugh.

His worried face collapsed into his puzzled I-don't-understand-girls-at-all face.

"Not the reaction I was looking for," he said finally, still sounding concerned, "but I guess it's better than pushing me in the pool and never speaking to me again."

The very thought of that sent Iza into another gale of giggles. She did try to stop laughing, but she couldn't seem to control the hysterical waves of mirth that had taken control of her.

"You've had a mental breakdown," Luke guessed, the contagious laugh starting to infect his voice. "You're about to snap and strangle me with your bare hands?"

Iza managed to get enough control of herself to shake her head, still giggling.

"So you're not mad?" he asked hopefully.

She shook her head again.

"Well, clue me in then," he said, "because this is not any of the reactions I prepared myself for."

Instead, she gave in to the mad spirit that had infected her with its wild laughter and leaned in to kiss him. It was the first time, she realised, that she'd ever kissed him first. It caught him by surprise, but soon his arms were wrapped around her, drawing her close.

After a long minute, she let her head drop to his shoulder and snuggled close.

"So I guess you're really not mad at me?" Luke ventured.

"Of course not," she said against his chest. "It's sweet of you to have even tried to get out of a concert for me."

"So why the giggle fit?" he asked. "Not that I didn't thoroughly enjoy it."

She felt suddenly shy. Like if she pointed out what he'd said, he might take it back. But shy was the old Iza.

New Iza could do anything.

"You called yourself my boyfriend," she said, pulling back to look up at him. "That's the first time you've said that."

"And you find it hilarious?" He looked stung at the thought.

"No," she said quickly, "I find it marvellous. That's why I was laughing, I think. I was just too happy to do anything else."

A slow grin spread over Luke's face. Almost as big as the one Iza could feel tugging at her own lips.

"Oh," he said. "That's okay then. That's more than okay. Marvellous, huh? I like that word."

She snuggled against him again and stared up at the dim LA stars. She was having a thought. A thought she didn't know if she was brave enough to say out loud, even now.

"What's going on in there?" Luke asked, running a soft hand over her hair. "I can hear you thinking from here."

Oh God, could he really? Iza buried her face against his shoulder, sure she was turning pink.

"You can tell me," he said gently. "Whatever it is. There isn't anything you can't tell me."

"Well." She took a deep breath. The worst he could say was no, right? He wouldn't think less of her. This was Luke, after all. Her boyfriend. Her real, honest-to-goodness boyfriend. "Well, I was thinking... I was thinking that I don't want you to go home. Tonight, I mean."

He pulled back a bit so that he could look down into her face.

"Really?" he asked. "Are you sure... I mean, I had assumed you were..."

"Oh, I didn't mean..." Her face was positively burning now, but she ploughed ahead. "I didn't mean like that... I mean, someday, I hope, like that..." She couldn't believe she was saying this out loud. "But I am. I mean, I am... a virgin, that is. And I'm not ready to... um... not be a virgin. I just thought... I just don't want you to leave, that's all," she concluded, feeling suddenly thoroughly lame.

"I don't want to leave either," Luke said, grinning. In fact, he wasn't only grinning, he was blushing as well. As brightly as she must be.

Iza couldn't help it. She started to laugh again. The wild, irrepressible happiness just couldn't come out any other way. Luke rolled his eyes, but he was starting to laugh along with her. Soon they were both lying on their backs, feet still in the pool, laughing so hard they could hardly breathe.

"Hey, can you give us a minute?"

Toni braced herself when Jason's voice intruded on her quiet perch at the end of the upstairs hallway, overlooking the raging party below. She'd known this was coming since Jason had appeared at the house that morning three weeks ago. She'd told herself she was ready for it when it did.

She wasn't ready.

Toni turned to face him, heart in her throat. The cameraman tasked with following her that night was already walking away up the hall at Jason's request for privacy. She and Jason were alone.

And the last time they'd been alone together...

"Toni," he said, reaching out to take her hand. "Toni, I'm so sorry."

He looked quite miserable, Toni noted with surprise. Like he hadn't slept in days. She didn't know what she'd expected, but certainly not the look of sheer torment in his eyes.

"You don't have to say anything," he continued. "I don't deserve... Toni, I can't tell you how sorry I am. You have every right to report me to Alexander and Sir Peter. Sir Peter will probably fire me, but I deserve that. I did everything wrong with you, and with Crush. And I just wanted to tell you, I'm sorry."

"You're married," she said, so quietly she wasn't sure he could hear her. "How could you do that? Why? Why would you... kiss me?

"You didn't know?" Jason said, shock filling his voice. "I thought... I... of course you didn't know."

Toni had spent the last three weeks wondering how she could possibly have not seen it. Everything seemed so perfectly obvious now. The quick phone calls he always took, no matter what was happening, when his mobile chirruped that one particular ringtone. The pink and purple striped yoga mat in the back of his car. His plea for Toni to leave that night before something happened between them. He'd been trying to stop what was happening before it was too late, and she'd just ignored him. How could she be the sort of person who would do such a thing?

"Toni?" Jason's voice punched through the suffocating bubble of shock. "Toni, are you all right? Oh, kiddo, what have I done to you?"

She tried to speak, but found that there was no room for words in her throat. The magnitude of her own stupidity was filling up all the space between them, sucking the air out of the room.

"Jason?" Skye stood at the top of the stairs. "The reporter from *Vogue* is looking for you, he... Toni, are you all right?"

"Toni," Jason said. "Are you okay?"

Toni opened her mouth, then closed it again. Was she all right? She had absolutely no idea. All she knew was that she had to get out of there. Now. So Toni did the only thing she could think to do.

She ran.

Down the stairs, through the masses of celebrating fans and out into the cool Los Angeles darkness.

11. SHARP things

The concert was over, but the party was just getting started and Harper could hardly believe her luck. Skye had just blown Rafe out to find Jason about a work thing. Again. It was the fourth time in about fifteen minutes that Skye had brushed Rafe aside to deal with some business nonsense or other, or network with some teen star. If Skye had put on a sandwich board that read *I don't give a crap about my boyfriend*, the message couldn't have been clearer. And Rafe wasn't missing it. Not this time.

He'd been a little distant with Harper since Toni's little outburst at The Echo, at least in public. His texts told a different story. Rafe and Harper were talking now like they hadn't in ages – like they hadn't since they'd been together. And now Skye had given Harper the perfect opportunity to finally make her move.

Harper took a big slurp of the chocolate milkshake she'd dosed with Jack Daniels, exactly the way Rafe liked it. Not for courage, but just to make sure it was strong enough.

Officially, there wasn't any alcohol in the house. Unofficially, she and Toni had been stocking up their rooms on a regular basis after they'd arrived in LA. Sneaking in the booze past the house cameras had been fun, like they were in a heist movie. And tonight she was going to pull off a heist for real. She was going to steal Rafe Jackson's heart.

He was sitting deep in the corner of one of the sofas that had been pushed back against the walls, brooding. She dropped down beside him, letting the sag of the cushions under his greater weight slide her to his side.

"Why the long face, cowboy?" she asked. "Not having fun?"

"Not especially," he grumbled. "Skye's run off again and I'm not about to bust in on Luke's game right now, am I?" He waved in the direction of Luke and Iza who were across the room, bouncing along with an upbeat tune, making funny faces at each other and generally being sickeningly adorable. "So here I am, sitting around by myself. Great."

"Drink this," Harper said, depositing the milkshake in his hand, "and follow me. I guarantee that you will shortly find yourself having a fantastic night."

"Guarantee, huh?" Rafe said, studying the shake and then Harper. "What are you up to, Harp?"

"Up to?" she said, letting her voice sparkle with feigned

innocence. "Why would I be up to something just because I want your sad-sack backside off my couch and having a good time at my party?"

He wasn't buying it for a second and she knew it. Then again, she wasn't trying to hide the fact that she wanted him. The question was whether he wanted her back.

"Fine then," he said, taking a long swallow of spiked milkshake. "I guess I have no choice but to obey your every whim."

"No," she said, allowing a satisfied smirk to spread across her face. "You really don't. After all, I'm a superstar, and this is my house."

"Well, technically it's my father's house," Rafe pointed out. He took another big slurp of his drink and reached out to teasingly muss her hair. "But I suppose I'll let you lay claim to it. You girls did just send us all to rock and roll heaven, after all."

"Exactly," Harper said, allowing herself to revel in the memory. "We were absolutely incredible, weren't we? Being up there... it's like flying. I've never felt anything so perfect in my whole life."

"You really love it, don't you?" Rafe asked.

"Yeah, I really do," she said. Harper hadn't realised it until she'd said it out loud, but it was true. Crush had been a means to an end before, and now... it was much more than that.

"Come on." Harper shook off her attack of deep thoughts and started towards the back door.

And then it happened.

Rafe reached out and took her hand. All on his own.

Harper had to fight not to overreact as he led her out to the patio. It had been almost a year since he'd broken her heart. A year of struggles and work and sweat and tears to get Crush this far. To get herself this far. And she was finally here. Holding Rafe's hand again.

"I dare you," he said, pointing to the pool.

"Dare me what?" she countered.

"Jump in," he said, eyes sparkling with mischief. "Fancy sparkly number and all."

He was talking about the sequined Miu Miu minidress Harper had changed into for the party. It was hot pink, it was beyond sexy and it was Harper's favourite dress. There was no way it was going in the pool.

But there was also no way Harper was turning down a dare from Rafe Jackson.

"Nope," she said, matching his devilish grin. "The dress is not going in the pool."

"You're no fun," he said, pouting into his milkshake.

"I said the *dress* wasn't going in the pool," Harper continued, reaching down to hook a finger under the stretchy hem. "I didn't say anything about me."

It was a good thing she'd decided on a set of cute but substantial underwear, she thought as she stripped the dress off, tossed it on a lounge chair and cannonballed into the pool. Otherwise Jason would *kill* her when the inevitable pap photos made it to page six.

"Pool party!" someone yelled, and soon underwear-clad bodies were raining down into the water around her. Harper grinned up at Rafe as he waded in beside her.

"Only you," he said, laughing as he pushed her wet hair out of her face. "Only you could strip your clothes off in the middle of a party and get away with it."

"That's why you love me," she said, grinning. And then she froze in horror. Had the l-o-v-e word really just come out of her mouth? Oh crap. But before she could panic further, Rafe let his hand slip through her hair to cup the back of her head, drawing her closer.

"You're right," he said. "It is one of the things I love about you."

Then his mouth dipped down to hers for a long, breathless kiss.

Harper leaned into Rafe and let the kiss unwind, basking in the awesomeness of their limbs tangling in the bright blue water like they would never let go, as they were buffeted by the splashing of the other partygoers.

That was when she heard the sirens.

Lucy needed a moment of quiet.

She was nearly positive that she'd talked to more people tonight than she had in her whole life. Reporters. Fans. Boys. She wasn't sure which she found more shocking – the adoring boys or the adoring fans. Eight months before, she'd felt lucky to have mates to eat lunch with at school. Now she couldn't seem to find a moment alone.

The soft footsteps of the camerawoman assigned to Lucy for the evening reminded her that she hadn't had an actual moment alone since June. If she wasn't home, where she was inevitably on camera, she was being filmed at a rehearsal, gig, or out with the girls.

Lucy pushed open the door to the nearest of the bedrooms. Everyone else would be downstairs. It didn't matter which bed she collapsed on, just so long as she found a soft place to land.

One glance through the open door, however, had her yanking it closed again. Holy Jesus. She couldn't let her camerawoman catch a glimpse of that. Or anyone else, for that matter.

But how was she going to get rid of the camerawoman without looking suspicious? She could insist the lady stayed in the hallway, but the camera crews had a tendency to summon producers when things like that happened. If any of the producers saw this, Crush would be royally screwed.

"Um, I, ah..." Lucy stammered. "I need to use the loo. Just a sec..."

She shot the camerawoman a smile she hoped was convincing and ducked into the big double bathroom that she and Robyn shared. She slid across the bolt on the door into the hall, and then the one on the door that led to her room, just for safety.

Then she turned and walked into Robyn's bedroom,

where Robyn's creepy friend Tomas sat on the bed surrounded by drugs and cash.

"Tomas," Lucy breathed. "What the hell?"

"Nothing to worry about," the pale Swedish boy oozed up at her with a casual smile. "I'll be done in a few. Just taking inventory."

"You're done right now," Lucy snapped and then tried to lower her voice. "Tell me you haven't been selling that stuff in our house."

"Why else would I be here?" Tomas said calmly.

"To support your friend Robyn?" Lucy said.

"Robyn doesn't mind," Tomas said.

"Right, well," Lucy said, grabbing a handful of pills and stuffing them back into the red canvas bag that lay empty on the bed beside them. "*We* mind and the producers of *Project Next* are bloody well going to mind, believe you me. That means you're going to gather up your gear and get out. End. Of."

"That's unlikely," Tomas said, a dangerously mild look on his face as he finished counting bills and stuck the roll of cash back in the pocket of his white jeans. "I've still got product to move, Shortie, and you wouldn't want any of the reporters here finding out that your dear sweet Robyn was one of my best customers, would you?"

On cue, a soft snore drifted up from somewhere beyond the edge of the bed. Lucy peered around it to see Robyn curled up between the bed and the wall.

Totally plastered. Or was it not alcohol that had her in this state?

"No," Lucy said, keeping her voice quiet. "I don't believe you. Robyn wouldn't—"

"Oh, yes she would," Tomas said. He reached for the red bag still clutched in Lucy's hand. "Now, if you don't mind."

But before he could take the bag from her, the bedroom door swung open and Alexander stepped into the room.

"Lucille," he said. "Your camera team were worried, said you'd been in the—"

Then he saw Lucy. And the open bag of pills clutched in her hand.

"Lucille?" he said, so quiet she could barely hear him. "Oh, Lucille. I thought you were better than this."

The disappointment in his voice was more than she could bear.

"It's not what it looks like, Alexander," she said in a rush. "I was just—"

"I've heard all the excuses," he said. "I don't want to hear more."

He turned and walked away.

Before Lucy could run after him, the high whine of sirens cut through the room.

"You called the police?" Tomas demanded, enraged.

"No, but I'm glad someone did," Lucy snapped. "That's what happens when you run about at a party selling drugs.

Someone is bound to notice you. I hope they throw you in jail for life."

"Not going to happen," Tomas spat back at her. He reached behind him, fumbling in the waist of his jeans for something.

When he pulled his gun free, Lucy thought her heart might stop. She was on the verge of dashing for the bathroom when Harper burst through the door to the bedroom, Rafe on her heels.

Harper pulled up short at the sight of the gun.

"What the f—" Rafe blurted, barrelling into the back of her.

"Shut up, Rafe," Harper snapped, gathering herself instantly. "He's got a gun."

"Smart girl," Tomas oozed, brandishing the gun far too casually for Lucy's comfort. "Kind of a brat, but undeniably bright."

Harper's hands were shaking as she reached behind her, clutching for Rafe. "We don't want any trouble, Tomas."

"Oh, honey," Tomas shot her a predatory grin and levelled the gun directly at her. "You've already got plenty of trouble. It's really just up to you whether the press downstairs know about it or not."

For a long beat, no one said a word. Lucy was so terrified, she was having trouble remembering to breathe. She'd never seen an actual gun up close, much less seen one pointed at her best friend.

"That dress really is delicious," Tomas said, eyeing Harper with casual cruelty. "I'm going to enjoy it when you snuggle up to me while we walk out of this place. But don't worry, all you'll have to do is get me past the police. What we do when we get to the car is quite up to you."

Lucy felt sick at the very idea. She couldn't let him take Harper hostage, but what was she meant to do to stop him?

To her surprise, Harper suddenly smiled at Tomas.

"You're right," Harper said. She took a step towards Tomas, smoothing her long, wet, blonde hair back from her face and tilting her head into what Lucy recognised as her give-me-what-I-want flirting pose. "It is up to me, isn't it?"

"You were a real bitch to me at Darkroom, you know that, Harper?" Tomas said. His voice was still coldly aggressive, but his shoulders had relaxed in response to Harper's soothing tone. "You're going to have to make that up to me if we're going to be friends."

"I can do that," Harper said, taking another step closer. "We'll be good friends, won't we, Tomas?"

"Harper!" Rafe said. "You can't be serious about this."

"I can," she said, running a finger down Tomas's chest lazily. "And I will."

Then, before anyone including Tomas had time to react, Harper threw her shoulder into his solar plexus, knocking him backwards. The icy-blonde drug dealer went sprawling over the corner of the bed and the gun skittered out of his hands and straight into Lucy's purple Converse.

"Luce!" Harper called as Tomas scrambled towards his weapon.

That snapped Lucy out of her freeze enough to lean down and scoop up the gun before Tomas could reach it. *Guns are bloody heavy*, she thought. *Far, far heavier than they seem in films.*

Harper blew out a big breath, like she'd been holding it in from the moment she burst into the room. Then she crossed to Lucy and took the gun.

"Tomas Angerman, I told you to stay away from my friends," Harper said, aiming his own gun at him.

She was quite calm, Lucy thought, for someone holding a drug dealer's gun with the sound of policemen echoing up the stairs behind her.

"Lucy, zip up that bag please. Our friend's lift has just arrived," Harper said.

"Wait," Rafe said. "You don't want him getting arrested carrying enough gear to sell here. Having a drug dealer get caught working the party isn't going to look good for Crush."

Harper nodded, still pointing the gun at Tomas. "You're right, baby. We'll have to find a place to toss this crap so the police don't find it. We can't have Crush looking like a bunch of drug addicts."

"It gets worse, Harp," Lucy said. "Robyn's over there, passed out. I think she might have taken something."

"Give it here," Rafe said to Lucy, reaching eagerly

for the bag. "I'll sort it. You girls see to Robyn."

"No," Harper said, taking the bag herself. She fished out a smaller bag containing three tiny white pills from inside and stuffed it into Tomas's pocket. Then she reached into his other pocket and pulled out the roll of cash.

Tomas snarled, but Harper just waggled the gun at him.

"None of that, Tomas," she said brightly. "I told you not to mess with Robyn again and you didn't listen. Now you have to learn your lesson. Really, you should thank me for taking these off your hands. I'm sure your daddy can make a simple possession charge go away, but possession of all of this? With the obvious... what do they call it? Oh yes, intent to sell. I think that's hard to get out of, isn't it?"

Harper stuffed the cash and the gun into the red bag and zipped it closed.

"Rafe, you see to it the police find Tomas. Lucy and I will find a place to stash this junk."

"Harp, I really think you should let me handle the drugs," Rafe objected sourly.

He was sulking, Lucy thought, amazed. Just like a toddler who'd had their toy taken away. He wanted to be the one carrying a bloody gun and a drugs stash past the police – and he wanted it badly. He was actually excited by the idea. Maybe he even thought he'd be able to keep the drugs. She wouldn't put it past him.

He'd get his way as well, Lucy was sure of it. Harper

couldn't resist him, and her weakness for Rafe Jackson was going to get them all banged up in prison.

But instead, Harper shook her head.

"Lucy and I know the house well enough to hide the stash and you don't, Rafe," Harper said, firmly. "I need you to handle Tomas. Now."

"Fine," Rafe snapped unhappily. "Come on you," he snarled, grabbing Tomas's arm and yanking him into the hallway.

"Harper," Lucy said, once the boys were gone. "I think we should call Jason and Alexander. We can't—"

"We can't risk throwing things off track again. Not now. We'll have to handle this ourselves."

Four hours later, dawn was quietly slipping into day.

Lucy was floating in the warm embrace of the infinity pool. There'd been no hope of sleep, not after the night they'd had. So instead of going to bed, she'd grabbed her suit and come out here to watch the sunrise.

Robyn was still passed out in her bedroom, in a deep sleep and breathing heavily. She had managed to stay hidden, curled behind her bed, through the entire hubbub with the police. She'd be livid when she found out what they'd done to Tomas, but that didn't matter. Harper was right. Tomas Angerman needed to be booted out of their lives for good.

Thankfully, Jason had managed to convince everyone, the press included, that this was just a sad example of a wholesome young people's celebration destroyed by the drugs trade. Crush, miraculously, had come off as the innocent victims in the whole business.

Harper padded out of the house in her hot-pink bikini.

"Sunrise?" she asked, yawning.

"Yep," Lucy replied. "No way I was sleeping, not after all of that."

"Seriously," Harper said, slipping into the steaming pool. "What a night."

"Jason is going to murder us all," Lucy said. "You know that, right? We finally get him back on our side and then this." *And Alexander is going to be so disappointed*, she thought.

"Nah," Harper said, paddling out to lounge beside Lucy in the warm water. "Have you checked the blogs? We were a huge hit. And the business with Tomas just made us front page entertainment news all over town."

"I'm not sure *Project Next* wants to be news for having a party busted for drugs."

"The party wasn't busted," Harper pointed out, yawning. "Tomas was. The cops had been watching him for a while, I guess. Predatory behaviour in selling drugs to minors, or something like that. And Jason isn't in any position to judge us, believe me. Stop fussing and just enjoy it. We had almost four hundred people here, and another three hundred that wanted to be. At a *house party*. We rocked that show and we're going to kill in Vegas. Everything is just... perfect."

"Perfect?" Lucy asked, incredulous. "Are you serious?"

"Yeah," Harper said, stretching out to float on her back in the water. "I am. I think... I think that Rafe told me he still loves me last night."

Just when Lucy had thought it couldn't get more complicated.

But when Lucy looked down at her best friend, blonde hair spilling around her in the water and the first rays of dawn tumbling across her face, she realised that Harper looked genuinely happy. Happy in a way she wasn't sure Harper had ever been before. However ridiculous Rafe was, obviously Harper loved him more than even Lucy could have guessed.

"I know you don't like him, Lucy," Harper continued, her voice a little more anxious now, "and I get that. But I love him... and I always will. After all of this, it turns out he loves me back, and that is just... that is perfect. The rest of it – Robyn, Toni's stupid thing with Jason – you and I can handle that."

She twisted in the water to smile at Lucy. "Just like we did Tomas. We can handle anything, as long as we do it together."

Lucy wasn't sure that was true, but she found she couldn't argue. Not now. Besides, right at that moment, with the two of them alone in the quiet of early dawn in their beautiful pool beside their rock star mansion, Lucy couldn't help believing her.

"Right. Whatever happens, we'll manage it. Together."

12. THE BEST BAD LUCK

No queues, no waiting around for hours... Airport security was brilliant when you were flying privately. Lucy still couldn't believe *Project Next* was flying each band to Las Vegas on its own private jet, but there Crush were, walking across the runway towards their very own Catch-22 G8.

As Lucy started climbing the staircase that was pulled up to the jet's door, she caught sight of a jeep with the *Project Next* logo parked alongside. Ash was leaning against it, chatting to a young woman in neon blue flats, skinny jeans, a long-sleeved black T-shirt and one of the familiar earpieces that the *Project Next* crew wore on duty.

Lucy couldn't help herself. She had to ask.

"Er, excuse me," she called, jogging over to the pair. "Are you dealing with our comp tickets?"

"Yeah, I've got it, Luce," Ash said. "Don't worry that curly head about it."

The girl in the neon shoes rolled her eyes, clearly annoyed with Ash's attempt to take credit for her job. "Actually, *I'm* handling the VIP guests," she said. "What can I help you with, Lucy?"

"I just wanted to know if two of the tickets requested by, er, Mr Holister… for Mark and Nina Gosling… Well, is there any word on whether they are being used?" Lucy asked.

The girl skimmed a tablet computer, zipping through a long list.

This was taking too long. If Mum and Dad were coming, the girl in the neon shoes would have known straight off. She'd be the person arranging things for them. In fact, they'd already be in Las Vegas.

Lucy wished she hadn't asked. Then she wouldn't know that her parents weren't coming. And as long as she didn't know, she could at least pretend that they were out there, that they'd read her letter and she'd been forgiven.

The girl in the neon shoes said, "I'm sorry, it doesn't look like any arrangements have been made. Actually, I think Jason told me to give those tickets to someone else because they weren't being used."

Ash put an arm around Lucy's shoulders and gave her a quick squeeze. "It'll be okay, I promise. Besides, we're going to be having way too much fun for parental supervision."

"Yeah." Lucy tried to smile up at him. "I guess."

She walked up the stairs and into the plane, feeling a little bit heavier with every step.

"Thanks for gracing us with your presence, Lucy," Jason snapped as she stepped into the cabin. The other girls were already sitting in a clump of plush captain's chairs and Jason and Alexander were standing by the door to the cockpit, glowering.

Oh great, Lucy thought. *I'm about to burst into tears and now I get to sit through a lecture.*

"We've been waiting for you," Jason said. "Before we take off, we need to have a little conversation."

"Jason—" Harper began, but he cut her off.

"Let me rephrase that. Before we take off, I'm going to talk and you're going to listen. You're going to listen like you have never listened to anyone or anything before in your lives, you get me?"

The girls nodded as one.

"Excellent," he said. "Now, I know we've had a rough time of it this summer, but I killed myself dragging you girls back up on top. I made you the face of an international charitable organisation run by one of the most powerful women in the world and I built you the best headlining debut that any band could ask for – an event at which you rocked so much harder than my greatest expectations and made everything we've been through worthwhile. And then, for some reason that I cannot fathom, one of you decided to invite a DRUG DEALER TO A CHARITY EVENT IN YOUR OWN HOME!"

Oh God, Lucy thought. *He knows about Robyn and Tomas.*

"You are the luckiest little brats in the history of rock and roll brain malfunctions, you know that? If that Swedish kid didn't have his daddy's lawyers swarming all over the LAPD right now claiming diplomatic immunity, he'd already have told them which of you invited him, and the press would be having a field day with *Project Next* playing host to a drug dealer at one of its events. But it's going to come out, eventually. He was on your personal comp list, which means that I need to know, right now, which one of you invited that kid to come and sell drugs at a party with Crush's name on it. With *Project Next*'s name on it. With MY name on it."

No one said a word.

"Well?" Jason said. "I'm waiting."

Lucy looked at Robyn. She was shrinking, Lucy thought. Visibly. She looked like she might melt into a teary blob beneath the seat at any moment.

Perhaps Lucy should tell Jason exactly how Tomas had ended up at their party. Robyn probably did need help. But what if Jason kicked her out of the band? What if she had a total meltdown and got Crush disqualified altogether? What if Robyn's mistake made everything Lucy had given up pointless? It wasn't as though it was their fault that Tomas had become a part of their lives. That had been due to Debra Z – and *Project Next* come to think of it.

"Now is the part where you start talking, girls," Jason prompted. "Who invited Tomas Angerman to that party?"

"No one!" Lucy blurted out, remembering what Robyn had told her. "No one invited him to the party. We met him through Debra Z. He goes to school with her daughter. He sort of followed us about for a while, and he seemed a nice enough bloke so we let him. He knows who to call to get on our list now. We'd no idea he was a drug dealer."

Lucy tried hard to look Jason straight in the eye as she spoke. He had to believe her. "We had nothing to do with the drugs, Jason."

Jason studied her for a long time. Finally he nodded.

"Thank you for the explanation, Lucy. You have proven yourself to be both responsible and devoted to your music over the last few months, so I'm going to take you at your word."

Lucy nodded back, relief and guilt turning her stomach to acid as she did so.

"And I will speak to Debra Z about the company she chooses to associate you with," he continued, reaching into the chair beside him and picking up an iPad. "But, in the meantime, I want you all to give thanks to the person who turned this disaster into a triumph – Patrick Nelson."

He flipped his tablet around to display a YouTube clip of Patrick Nelson, pretty much *the* hottest teen film star in the universe, stumbling down the middle of a street Lucy recognised as their block of Wonderland Avenue.

"I'lllll crrrrrrrrrrrrrrrrrroushhhh the woooooooorrllldddd to be with YOOOOOOOOOOOUUUUUU," he sang drunkenly. *"I'll gggggiiiiiiiiiiiiiiiiiiiivvvvvvvvvvvvvveee it ALL up to seeeeeeeeeeeeeeeee this tthrooouuuughhhhhhhhhhhh."*

He stumbled into the bushes, fell over a rock and, incredibly, landed in one piece halfway down the almost sheer drop into the canyon beside the road, the camera zooming in from above.

Lucy watched, jaw dropped, as he half fell, half climbed, down the rest of the hill. She'd have worried that he could have hurt himself, but he kept singing the whole way. He actually made it all the way through 'I'll Cross the World' before he was out of range of the camera.

"Dear, wasted Patrick has not only distracted the press from your friendly neighbourhood drug dealer, he has also brought Crush's first single into the homes, offices and mobile phones of half of America." Jason shook his head. "*Saturday Night Live* called this morning, asking for permission to use the song in a skit spoofing this video."

"*Saturday Night Live*?" Harper blurted. "That's brilliant!"

"It is," Jason agreed. "You couldn't be going into the final from a stronger position. Demand for 'I'll Cross the World' is so high that we're seriously considering releasing the song as a download before the final even airs. You've gone from dead last to the top of the heap, as far as the fans are concerned. And you've literally done it overnight. So, just this once, I'm going to hold off on tossing each and every one of you out of this plane at thirty thousand feet. If you ever, and I do mean *ever*, let someone like Tomas Angerman ride on your coat-tails again, I won't show as much restraint. And, even worse, I will fire you and see to it that you get dumped from the label and none of you ever get paid a single cent to produce so much as a note again. Is that understood?"

They all nodded.

"Good. Now relax. Be proud of yourselves for getting this far. I know I am."

With that, he turned and strode up to the cockpit.

"Like he has any right to lecture us," Robyn said, not nearly as quietly as Lucy wished she'd be. "After what he did to Toni."

"It's over now," Toni said quietly. "Bygones, right?" She shot Robyn a meaningful look. "For all of us. Let's just focus on ruling Caesars Palace tonight, shall we?"

As the other girls settled in around her, Lucy turned to look up the aisle, her eyes finding Alexander's. He pointedly turned away, raising his copy of *Billboard Magazine* between them. She'd tried to call him several times since the Crush benefit, but he'd never responded. Jason might believe that Lucy had nothing to do with the drugs, but Alexander had seen her holding Tomas's stash in Robyn's bedroom. He obviously wasn't buying their excuses. He couldn't have made it clearer that he'd joined the ever-expanding club for Adults Who Are Disappointed In Lucy Gosling.

Suddenly, Lucy was just too tired of it all to care. If it wasn't one thing, it was another. The moment she got the girls speaking to each other again, she lost Alexander. And her parents. It was just exhausting, the lot of it.

The moment the plane reached cruising altitude, Lucy dived past the others into the tiny WC at the back of the plane. She slammed the lock shut and sagged down onto the closed chemical toilet, tears running down her cheeks. All she wanted to do was play her drums. Why did the world seem determined to make that as difficult as possible?

Forty-five minutes later, a blast of bone-dry heat smacked Lucy in the face as they stepped off the plane and onto the Las Vegas runway, adding a coating of desert dust to her misery.

Harper linked her arm through Lucy's as they crossed the tarmac to the welcome relief of the air-conditioned buildings.

"Why the long face, gloomy? Jason barked a bit, but you were brilliant talking him down and blaming Debra Z! Everything's golden. The party was fantastic and we're a huge hit, and we haven't even played the final yet!"

Lucy swallowed back the tears that were threatening again. She had to stop being such a sap about this. "My parents aren't coming," she said quietly.

"Nobody's are," Harper said. "I thought they weren't allowed. Were we supposed to invite our families?"

"No," Lucy said, "but Alexander said I could invite mine. He thought maybe it would help mend things. He told me to write them a letter, to explain why I felt like I needed to be here and asking them to come and see... so they could understand. But they haven't replied and they're not here. They're never going to forgive me."

Harper stopped and pulled Lucy into a hug. She didn't say anything, just squeezed Lucy tight. Then she grabbed Lucy's hand and pulled her along towards the front doors of the airport.

"This, my darlings, is what we call a swag suite," Debra Z cooed a few short hours later as they stepped into the hospitality room *Project Next* was hosting.

It looked like a pirate's treasure trove, Lucy thought. If pirates really, really liked Prada.

"We can just take stuff? Any stuff?" Toni breathed, her eyes sparkling at the prospect of free designer baubles.

"That's the idea, my lovely," Debra said, grinning as the girls wandered into the room.

Toni hefted a bright red, patent leather clutch and tossed it to Lucy. "That's all you, Luce. It'll be perfect with that little white dress you've got, the one-shouldered thing?" She grabbed an oversized pair of sunglasses and popped them on her nose, twirling to one of the full-length mirrors that had been scattered about the room. "These, on the other hand, are all me."

"I want you ladies to pick out your victory outfits first,"

Debra called. "Then you can play with the toys."

Robyn was already pulling a short yellow tube dress over her head, and Iza was in front of a mirror trying on a bright pink skirt that looked like someone had chopped off the bottom half of a ballerina tutu. Harper seemed to be torn between a cherry red mini and a black sequined dress that was so laden with sparkles it looked like it might weigh almost as much as she did.

Lucy tried to be excited about the black-and-white striped top she was half-heartedly considering, but she just wasn't in the mood for fashion.

She mentally shook herself. She had to snap out of this gloom and get excited about tonight. She simply had to. That would be properly ironic, she thought, if she managed to be exiled from her family forever because she'd insisted on *Project Next* and then Crush lost the competition because Lucy was so distraught over it that she couldn't keep it together on stage.

The door to the suite swung open to reveal a thoroughly grim-faced Alexander.

"Lucille," he growled, not bothering to look at the other girls. "Come with me. Now."

Perfect, Lucy thought. *This will be fun...* Her mood was already disastrous enough, but she followed Alexander anyway.

Alexander didn't say a word on the twenty-storey ride down to the lobby, or the hike through the blaring casino, which seemed like miles. He didn't even look at her.

Lucy thought he would stop at the concert hall, but he didn't. He kept moving past the main stage, then down a back corridor.

He finally stopped at a smaller door and pushed it open, gesturing her impatiently inside.

It was a tiny theatre. With no more than forty seats and a low stage with no curtain. The chairs looked old. The floor looked worn. It hardly seemed to belong in the flashy, over-polished building outside the door that Alexander had just closed firmly behind them.

He stood there for a moment, looking around the room with a strange expression on his face. Then he turned and looked at Lucy.

"This was the first house I ever played," he said. "I was younger than you are now. Never finished high school. Did I tell you that?"

She nodded.

"I'd hitch-hiked to Nashville for the summer to try and get a job. Got a gig playing bass. The band were awful, but when we stood up there and started to play... I was hooked. The music just had me. At that moment, I knew I'd do whatever it took to stay on the stage. Stay in the music."

He sagged into one of the creaky, velvet chairs and waved her into another.

Lucy sat.

"I was playing at here at Caesars the night I almost destroyed it all too," he continued. "Life is funny that way.

It was ten years after that first gig. I was playing with Winding Road on the main stage by then. I had everything I'd ever dreamed of. But having a room in the penthouse didn't stop me from overdosing that night. And if it wasn't for my bandmate Pete Hanswell, it wouldn't have stopped me from doing it again."

He shook his head, wrapped up in the memory. "The music was my life, but the drugs... the drugs can take up so much space that there's no room for anything else. If Pete hadn't forced me into rehab, I wouldn't be here, Lucille. I would never have been able to stop on my own."

Lucy stared at her mentor. He had always seemed so solid. So confident. Like he didn't ask the world any questions and the world didn't dare ask any of him. But right now he looked almost fragile.

"Drugs are a part of the music business, Lucille. Always have been. But they aren't worth the price. I thought I could keep you from having to learn that the hard way, but then... after I saw you at that party... I thought you'd fallen into the same black hole I did when I was your age."

"Oh no," Lucy blurted. "I would never. I promise, I had nothing to do with Tomas. I'd only just discovered that he was there with those drugs when you walked into Robyn's room and saw me."

"You scared the stuffing out of me, frankly," Alexander said, "when I saw you holding that bag. Because I knew then that I couldn't protect you from that world. No matter what I did. You're going to have to make your own choices... and your own mistakes."

"I promise I'll try my best to choose right," Lucy said. "I really will."

"I know, dear Lucille." He smiled at her. "I didn't bring you down here to tell you what you should have done. I brought you here to tell you what I should have done. I should have had faith in you. And I do. I have faith in you and I have faith in your choices. And in your music. You are going to get up on that stage tonight and you're going to show the world that you're more than a rock star. You're a musician."

Lucy felt a bit tongue-tied. Alexander Holister had faith in her. In Lucy Gosling.

"You'd better have as much faith in yourself too," he snapped when she didn't reply, a little bit of his usual grumpiness sneaking into his voice. "After all the work I've put into you this summer, I will take it personally if you get on that stage tonight feeling anything less than bulletproof. You hear me, girl?"

Lucy felt a smile bubbling up from the pit of her stomach. Maybe, just maybe, if Alexander could believe it, she could too.

"I don't hear you!"

"Bulletproof," she agreed. "I'll be bulletproof. I promise."

"I expect nothing less," Alexander growled, pushing himself back up to his feet. "Now get out of here or you're going to miss the soundcheck."

Lucy couldn't help herself. She went up on her tiptoes and threw her arms around his neck. She was even more surprised to feel him wrap his arms around her and squeeze her tight enough to lift her feet off the ground.

When she turned and ran out of the door and down the hall, she was smiling again.

Harper stood on the slice of luminescent tape that marked her place on the Palace stage. She tried to focus on what the assistant director was saying, but she wasn't really hearing a word, and she knew it. She was too distracted watching Rafe, who was standing in the wings next to Skye.

Harper told herself she shouldn't be surprised that Rafe still hadn't broken up with Skye, despite the amazing kiss she and Rafe had shared in the pool at the benefit. It'd only been a few days, and everyone, Harper included, had been focused on the finale show. He'd leave Skye after Crush won *Project Next*. Harper was sure of it.

But still, there he was. Standing with Skye, looking tragically bored while she talked earnestly to a tall, rangy woman with a backstage pass strung around her neck. Rafe made eye contact with Harper and rolled his eyes, pretending to gag as Skye pulled a business card from the pocket of her jeans and handed it over to the woman she was trying to get in with. Harper tried not to giggle.

Harper walked through the next formation change on

autopilot, swapping places with Robyn and Toni stage left as the pair came forwards to do the guitar and bass guitar duet at the end of 'Teenage Tragedy'. She had felt like she was tipsy on good champagne for the last three days, ever since Rafe had kissed her in the pool. Rafe Jackson loved her. She'd hoped it was true but she hadn't had any proof until that night. Now she had. He really did love her.

"Okay, girls," the assistant director, a tall, bald man with thick black-rimmed hipster glasses, called. "I think you've got it. Do you think you've got it?"

"Yes!" Toni called before Harper could ask him to run over the last three marks again. "We've got it nailed! We're going to win this thing, just you wait!"

"Best of luck with that, kids," the assistant director said. "Now get the hell off my stage. Plastic Virgins? Where are the Plastic Virgins? Come on now, people, we're already running behind!"

Harper followed Toni off stage, making room for one of the American bands who were jostling each other to find their marks.

Robyn blew past Harper, deliberately avoiding eye contact as she flounced over to Iza and dragged the piano player away. She was still pissed off about the whole Tomas business.

At least Iza would keep Robyn from doing anything too dumb before the show, Harper thought, irritated. Robyn wouldn't want Iza to see her popping more pills, or throwing up her dinner or any of the other disgusting habits she'd picked up. Harper just needed Robyn to hold it together tonight. They could deal with the fact that she'd become such an epic disaster after they'd won.

"Gotcha!" Rafe cried, throwing his arms around Harper from behind and lifting her off her feet.

"Hey!" She giggled as he walked them further into the maze of curtains and wiring. She twisted free and darted ahead, ducking past a thick tangle of cabling to lie in wait for him.

"Har-pperrrr," he crooned. "Where areee—"

"Gotcha!" she crowed, jumping on his back.

He swung her round, somehow positioning her so she was trapped between him and a wall of blackout curtains.

They stood for a moment, almost nose to nose. Eyes locked.

He was going to kiss her again, Harper thought, her brain floating on a cloud of pure happiness.

"Harper." A deep voice snapped through her fog of joy. "I believe wardrobe is looking for you."

Rafe stepped back so fast that Harper had to struggle to keep her balance.

"Dad," he said, turning to face Sir Peter. "I was just—"

Sir Peter smiled at Harper, ignoring his son. "You should run along, dear; you'll love what they've got planned for you down there."

"Great," Harper said. Rafe was looking at her with pleading eyes. "Rafe, can you walk me—"

"My son and I need to talk, Harper," Sir Peter said firmly. "And you need to focus on the show. Hurry now."

Skye felt a little smile twitch its way to the surface as her iPhone buzzed in the pocket of her jeans. That would be a reply from Cesar.

Don't wish I was there. Wish you were here so we could sit on the roof and watch the stars tonight.

The smile grew. She tapped in a quick reply.

Could we order pizza too?

She wished she could snap her fingers and be home right now, sitting on a beach towel on the flat section of the roof that she and C had discovered was totally hidden from everything but the ocean view, planning to order the gooiest pizza they could dream up. She couldn't think of anything she'd ever wanted more.

She loved Cesar. She'd said it to him before, but she didn't think she'd really known it was true until today – not until the moment she'd seen Rafe chase Harper McKenzie through the backstage curtains.

She should thank Harper for being such a boyfriend-stealing skank. If Skye hadn't seen her run off with Rafe, she would never have known the difference between what she'd felt in the few minutes that she'd thought Cesar was flirting with Lucy and how she'd felt when she'd known that Rafe was about to go and make out with Harper.

It hadn't been jealousy, she thought. It had been pain. The idea of losing Cesar had been like being torn in half. C hadn't actually been flirting with Lucy, but she knew if Cesar ever did fall for someone else, he would leave her. And he might, if she kept up like this. That was probably why the only thing she'd felt when she saw Rafe chase Harper into the wings was relief.

Her phone buzzed.

> **Of course there'd be pizza. And the Monopoly board.**

Pizza and Monopoly and Cesar. It sounded like paradise.

"I've given up on the idea that you will learn to be the kind of man who will *not* be a disappointment to us, Rafe." Sir Peter's voice sliced through the curtains.

Skye slid into a darker spot, hoping they wouldn't see her. Sir Peter was always nice to Skye, but she'd seen him in this mood with Rafe before and she didn't want to catch any of the fallout.

"But that doesn't mean I'm going to allow you to make a fool of yourself, or that I'm going to allow you to embarrass this family." Sir Peter stepped out from the maze of curtains, Rafe on his heels. "We live our lives on a public stage, young man. If I have to make decisions for you to see that you live up to that responsibility, I will."

"Dad," Rafe said, "I told you, nothing's happened between me and Harper. But why would it be so awful if it did? She's a star. She's *your* star."

"And if it comes out that she's dating my son, it will reflect poorly on us if she wins tonight, won't it?" Sir Peter snapped back. "Particularly if she's just stolen him out of the arms of Skye Owen, daughter of Jennifer Owen, Chairwoman of Paramount bloody Pictures with whom I am on the verge of closing a major movie deal."

Skye's iPhone buzzed in her pocket and she clamped a hand over it to muffle the sound.

"That's what this is really about, isn't it?" Rafe snapped back at his father, resentment blasting in his tone. "Protecting your deal. Who cares what I want if it gets in the way of your precious business?"

"This has nothing to do with business, young man," Sir Peter snarled. "It has everything to do with legacy. You are my legacy and so are your actions. If your actions interfere with the potential success of my legacy, then I will modify your actions for you. Do you understand that?"

"What if I don't want to be your legacy?" Rafe spat out.

"You are, for better or worse," Sir Peter fired back. "Someday, you'll thank me for making you into the man I expect you to be."

Rafe punched the wall.

Sir Peter reached out and put a hand on his son's shoulder.

"Listen, Rafe," he said. "I know that you're frustrated. I know that I'm hard on you, but I have my reasons, son. I'm older and wiser, and I know what you need right now. I want you to see to your relationship with Skye because you need a woman like her – a strong, independent woman who will make you better than you are. Harper is a wonderful girl, but she can't do that for you. You'll just end up ruining her, and yourself in the process."

Rafe didn't say anything.

"Just think about it," Sir Peter said. "I expect you to make the right decision."

He walked away, leaving Rafe standing alone.

Come on, Skye thought. *Stomp off. Go find Harper and make out with her, just to prove him wrong.*

But Rafe didn't seem to be going anywhere.

She glanced down at the screen of her phone.

Where'd ya go? Must be making you work hard out there – hope it's going well!

Trust Cesar to be sweet, even when he was feeling ignored. Once she would have enjoyed playing hard to get, but not any more. She glanced up at Rafe again. He looked like he was settling into a sulk right there and, she knew from experience, Rafe could sulk forever. If she wanted to text Cesar back, she'd have to get out of here.

She reached out and deliberately shook the curtain that sheltered her from view, and then burst through as though she'd just walked up from the other side.

"Rafe!" she said, like she was surprised to see him there.

She almost felt sorry for him when he looked up at her. His eyes were brimming, open wounds.

"I'm on the hunt for Harper. Wardrobe is looking for her." She kept moving past him, hoping he would let her escape without a long-winded scene. "I'll just—"

But instead of letting her pass, he reached out and grabbed her, pulling her into his arms.

"Rafe," was all she managed to say before his lips closed over hers. She pushed him back after a moment. "Rafe, I'm here for work, I really need to—"

"Screw work," he said, pushing her back into the curtains. His lips closed over hers again and she found herself wrapping her arms around his neck on reflex. He'd always been an amazing kisser.

Her phone buzzed again. Cesar. She was ignoring Cesar to kiss Rafe Jackson, a boy who had been on the verge of cheating on her only minutes before. What was she doing?

But the kiss was deepening, making it difficult to think. Making it hard to remember that Rafe wasn't the guy she wanted him to be and Cesar... Cesar was...

And then she couldn't seem to remember who or what Cesar was. All she could think of was the feeling of Rafe's lips on hers.

13. WORTH IT (FT. TRENT EISNER)

"Are you worth it? Do I care?
If I don't, what am I doing this for?"

Trent Eisner couldn't stop himself from bouncing a little in time with the pounding beat of Lucy Gosling's drums as it drove Harper McKenzie's voice outwards to fill the Caesars Palace auditorium. It was hard to believe that five teenage girls from London could dominate the Caesars stage this way, but they were doing it.

"Are you worth it? Just a little bit,
But you'd better know how lucky you are.
I'm gonna go far, but if you're worth it,
I might let you ride in my car."

They were good, Trent thought. They were better than good. Even the camera crews that surrounded him in his perch in the eagle's nest were having trouble resisting the driving beat that pulled them into the music.

Harper sashayed over to Robyn, the two girls moving effortlessly in time with each other and their music. Robyn picked her way through a long riff that sounded a bit like flamenco guitar but somehow melded perfectly into the rapid fire punk-pop melody, then Toni ran to the front of the stage and took the mic for a line or two as Harper dashed across the stage to sit next to Iza, picking out a few notes around Iza's playfully elaborate piano line.

"You say you're worth it, but I don't know,"
Toni's alto throbbed out.
"I'm worth a little more with every step I go.
Can you keep up? For your sake, I hope so."

Oh yes, these girls were good. And gorgeous, he thought. Every single one of them. Their monochromatic white outfits were a perfect choice – from Lucy's all-white Converse to Toni's white bustier and skinny jeans, they looked striking, sophisticated even, but they were still their unique, original selves. And as for Harper McKenzie – she could have been dressed in her pyjamas and still look like a superstar. Harper McKenzie was the kind of girl born for the spotlight.

But Harper wasn't the one he couldn't stop staring at.

That was Lucy.

Her long curls tied back in a dark starburst behind her head, Lucy's sticks flew like they had a life of their own, even though Trent knew that she had absolute control of them for every second of every song. She made it look easy. And that smile. God, that smile. It was like an arrow to the heart, designed just for him.

He mentally smacked himself. Melodrama was good for ballads but not for real life. Lucy wasn't smiling for him. She didn't even know he was there. He was going to surprise her after the show and sweep her off her feet the way he'd wanted to at Blvd3. Or at least, that had been the plan. He hadn't thought Crush would be so damn awesome. He hadn't even considered the possibility that they'd win. He hadn't thought much beyond being with Lucy again.

But that was the problem. When he looked at Lucy Gosling, he heard nothing but love songs. It was embarrassing but it was true. He was such a walking cliché. He'd met a girl and suddenly the love songs he'd always thought were ridiculous sounded... Well, they sounded true. They sounded like all the feelings that were jammed into every corner of his brain.

"Are you worth it? I don't care.
I say you're worth it, so you better be worth it.
It's only fair,"

Harper blasted.

"I'm worth a little more every step I go.
If you're worth it, you better show me it's so."

Oh yes, he could fall in love with Lucy Gosling, if he let himself. But did he want to? Was she worth it? He couldn't see her, he thought, until he'd made up his mind. It wouldn't be fair. Should he go backstage and surprise her as he'd planned? Or should he just leave, get on a plane back to LA and try to forget the drummer girl forever? If Crush won *Project Next* they'd be on tour for a year. And he'd be on tour at the same time. He and Lucy would be in a different city every night. How much did he want to give up just for the chance of a few minutes of Skype time with her every day? How much did he want to make her give up? Was *he* worth it? Or would falling in love with Lucy Gosling be an express ticket to a broken heart?

"I'm worth it,"
Crush belted out in chorus.
"Are you?"

It was so quiet in the auditorium that Lucy could actually hear the stiff white envelope tear as the *Project Next* host Liam Michaels ripped it open.

Lucy Gosling's destiny was in that envelope. And it was about to be set free.

If she could, she'd freeze time in this moment, the

tingle of an amazing show still sparkling across her skin. There was no failure here and no success; only potential.

But potential can't last forever.

"Are you ready for this, kids?" Liam Michaels asked the four bands, gathered in bunches behind him on the massive stage at Caesar's Palace.

"YEAH!" the bands around her crowed. Harper grabbed one of Lucy's hands and Robyn grabbed the other as Crush huddled together. Lucy felt like the only fixed point in a world of colour and movement and sound that made less and less sense with every second that Liam drew out his dramatic pause.

"Okay, straight to the point then. The winner is..."

The auditorium seemed to hold its breath.

"CRUSH!"

Fireworks, Lucy thought, abstractly, as she felt her body joining in the bouncing tangle of arms and legs and screaming girls that Crush became as the hovering cameras moved in for a close-up. It was like fireworks going off in her brain. An explosion of emotions and sensations she couldn't give proper names to if she tried.

They'd won.

Lucy suddenly found herself sitting in a make-up chair, being dusted and powdered by a large black man wearing a sequined sweatshirt who sternly instructed her to, "Sit still and keep those peepers shut!" as he carefully glued false eyelashes to the far corners of her eyelids, one sprig of lashes at a time.

It felt as though she blinked once, cautiously hoping that the eyelash glue would not end up sticking her eyes shut forever, and then found herself standing in front of a bank of mirrors in her pants and bra, as Debra Z rained designer clothes down on her. Debra was chattering about something, but the adrenaline-fuelled blood rushing through Lucy's ears was too loud for her to hear anything past it.

Another blink and she was on the stage of the now empty Caesars Palace theatre, clinking champagne glasses with the girls, Sir Peter, Jason, Alexander and half a dozen people she didn't recognise as camera flashes exploded all around her.

A blink again, and she was in a limousine, watching the neon outlines of Las Vegas pass on the way to some place called The Ends that Ash said was the latest hotspot.

They'd won.

Crush had won *Project Next.*

If Lucy Gosling had ever wanted to be a boring human being, she was out of luck. She would never be normal again.

"Lucy?" Harper's voice was so quiet compared to the decibel level the whole world had been set to since Liam Michaels said the word 'Crush' on stage hours ago that Lucy almost didn't hear her.

"Um, yeah, Harper," Lucy said, shaking herself out of the fog of shock. "What's up?"

"We are," Harper said with a grin. She topped up the champagne flute that had somehow made its way into Lucy's hand, and then clinked her own against it. "To us."

"Yes," Lucy said, with a smile. "To Crush."

"Nah," Harper replied, settling back into the plush seat beside her. "There'll be plenty of that later. That one was just for you and me. I couldn't have done this without you, Luce. We wouldn't be here. I wouldn't be here."

Lucy twisted to look at Harper. She wasn't mucking about. She was serious.

"Well, I wouldn't be here either, obviously," Lucy said. "Without you, I mean. You changed my whole life, Harper."

"Hopefully not in a totally-ruined-it sort of way," Harper said. She laughed, but Lucy could see she wasn't entirely kidding.

"Of course not," Lucy assured her. "Look at this! Look at where we are! You were right before. Together, we can do whatever we want. As long as there's you and me, and we've got each other's back, nothing can stop us."

"BFF, right?" Harper said, jingling her charm bracelet.

"Quite right," Lucy said, in a mock posh voice. "BFF for good."

They grinned at each other and Lucy finally felt the world coming back into focus around her.

"We're here!" Toni crowed from the other end of the vast limousine.

"YEE-HA!" Iza yelled. Then she burped a tiny Iza-sized burp and collapsed back into her seat in a fit of giggles.

"Oh my God," Robyn said, shaking her head. "Iza's lost the plot already and we're not even at the party yet."

"I have not," Iza said, crawling to the door the chauffeur was holding for them.

"Have too," Harper said, nudging her affectionately. "But it's about time we got you properly trashed. Out you get."

Lucy slid out next and stood beside the limo, blinded for a moment by the explosion of camera flashes that echoed around them. This couldn't all be for Crush. But it was, she realised. This was all for Crush. All for Lucy Gosling and her four best friends. How amazing was that?

Just out of the corner of her eye, Lucy saw a familiar figure that made her heart thump double time. Could it be? Had Trent Eisner come to their show? Was he really here?

Lucy craned her neck, allowing herself a few seconds of crazed optimism as she searched the crowd for floppy brown hair and chocolate eyes. But after a moment, she felt the little spark of hope die. She'd been imagining it. Of course. Why would Trent bother to come? He barely knew her, and he certainly wasn't interested in getting to know her better. He'd made that abundantly clear.

"Come on, Luce!" Harper called, reaching out to grab Lucy's hand and pull her along. "Let's do this!"

Lucy followed Harper out into a lightning storm of flashbulbs.

"Look over here, Lucy!"

Worth It (ft. Trent Eisner)

"This way, Crush! Look at me!"

"Harper! Over here!"

Lucy hooked her arm through Harper's and struck one of the poses Debra Z had taught them, then another and another. The hail of light and voices battered her relentlessly, but with her arm through Harper's, she found that she wasn't as overwhelmed or frightened as she'd expected to be. Together they could do this. They could do anything. They'd walk the red carpet like they belonged there, because now... they did.

Skye Owen shifted her weight, trying to ease the pressure on the blister that was forming under her right big toe. Her white snakeskin four-inch heels looked amazing, but they were sample size, so they didn't fit at all. Standing on the unforgiving slate tiles of the pool deck at The Ends didn't help.

Like so many clubs in Vegas, The Ends had an indoor dance floor with a bar and a second bar outside. This one happened to be on the thirtieth storey of the casino tower that housed the club. It was a beautiful view. Skye might even have enjoyed standing at the railing, looking out over the sparkle of the Strip, if she had been alone. But she wasn't.

Rafe had stuck to her like glue since their impromptu kiss backstage before the *Project Next* final. And now, just to make things even more awkward, they were stuck at the hottest club in Las Vegas with their parents.

"I'm so glad you thought to ask us to come out for the show, Peter," Jennifer Owen simpered. "It's wonderful to see what Rafe and Skye have been working so hard on all summer."

Skye wondered whether Sir Peter could hear how fake her mother's coo was.

"I'm sure Skye has put in much more work than Rafe," Sir Peter said, returning her mother's smile with just as much genuine emotion as Jennifer had given him. "I'm so glad her influence is getting Rafe involved in the family business."

"Not just involved, Dad," Rafe grumbled. "I've put in a massive amount of work this summer, just like Skye."

"He really has," Skye cut in. She'd rather lie than deal with the fight she could see brewing. "Thank you so much for the opportunity, Sir Peter."

"Of course, dear," he said. "You two are going to have to learn the business from the ground up if you want to run Catch-22 someday."

"Our very own future movie moguls," her mother threw in, not one to be left out of a hyperbole competition. "Aren't they adorable?"

"Quite," Sir Peter said, shoving Rafe closer to Skye. "In fact..." He turned and waved a photographer over. "Jack, take a few of this pair, will you? This is young Hollywood royalty. This is a dynasty in the making."

Rafe draped his arm over Skye's shoulders and she leaned in, letting the momentum of all the staring eyes push her in the direction they wanted her to go. Towards Rafe.

"My little princess and her prince," her mother gushed convincingly.

Skye felt the buzz of her phone, where she'd tucked it into the pocket of her skintight jeans. That would be a text from Cesar. She'd told him she'd call when the show was done.

She hadn't.

After she'd nearly let Rafe tear off all of her clothes backstage at the show, calling Cesar and pretending nothing had happened felt... wrong. It was unsettling. It wasn't like Cesar didn't know she was still dating Rafe, but somehow all of the things that hadn't bothered her before about being with both of them now made her skin crawl. She didn't want Cesar having to think about Rafe's hands on her, just like she didn't want to think about another girl being with him.

Except, of course, Rafe's hands *were* all over her right now. And they'd be all over her in every magazine that covered the *Project Next* final. On every website. On freaking *Entertainment Tonight.*

The thought very nearly made her shove Rafe away. She didn't care how big a scene she made, but then Skye caught the thrilled smile on her mother's face as she watched her daughter in the limelight. For once, Jennifer Owen was completely happy with her and Skye just couldn't ruin that.

"This way, kids!" called another photographer. Skye followed their directions, resting her head on Rafe's shoulder and letting the flashbulbs blind her.

When Toni had caught sight of Jason's tousle of blonde hair moving through the crowd, she had to stop herself turning and running in the other direction. She couldn't do that. Jason was going to be their manager for a long time. She couldn't just avoid him forever.

It wasn't as though he was the only one who'd made a terrible mistake. He might have broken her heart, but she couldn't blame him for it, not really. She'd been the one who'd thrown it at him, not realising how breakable it really was, and nearly ruined his life in the process too.

It was time. Time to get on with her own life and let Jason get on with his.

"Jason," she called. "Over here."

He had a strange look on his face when he turned to greet her.

"Toni," he said. "Shouldn't you be with the girls?"

"You did a fantastic job tonight," an unfamiliar woman said, stepping up beside Jason and weaving her arm through his. "Jason is right to be so proud of you girls."

She was gorgeous, Toni thought. Slim and graceful, with a brilliant shock of red curls that gave her a look of unintentional perfection that made her all the prettier.

She was also immensely pregnant.

"I don't know how you girls put up with him," the

beautiful woman said with a conspiratorial grin. "Always watching you like a hawk when you're supposed to be having fun. I'm Leah." She stuck out a hand. "Jason's wife. You must be Toni. I recognise you from the publicity shots that Jase showed me when he was picking his band for the show."

"We wouldn't be here without him," Toni said quietly, managing to return Leah's smile.

Leah Darrow bore no resemblance at all to the picture Toni had constructed in her head during her weeks of obsessing over the subject of Jason's wife. She couldn't be further from the polished elegance of her husband, but the chaotic brilliance of her wild hair and simple white maternity dress accessorised with an antique pocket watch on a delicate chain fitted with him somehow. Like the last piece of a puzzle whose shape Toni would never have been able to guess without holding it in her hand.

Jason looked positively stricken, staring at the two of them standing together. Any other time, Toni might have enjoyed tormenting him a bit. Not that she'd ever give the game away to his wife. This woman didn't deserve that.

But right at that moment, there was something else she needed to do.

"I won't take up your night," Toni said, rushing the words before she lost her nerve or burst into tears, both of which felt possible. "I know Jason's been with us constantly the last few weeks, so you must be dying to have him to yourself. I just wanted to thank you," she said, turning to look Jason in the eye, "for everything. We couldn't have done this without you. And I... I've learned a lot from you this summer. And I know I haven't always been easy to get along with, but thank you for not giving up on us and making this happen."

Jason opened his mouth, as though to speak. Then he closed it again. Leah looked up at her husband, amusement blending with concern on her expressive face.

"You'd think you'd never met a gracious musician before, babe," she said, elbowing her husband gently. Then she turned back to Toni with another of her warm smiles. "Congratulations, Toni, I think you've done the impossible. You've left Jason Darrow speechless."

"Quiet you," he said, shaking himself from his trance, like a dog shaking water from its fur. "You're not supposed to mock me in front of the talent."

Then he smiled at Toni. "Thank you, Toni. I hope you're excited for everything that's coming. I know I am."

"Right," Toni said. She felt lighter, she realised. Literally lighter, as though she'd been living underwater for the last three weeks and suddenly she'd been lifted up into the air. "Absolutely. Me too."

Leah grinned. "Now, enough of all this gushing, you two. I think it's time Toni enjoyed her party, don't you?"

"Couldn't agree more," Toni said, tossing her hair over her shoulder and looking around at all the people filling the sleek, all-white interior of The Ends with renewed interest. "High time, actually."

With that she strode off, head high, just like the rock star she was.

Lucy was tired. She'd been having a blast until Harper had shifted into mad-for-Rafe-Jackson mode, which had happened pretty much the second that Sir Peter and Skye's parents had left.

Normally, Lucy wouldn't have been overly bothered. She knew Rafe, in his own way, seemed to be quite mad for Harper as well. He was semi-cheating on his girlfriend, of course, but Skye was also completely cheating on him, so did it really count?

But tonight of all nights, shouldn't Harper have wanted to celebrate their victory with her best friend? Without Harper, Lucy was having a hard time forgetting the fact that when the others went home for a month before they started touring, Lucy would have nowhere to go. Dancing with the other girls had helped distract her for a while, but now they'd gone AWOL as well.

If Harper hadn't disappeared, Lucy would probably have carried on dancing and had a few more cocktails and stopped worrying about the future. But on her own, Lucy had started feeling tired. And worried. And sad. Now all Lucy wanted was to go home. Not to the hotel room upstairs, but to her bedroom in Greenwich where her annoying older brother would be waking her up at the crack of dawn to play tennis and her brat of a sister would steal her stash of sweets and tell on her for having it at the same time. But she couldn't go home, so their luxurious hotel suite would have to do. She'd just text the others that she was leaving and go upstairs.

Lucy was fishing her phone out of her green patent clutch when she heard a familiar voice.

"Wait, wait, wait. I want to take the shot of Death Juice, *then* the shot of vodka to wash it down."

That was Iza, Lucy thought, craning to see the pianist through the crowd that towered around her. But that wasn't something Iza would say. Ever. Iza hated vodka, and she most definitely did not drink mystery booze called Death Juice.

But there she was – leaning against the poolside bar, holding court with four or five guys, all of whom seemed eager to put another shot in her hand, and two of whom had cameras. Christ.

"Excuse me," Lucy said, trying to squeeze between two of Iza's admirers. She had no luck. She might as well have been talking to a brick wall.

"To Crush!" Iza proclaimed, downing another shot.

"Excuse... me..." Lucy found herself moving backwards instead of towards Iza. It was like she wasn't even there. Maybe she should just give up. Iza seemed to be having a good enough time. Lucy was probably overreacting. In fact, it was probably out of order of her to stop Iza's party. Iza was a big girl.

"Body shots next!" one of the guys called.

"Ye-ah!" Iza hooted.

Okay, that was it. Iza Mazurczak did *not* do body shots. She didn't even like to drink all that much. Not to mention the part where Lucy had no desire to see the look on Jason's face tomorrow if Crush made the headlines for its underage keyboard player doing body shots with a gang of drunk men in a bar.

Lucy pushed into the group, ducking under the arm of a fat man who smelled terrible, to grab Iza's hand.

"Lucy! You're here! You're my favourite, do you know that?" Iza gushed drunkenly, throwing her arms wide and smacking more than one of her suitors in the face in the process.

"Yeah, hi, boys, give us some room, can you?" Lucy said, throwing an elbow hard into the gut of the one on her right, just to make her point.

He moved, finally, giving Lucy room to duck to Iza's very wobbly side.

"Try this," Iza said, handing Lucy a sloshing shot glass. "It's blinding."

"I bet it is," Lucy replied, setting the shot carefully on the counter, "but right now I think we'd better leave it be, yeah? I'm pretty sure we've both had enough."

"But we *won*! Why would we have had enough?"

"We'll buy you one too, babe, don't worry," said a tall guy who was way too old to be buying underage girls drinks in bars.

"Yeah, don't be a buzzkill, sweetie," said another twenty-something guy. A twenty-something guy with a camera in his back pocket that he was clearly trying to keep hidden.

"I'm not a buzzkill," Lucy said sweetly. "But Ash is."

She turned and called to Ash, who was sprawled in a pool chair nearby, tapping away at his iPhone. "Hey, Ash, how would Jason feel about me taking this scumbag's camera and stomping on it?"

"He might not encourage it," Ash drawled. "What's giving you the urge?"

"This lot are feeding Iza shots, I expect with the hopes that she'll do something page-six-worthy," Lucy said, eyes narrowed at the guilty photographer.

"Oh, well in that case, don't worry about it," Ash said, straightening up. "The Catch-22 lawyers love lawsuits. This will give them something fun to play with."

And just like that, the whole crowd of guys made themselves scarce.

"Thanks for that, Ash," Lucy said, reaching out to steady Iza as she wobbled against the bar.

"Thanks for nothing!" Iza pouted. "You've made them all leave now."

"Yes and we're very thankful for that," Lucy said, patting her friend's shoulder. "Come on, Iz. Let's go upstairs and drunk-text Luke, shall we?"

"Oh! I like Luke!" Iza said, brightening again.

"Yes, yes you do," Lucy said, half smiling. Trust Iza to be a ray of sunshine, even when completely destroyed with drink. "Come on."

But Iza wasn't as good at walking whilst drunk as she

was at being happy whilst drunk. Ash reached out to steady her other arm.

"Little help, here?" he asked, eyebrow raised.

"Thanks," Lucy said.

Iza might have been small, but she was still bigger than Lucy and quite a lot heavier after she passed out in the lift. Lucy and Ash were both struggling for breath by the time they deposited Iza in her room in the penthouse suite where Crush had been moved after they'd won.

"Thank goodness you were there," Lucy breathed, collapsing next to Ash on the oversized leather sofa in the living room. "I don't think I could have got her out of the lift alone."

"That's cute," Ash said, shifting to smile down at her.

"What is?"

"The way you say that." He reached out to tuck a curl behind her ear. "Lift," he repeated in a horrible imitation of Lucy's accent. "It's adorable."

"Lift?" Lucy said, giggling. "That's what it's called, that's all; nothing adorable about it."

"You're right," Ash said, leaning a little closer. "*You* must be the adorable part then."

Then he was kissing her.

He wasn't a bad kisser. In fact, it didn't feel bad at all. Being here. Letting him kiss her. Letting him trail his lips down her neck.

Trent Eisner might not have wanted to kiss her, but Ash did. Ash always had, she thought. Since the day they'd met. Why shouldn't she let him now? Why shouldn't she keep her arms wrapped around his neck as he scooped her up and started walking towards her bedroom at the back of the suite? Why shouldn't they go inside and do all sorts of things that would let her forget about her humiliating kiss with Trent and her parents and Harper and everything else?

Lucy even surprised herself when her foot came up to wedge between them and the door to her room, stopping Ash in his tracks.

"Ash," she said, freeing her lips.

He just kissed her again and tried to manoeuvre her through the door once more. She shifted her weight, making it impossible for him to get past.

"Ash," she tried again. "Stop!"

"Don't worry, babe," he muttered, trying to kiss her once more. "Don't worry so much. I'm going to take good care of you."

"Ash, wait. Put me down."

He didn't.

Lucy tensed and twisted, breaking his hold and managing to catch herself before she went crashing to the ground. She backed off a few paces, just to give herself a moment to think.

"I need to take a breather. I'm not really ready to—"

But he was already reaching out for her again.

"I've been waiting so long for this," Ash murmured, wrapping his arms around her again. "Don't let me down."

"I'm not letting you down," Lucy said, trying unsuccessfully to shove him away. He was so much bigger than she was. "I just need a moment. ASH!" she half yelled, as he pushed her back against the wall. "Stop that."

He didn't.

Lucy shot a hard elbow into his abdomen, then twisted out from under his arm and shoved him backwards, over her extended leg. Thank God John had insisted on teaching her a few of his judo moves, even if he'd only done it because he wanted to use her as a practice dummy.

"Way to be a loser, Lucy," Ash groaned from the floor.

"Way to be a psycho," Lucy shot back. "Get out, Ash!"

"Oh come on, Lucy," he said, gathering himself. "You're overreacting. We were just having some fun. Don't be such a drama queen about it."

"I'm not a drama queen," Lucy snapped, "but you are a disgusting, wannabe sex pest and a drunk, and you need to leave now – or I'm calling Jason."

"Fine," Ash snapped. "Be a crazy bitch. See if I care."

Lucy didn't bother to reply, she just stepped through the door to her bedroom and slammed it in his face.

14. Sucker Punch

"We've officially got to do something about Robyn," Lucy said, dragging the heavy door of the beach-side Ladies' loo closed behind her. "And Iza."

Coming back from Las Vegas, Crush had gone straight from LA airport to Skye's house in Malibu. Harper had suggested it as a way to avoid the cameras at the Crush house, but Lucy was sure she was just looking for excuses to be around Rafe. After a morning of Rafe and Harper flirting with each other while the others moped about, Lucy had wholeheartedly agreed with Skye's suggestion of a trip to the beach. She didn't blame Skye for insisting that she and Rafe drive separately either.

They'd arrived to find Skye already setting up a picnic on the expensive beach mats she'd spread by one of the Venice Beach volleyball courts. Judging by the determined look on Harper's face, Lucy reckoned Skye would have her hands full if she wanted to hang on to Rafe.

Why she'd actually want to do that, Lucy hadn't a clue, but Lucy hoped for Crush's sake that she would.

"Oh come on," Harper said, poking at her lashes again with her mascara wand. "We just won *Project Next.* Can't you relax and enjoy that for five seconds?"

"Relax? You want me to relax, with Robyn looking like she's escaped from an anti-drugs ad and Iza somewhere, crying I'd imagine, trying to explain to her lovely boyfriend how she ended up plastered all over the internet under headlines like *Crush pianist hooks up with manager's assistant.*"

"If she didn't want to make headlines, she shouldn't have got trashed and left with Ash," Harper snipped.

"She *didn't,*" Lucy said. "She left with me *and* Ash, that gossip site cropped me out of the pictures, then sold them to every magazine who'd buy. And she got trashed because those awful journalists were pouring shots down her throat and she was already too drunk to stop them. We should have been there, Harper. We should have stayed together last night, or at least kept an eye on her. She'd already had more champagne by the time we got out of the limo than she's had all summer. And we all knew it."

"She's a big girl," Harper said.

"So are we! And we're her friends. We let her down, Harper," Lucy said.

Once upon a time the look of put-upon annoyance on Harper's face would have shot stabs of anxiety up

Lucy's spine, but now it just irritated her. Harper was free to be annoyed but Lucy wasn't going to let her get away with mooning over Rafe all day and forcing the others to deal with the real problems. Not today.

"Fine," Harper relented. "We should have stuck together. But I had to find Rafe, Luce. You don't understand. We're so close—"

"I can't believe Rafe Jackson is still more important to you than we are."

Harper's eyes went wide, as though Lucy had just slapped her.

"I would never—"

Harper's mobile rang, cutting her off. She snatched it up and connected without even looking at the screen.

"I told you, Tomas," Harper snapped into the phone. "I told you not to mess with my girls and you did it anyway. You're lucky I haven't flushed your stash and put a match to your money."

Lucy stared at Harper, horrified. She started to open her mouth but Harper held up a finger for quiet.

"No, Tomas, I'm not afraid of you. You want us to think you're all gangster but you're so not. You're an embassy brat who's going to get out of jail in a few days and get tossed on a plane back to wherever the hell you come from. Trying to act tough just makes you sound pathetic."

"Harper," Lucy hissed. "What are you doing?"

"Making it crystal clear to at least one of our problems

that he'd better not mess with Crush," Harper said loudly so that Tomas could hear her at the other end of the phone. "I promised I'd destroy him if he came near us again and I meant it."

She clicked off the phone and dropped it into her bag. "That's settled."

"*Settled?*" Lucy gasped. "You're holding a drug dealer's stash hostage and he's threatening to do goodness knows what to you and you think that's *settled*?"

"He's a spoilt high school kid with too much time on his hands, Lucy," Harper said, pulling her long hair into a loose ponytail. "Not a drug dealer. I told him to stay away from us and he didn't, so now he's got to learn his lesson."

"We have to call Jason," Lucy said. "Right now. We can't just—"

"We're big girls, Lucy," Harper said. "You said it yourself. We don't need Jason."

"Yes, we do."

"It'll just get Robyn in trouble. What if she ends up in jail? You don't want that, do you?" Harper pointed out.

"No," Lucy said, reluctantly. "I don't... but don't you think—"

"I think it's going to be fine," Harper said firmly. "Just fine." She pulled off her cover-up and surveyed her white bikini in the warped full-length mirror. "Now, I'm going to go knock Rafe's socks off. Care to join me?"

Lucy sighed. The last thing she wanted to do was

watch Harper make a fool of herself over Rafe. In fact, she didn't want to deal with anyone else right now. She needed some quiet.

"I'm going for a walk," she said, pulling out her iPod. "I'll be back to the volleyball courts in a bit."

As Lucy struck out over the burning sand, she pulled her mobile from her pocket. She wanted to call home. She needed her parents. She'd never realised how nice she'd had it before. Having parents who cared, parents who wanted to help and made sure life never got over her head.

She wasn't sorry she'd come to LA. She couldn't be. No matter how hard she'd tried to think that all of this was a mistake, she knew it wasn't. The mistake had been lying about it. The mistake had been thinking that she wasn't strong enough or smart enough to make her parents see why she needed this. She could have made them understand, if she'd talked to them about it properly in the first place. Maybe, now she knew that, she could find a way to talk to them.

Lucy hit call.

The phone rang. And rang. And rang.

"Hello, you've reached the Gosling family," Emily's recorded voice piped through the thousands of miles of digital airwaves. "We're not in at the moment, so leave us a nice message and we'll call back – we promise!"

Lucy listened to the beep, then the dead air of the answerphone waiting for her to say something. Anything.

They wouldn't call back.

But maybe that wasn't the point.

"Hi, guys," she began haltingly. "I just wanted to say... I know, I said it in my letter, but I wanted to say... I'm sorry. Not that I joined Crush. Or that we did *Project Next.* I needed to do both of those things and I hope you'll understand that one day. But I'm sorry I lied to you about it. I'm sorry I didn't give you the chance to understand. I should have. I should have been grown up enough to do that. You deserved that. Because all of this... everything that's happened. It's so much. There's so much going on and I need you. I need my family. And I didn't know it when I left. But I know it now. I need you. So please call me. Please."

Lucy ended the call and tucked the phone back into her pocket. That's when she heard the crying coming from the other side of a rocky outcrop.

Iza couldn't see Lucy from her spot amongst the smooth, high rocks, but she could hear her talking to someone on her mobile. Part of Iza wanted to go to her friend and tell her everything, but it was just too humiliating. How could she tell Lucy what she'd done?

"Iz, what's wrong?" Lucy's head poked over the rocks that sheltered Iza's hiding place from the rest of the beach.

"Nothing," Iza said, desperately trying to swallow enough of her sobs to sound normal.

"I don't believe you," Lucy said, plopping down beside her. "You're upset. What's happened? Spill."

Iza tried to force the words out of her mouth, but they just wouldn't come. Finally she simply held out her iPhone.

Lucy took the mobile from her and looked down at the screen where Luke's latest text was displayed.

Pls stop calling. Don't want to talk to you right now.

"He's going to hate me forever," Iza burst out, tears spilling down her cheeks again. "He saw the videos and the bloody pictures in the bloody magazines and now he'll never speak to me again and he's every right not to. I'm horrid."

"Those guys were pouring shots down you, Iz, when you were already too trashed to know what was really happening," Lucy pointed out. "It wasn't your fault. Luke will calm down eventually. Then you can explain that the photo of you getting into the lift with Ash was edited, that I was there too. Nothing happened. It'll be fine."

"That's just it, Luce," Iza whispered. "Something *did* happen."

"What? When?" Lucy demanded. "Did one of those guys—"

"No. It was later. I woke up... in our suite," Iza said, swiping at her eyes, trying to clear the tears away.

"I woke up and no one else was there but Ash. He was watching telly on the couch. And I was still so drunk... I kissed him."

"Oh, honey," Lucy began, but Iza wasn't finished yet. If she didn't say it now, to Lucy, she'd never have the guts to tell anyone ever.

"The next thing I remember... I was in bed. Naked. I don't remember him leaving, Lucy. I don't know what... what we did. I haven't before... done that, I mean. I thought it would be Luke. I really did. And now I've just... I've just thrown everything away."

There.

She'd said it.

Funny. The words had been so ugly that the taste of them in her mouth made her want to vomit, but now that they were out she felt a little better – like forcing the awful night out of her memory and into the light of day had cleared some of its toxins from her body.

Lucy had gone dead white when Iza had begun the story, but now a dark red flush was burning across her cheeks. Iza had never seen her usually easy-going bandmate so furious. In fact, she wasn't sure she'd ever seen Lucy truly angry. Not like this.

Lucy reached out and gripped Iza's hand for a moment, lips pressed together like the very muscles of her body were too enraged to allow speech. Then she pulled her mobile from her pocket.

"I'm calling Alexander," Lucy said, already dialling.

"And then we're going in to Catch-22 and calling the police. I was willing to let Ash get away with being a pushy bastard to me, but this, this is out of order. Just... out of order."

"No," Iza cried. "Please, Lucy. I'm glad I told you, but I don't want to make a big deal about this and I certainly don't want to tell the others. That would just be... I mean, I don't want everyone to know. And my parents... What if my parents found out? I'm okay. I'll be okay. Really. Let's just go back to the others, all right?"

"I really think—" Lucy began, but Iza shook her head furiously.

"It's over now. I just want to forget about it," Iza insisted. "Honestly."

Lucy studied her intensely for a long moment. Iza did her best to look like someone who knew what she wanted.

Finally, Lucy nodded. "Okay. We'll leave it be for now. But, Iz, he didn't have any right to do that, and you mustn't blame yourself for it. It's up to you whether we do anything about it or not, but don't let him get away with making you feel like someone less than you are, okay? He doesn't deserve that - and neither do you."

Skye dragged another towel out of her oversized beach tote and tried to pretend that tears weren't dripping down her cheeks. What was wrong with her? What did she care if Rafe was too busy chasing Harper around to play a decent game of volleyball? In fact, why hadn't she just stormed off, jumped in her car and driven home to spend the afternoon with Cesar instead of staying here watching them?

But that was a stupid question. She knew why not.

Why's name was Jennifer, but it preferred to be called Mother.

Her mother just couldn't stop talking about how excited she was about Skye and Rafe ending up on page six, in *People*'s Style Report and about ten other magazines as the next Hollywood it-couple. Jennifer had already had dozens of texts and emails from business associates congratulating her on her darling daughter and her adorable boyfriend. She was even in talks with Graydon at *Vanity Fair* about doing a feature on Skye. What would she do if her little Hollywood princess told her she was actually in love with the gardener?

Jennifer would kill her. Or maybe disown her and adopt a few Somali orphans in her place. Better PR.

She should take the damn interview and tell *Vanity Fair* all about how she'd been sleeping with the help, Skye thought. If she was going to get disowned, she might as well go out with a bang.

But Skye knew she wasn't going to do that. Just like she knew Rafe wasn't really going to flout Sir Peter and dump her for Harper McKenzie. They'd stay together through college. Have a 'fairytale' wedding. Maybe have their own reality show for a few seasons before he got some starlet pregnant and left Skye a disgraced divorcee.

And it would all be over before she turned thirty. She could see it, laid out in front of her like it had already happened. No one would ever take her seriously again, but it would be great publicity for dear old Mom.

Just thinking about it made it hard to breathe.

Then another picture formed in her mind. A bungalow in Hollywood somewhere. Small. Probably rented. A laptop and a pile of scripts on the dining room table. A couple of kids' bikes in the backyard. A barbecue pit with *tamales* and *carne asada* heating on the open flame. Loud voices and laughter in the background.

A future where she could breathe.

Why did she care what Jennifer Owen wanted? Jennifer Owen didn't care what her daughter wanted, that was for damn sure.

And what Skye wanted was Cesar.

She turned to look at Rafe who, in between slurps of spiked lemonade, was batting the ball back and forth over the net with Toni while Harper stretched out strategically in the sand beside the court, artfully applying sunscreen to her long, graceful legs.

She'd talk to him as soon as the girls went home. She'd tell him it was over. Then she'd be able to tell Cesar, in complete and total honesty, that she was all his.

By four, Lucy was beginning to think the day might not be such a disaster after all. Toni and Iza were having a blast bodysurfing in the soft waves, and Robyn had even had a few snacks before dozing off on her towel beside the volleyball court. Harper and Rafe seemed to have cooled off with a volleyball net between them, despite Rafe's obvious tipsiness. Even Skye seemed to be at peace with the world.

Lucy checked her mobile for the seven-thousand-and-first time. Her parents still hadn't returned her call. Surely one of them had come home by now – it was just after midnight in London. That meant they'd listened to the message and chosen not to call her back.

"Hey, babe. Nice bikini."

Lucy looked up from her mobile to find Ash strolling through the sand towards their court.

"Who invited Ash?" Lucy breathed to Harper.

"I did," Harper said. "Why not?"

Oh Christ. Harper didn't know. Lucy hadn't had a chance to tell her.

"Just stay here and keep the others away from him, yeah? I'll explain later," Lucy said, racing up the beach towards Ash.

"I knew you'd be happy to see me." He grinned at her just like nothing had happened with Iza. "You must have been pretty wasted last night to kick me out that way."

"I must have been," Lucy agreed, grabbing his arm and towing him down the beach, away from the other girls. "If I'd been seeing straight, I would have kicked you all the way out of the suite and locked the door. Maybe then you wouldn't have *assaulted* Iza."

"Hey," Ash said, stopping dead. "I didn't assault anyone. *She* came on to *me.* What was I supposed to do?"

"What were you supposed to do with an incredibly drunk, incredibly sweet virgin?" Lucy snapped, spinning on him. "You were supposed to be a gentleman. And a gentleman would have put her back into bed and *not stayed there with her.*"

"Whoa, whoa," Ash said. "I didn't do anything to her. She's still an incredibly sweet virgin. Sure we made out a little bit, I could barely stop her, and yeah, maybe I shouldn't have even let it get that far, but you had just completely rejected me. I was upset."

He put his hand on Lucy's shoulder as he continued.

"I really like you, Lucy. I have since the moment I saw you, and last night, I thought you were finally interested. Then you kicked me out. That was cold, Lucy. It really messed me up. I'm only human."

Lucy shook his hand away. "Very nicely done, Ash. Apologise just enough to make me feel like this is my fault in the hope that I'll feel guilty, right? I don't think so. You did this all on your own. Iza's a wreck. She'd had enough guys trying to take advantage of her last night, she didn't need you to have a go too. And if you can't be trusted to watch out for her, or any of us, then we can't have you on tour. I'm going to have to talk to—"

"No!" Ash grabbed her shoulder again, this time not in a friendly way. "You're *not* going to tell Jason. I'm not going to have a couple of British sluts ruin me just because they don't feel like facing the consequences of what happens when they drink themselves into a coma."

"Yeah, I'm pretty sure you are, actually," Lucy shot back, a little amazed at how completely not intimidated she was by him. She really had changed, she thought, abstractly.

"You are going to regret this," he growled, yanking his iPhone from his trouser pocket.

"Why, because you're going to tweet me to death?" Lucy asked.

"No, because I'm going to tweet this *everywhere*," he replied. He flipped the screen around to show Lucy a grainy but still perfectly identifiable video of Iza lying in bed, half naked and giggling.

"Come on in!" a drunken Iza hiccupped. "Room for a little one!"

"You didn't," Lucy breathed.

"I did. And if you bitches don't treat me with respect, I'll share it with the universe."

"Go ahead."

Lucy and Ash whirled to find Iza standing behind them, still soaking wet in her bright blue spotted one-piece, short hair slicked back to her skull.

"Go ahead and post it, Ash," Iza said, voice unwavering. "I'm a rock and roller now, aren't I? A little light nudity isn't going to hurt my career. In fact, my guess is that will be the thing that stops me being 'that girl at the piano' and makes me a real Crush vixen and general bad girl.

You, on the other hand, will be just that guy that Iza Mazurczak slept with once in Vegas."

Lucy felt a huge grin growing on her face. Iza had done some growing up this summer as well.

"That's what you think, little girl," Ash hissed. "Twitter rumours have killed more careers than they've helped."

Little girl... Ash was right about at least one thing, Lucy thought. And it was going to end this conversation, for good.

"Actually," Lucy said. "I believe she's right. But I also believe she's not going to have to worry because you're never going to say a word about that video. In fact, you're going to delete it. Right now."

"Oh, you think so?" Ash spat.

"I do. That video won't just make you that guy that Iza Mazurczak slept with once in Vegas. It'll make you that guy who Iza Mazurczak slept with once in Vegas who is also in jail."

"What?" Ash said, startled out of his blind rage.

"Iza's under eighteen," Lucy said. "You are over twenty-one. They have a name for that here, don't they? Oh yeah... statutory rape."

"But nothing happened!" Ash blurted. "I barely touched her, I didn't—"

"You didn't?" Iza demanded. "But I thought—"

"He's mucking about with us, Iza. He always has been. You never slept with him. Or anyone else," Lucy assured her.

"Really?" Iza looked so relieved that Lucy felt her heart break a little bit for her friend.

"Really. Just like Ash is *really* going to delete his little video and leave us alone. Right, Ash?" Lucy shot him a hard look.

He looked like he wanted to punch her in the face, but instead he reached down and tapped at his phone, bringing up a prompt that read *Are you sure you want to delete this video?*

He slammed his finger down on *Yes*.

"Satisfied?" he snarled. "Let's just forget this ever happened, shall we?"

"Maybe," Lucy replied. "We'll see."

"You'll be sorry, Lucy Gosling," he said, his voice suddenly icy calm. "You could have just been nice to me, and things would have been so different. But now... now you'll be sorry."

With that he was gone.

"Lucy, what if he—" Iza began, her sudden burst of aggression fading into anxiety.

"He won't," Lucy said, quite sure of herself for some reason. "He's the one with something to hide, not us. And he may not have actually done anything we can get him arrested for, but we can still get him fired. That'll be highly satisfying, don't you think?"

But Iza looked as though she was on the verge of bursting into tears.

Lucy started back towards the volleyball courts,

tugging Iza along. "Cheer up," Lucy told her. "Your virtue is reserved for a certain sweet violinist at a much, much later date."

"I don't think he's going to be interested in that," Iza said, sighing.

"Well, if that's true, it'll be his loss," Lucy said, slinging her arm through Iza's as they walked. "Because you, my friend, are both gorgeous and an amazing Hollywood-jerk-slayer of the first order."

"I was pretty fierce with Ash there, wasn't I?" Iza said, almost managing a real smile.

"Without a doubt," Lucy agreed.

That's when they heard the screams.

15. TERRIFYING THINGS

Lucy was at a full sprint with Iza just on her heels when they crested a dune to find Harper and Toni crouched over Robyn, who was lying crumpled in the sand.

She was so still. Was she dead?

"Clear out," Skye urged Harper and Toni. "I learned CPR last summer."

"Come on," Lucy said, hurrying over to drag Toni and Harper away. "Let her in."

Skye reached down and felt Robyn's neck for a pulse.

"Her heart's beating. But she's barely breathing. Her pupils are fixed... Lucy—"

"I'm already dialling 999."

"It's 911," Harper said. "911! We're in America, remember?"

Lucy stopped dialling and started again, fingers shaking.

"Hello? Yes, I have an emergency. My friend has collapsed. Venice Beach. At the volleyball courts."

It felt like hours before the blare of sirens burst through the chatter of the beachgoers who had clustered around them, offering advice and talking nervously amongst themselves.

"What did she take?" the taller of the two medics demanded.

"Take?" Rafe said, shooting Skye a warning look. "She hasn't taken anything."

He was lying, of course. Bastard. Lucy shook her head. "She's taken something."

"Lucy," Rafe cut in.

"Shut up, Rafe," Lucy snapped. Then she turned back to the paramedic. "We're not sure what it is exactly, but she's been taking something to lose weight. But she may not have taken it for the last day or two. The person who was giving her the pills was arrested recently."

"Thank you for being honest," said the shorter paramedic. "We can't treat her if we don't know what we're facing."

"Withdrawal," the taller one said, slipping an oxygen mask over Robyn's face. "Her pulse is racing."

"I don't think she's eaten much either," Iza said. "We've been trying to get her to eat but..."

"Anorexic?" the shorter medic asked.

"Bulimic," Skye said.

"The perfect storm," the taller one grumbled.

Robyn moaned on the stretcher.

"There she is," the shorter one said. "Can you hear

me, honey? I need you to nod if you can hear me."

Robyn nodded blearily, squinting her eyes against the sun. Lucy sagged in relief.

"Okay," the taller paramedic said. "We're okay. We're going to get her to UCLA Medical Centre. Do you know how to get there?"

"I do," Skye said.

"Good," the medic said. "Go straight to the ER and ask for your friend. They'll help you find her."

Then they bundled Robyn away and were gone, sirens roaring up the beach road and out of sight.

The girls just stood there for a moment, stunned.

"I'll drive," Skye said. "It'll be a squeeze but we can take the SUV and leave my car here."

"I'll take yours," Rafe said. "That way there'll be no need to come get it later."

"I don't think that's a good idea," Toni said. "You've been drinking, Rafe."

"I'm *fine*," Rafe insisted. "Skye, you take Iza and Lucy in the SUV. Harper, you come with me."

"Whatever, Rafe," Skye said. "We don't have time to argue. We'll see you there."

Lucy's eyes darted to Harper's face. *Please*, Lucy prayed silently. *Not now, Harper. Please tell him to stop being such an unbelievable wanker and get in the SUV with the rest of us.*

But the look of stunned joy on Harper's face told Lucy all she needed to know. Harper wasn't seeing Rafe as he was – belligerent and bleary with drink – she was seeing Rafe as she wanted him to be: the tall, handsome athlete who'd swept her off her feet two years before.

Lucy opened her mouth to protest when Skye tossed Rafe her keys and turned to Lucy. "Come on. Robyn needs us."

Lucy watched Skye walk towards the SUV, completely abandoning her designer beach bag and the bundle of towels Lucy swore had Hermes logos on them. Just as she was abandoning her boyfriend. This was not the girl she thought Skye Owen was, Lucy considered, but perhaps she had been altogether wrong about Skye.

"Come on, Harp," Rafe said, pulling Harper in the other direction.

"No," Lucy replied, reaching out to grab Harper's hand and holding on. "Harper should come with us."

"It's not your choice, is it?" Rafe shot back. "I need to talk to Harper about something privately. So you just run along and we'll see you at the hospital."

"Harper," Lucy said, turning to her friend. "Come with us. Please. He's had too much to drink."

"It'll be fine, Luce," Harper said, squeezing Lucy's hand without even bothering to turn away from Rafe and look at her. "I'll see you at the hospital."

"Harper—" Lucy began, but Rafe cut her off.

"She said she'd see you at hospital, right? So leave her alone."

"Harper," Lucy insisted, ignoring him. "Please don't

go with him. Not now. I can't handle this without you. Together we can do anything, remember? But we have to stay together."

"You're right, Luce," Harper said. "And we'll be together at the hospital in, like, thirty minutes. I'm just getting a lift with Rafe, that's all."

Then she let go of Lucy's hand.

16. I ♡ BAD CHOICES

Harper tried not to be too obvious about hanging onto the door handle as Rafe wove through traffic on the Pacific Coast Highway. He was going so fast. Too fast. Maybe the others had been right about Rafe driving.

"Babe," she said, as he shot through an amber light. "Do you want me to drive? I'm totally fine. I haven't had anything but that mojito at Skye's..."

"Don't worry so much, sexy," Rafe said, shooting her a quick grin. "I'm cool. But if I'm making you nervous, I'll slow down."

He did too. Harper smiled, relaxing against the seat. The others didn't see it, but she knew him. She knew the real Rafe.

"Harper," he began as they slowed to the inevitable crawling speed of the coastal highway traffic, "this whole thing today with Robyn... It's made me think."

"Think about what?" Harper said, twisting in her seat to face him.

"It made me think that life's too short to worry about what my father thinks," Rafe said, reaching out to squeeze her knee. "I was planning to tell you something completely different before. I was going to tell you that Skye was a better fit for me. That I love her and we have the same goals and all that noise. But that would have been a lie, Harper. She isn't what I want. She's what Sir Peter the Great wants. He thinks she'll be the making of me, but the person she's going to make me..."

"Is not who you want to be?" Harper breathed, her heart thudding in her ears.

"Exactly," Rafe said, inching the car along with the traffic. "I don't want to be just my dad's heir apparent. I want to be me. And you... you're the only girl who's ever made me feel like me. Like Rafe. You know?"

"I know," Harper said. She felt light-headed. She'd always thought being dizzy with happiness was just a saying, but now she knew it wasn't.

"So I've decided. I don't care what he wants. I want to be with you."

"That's all I've ever wanted, Rafe," Harper said.

"I should never have broken up with you," he said. "I love you, Harper. You know that, right?"

"I do now," Harper said. It was really happening. Finally. She'd done it. She'd made Rafe love her again. "I love you too."

"Of course, now I have to deal with Skye," Rafe said.

"I guess you do," Harper said. "I doubt she'll mind

much; she does nothing but network and talk about business anyway."

"She's been cheating on me with someone too," Rafe said. "I know that. Maybe it's Ash. Actually, you know what?" he said. "I'm not going to deal with Skye. If Dad wants her in our lives so much, he can play all nicey with her. I'm going to get my car from Skye's place and we're going to Santa Barbara for a few days. We'll just hide out until the dust settles."

"Rafe, I don't know. I need to go check on Robyn," Harper said, forcing herself not to shriek when he swerved across two lanes of traffic and screeched into a u-turn with only seconds to spare before oncoming traffic caught up with them.

"That's what cell phones are for," Rafe said, pulling into traffic going in the other direction. "Please, Harper. I need to get away and I want to get away with you."

Harper didn't want to go. She knew Lucy needed her, maybe Robyn too. But she'd waited so long to have Rafe back... Could she really say no to him now?

"Come on, Harp," he pleaded again. "I need you."

She couldn't say no.

"Okay," she said, letting an enormous smile burst through. "Let's do it!"

"Wicked!" Rafe grinned back at her.

Then he gunned the engine and swerved through the traffic ahead of them.

Cesar was in a hurry. Once he'd finished the pruning and mowed the lawn, he'd be done with the garden and he'd have the whole afternoon to write. He was almost finished with his new screenplay. He hadn't wanted to write the exuberant gore fest, but reading it over last night he'd known that Skye had been right to push him on it. It was one of the best things he'd ever written.

They'd release it on Halloween, he thought, letting himself daydream a bit as he clipped back the bougainvillea around the driveway. Skye would be with him at the premiere, of course. She'd wear a slinky silver dress, her hair all free and loose down her back and maybe the funny little plastic spider earrings he'd found in a charity shop for her last year and she'd worn at least once a week until Christmas.

The future was so close he could taste it.

A smile spread across his face when he heard the roar of a familiar engine. Skye's car. She was back. Had she actually had the guts to blow Rafe off at the beach and leave him to his blonde so that she could come home to him?

Cesar stepped into the driveway, looking up at the private road.

Maybe it would have been different if he hadn't been imaging her coming around the curve, her face brightening the way it always did when she first saw him, like a flower blooming at dawn. Maybe then he would have realised that whoever was driving Skye's car was coming in the wrong way around the driveway, and moving too fast to stop. Maybe then he could have moved out the way.

Maybe.

Harper wasn't sure she could breathe. Rafe took the twisting road like a rollercoaster. Hurtling downwards as though, if he drove fast enough, he could spin the Earth backwards, reverse time and change what had happened in Skye's driveway.

She hadn't even seen it, the moment the car connected with the gardener's body. But she'd heard it. Harper couldn't stop hearing it, in fact. That awful, dull squishy sound of car meeting flesh. She thought she'd never stop hearing it.

She fumbled in her bag for her mobile, yanked it free and swiped the screen to life. Then she started to dial 911. Or at least, she tried to. Her hands were almost shaking too hard to hit the buttons.

Rafe reached out blindly and knocked the mobile from her hand.

"No, Harper," he cried. "We can't."

"We have to!" Harper sobbed, finally finding her voice. "We have to call someone and we have to go back. He was hurt, Rafe. Oh, God, he was so hurt."

"He's not hurt."

"Yes, he was!" Harper cried. "He was lying on the ground. He wasn't moving. Please, Rafe, we have to go back."

"He wasn't hurt," Rafe said grimly. "He was dead. There's nothing we can do for him now."

"We have to try, Rafe," she said.

There were tears running down Rafe's face. "If we go back, Harp, this will ruin my life. They'll send me to jail. For a long, long time. I'm Sir Peter Hanswell's son. They love to make an example of celebrities' kids."

"We might be able to save him," Harper cried. "Then it wouldn't be so terrible. It was just an accident, Rafe."

"They won't see it that way," he said. "Please, Harper, please. You have to help me. If you love me, you'll help me."

She thought she was going to throw up. She couldn't do this. She'd loved Rafe Jackson so long, but she couldn't do this for him. She couldn't let that boy die for Rafe.

But she couldn't destroy Rafe either.

"Let's stop at the gas station on the corner. They have a phone, I think. I'll call 911 from there. That way, if he's alive, they'll help him, but they won't have to know it was you."

Rafe took a deep breath and nodded, swinging around the last corner and coasting down the hill.

The flashing cameras and clashing voices of the paparazzi blinded and deafened Lucy. Skye's hand, dragging her through the crowd, was her only guide.

"No comment!" Skye said firmly. "Please, just let us

through. Catch-22 will release an official statement when there's something to say."

"GET OUT OF OUR WAY!" Toni bellowed, finally clearing a path through the writhing mass of reporters.

Someone at the beach must have recognised Crush. That was the only way this crowd of vultures could have been waiting when they'd arrived.

"I'll go track down the admin nurse and find out where Robyn is," Skye said, yanking her mobile from her purse. "Lucy, call Jason and Alexander. We need them here, like, yesterday."

"Ladies, are you here for Robyn Miller?" The doctor was no taller than Lucy, and didn't look much older, but there was something about her simple black ponytail and rolled up scrubs that made Lucy feel certain she had everything well in hand.

"Yes, we're her bandmates," Lucy said, stepping forwards. "I'm Lucy Gosling."

"I know, I'm a big fan of *Project Next*. My name is Dr Rashid," the young woman said, holding out her hand to shake. "And your friend is going to be just fine."

"Thank goodness," Iza cried. "What happened to her? What made her collapse that way?"

"She's very lucky that you ladies got her here so fast, and that whoever did CPR and took care of her before the ambulance arrived clearly knew what they were doing," the doctor continued. "She's dehydrated and malnourished, and suffering from severe withdrawal syptoms. She isn't sure what she's been taking, but we're running tests now."

"I hope they lock Tomas up and throw away the key," Toni muttered.

"Thank you so much, Dr Rashid," Lucy said. "We had no idea she was in such a bad way."

The young doctor studied them for a moment, and then nodded. "I believe you. It's at our discretion whether this becomes a police matter. I'm going to hold off for now. I will, however, need someone who isn't a minor to sign some paperwork. I'm also going to need to speak to her parents to be sure that they'll continue a treatment plan. This is going to be a long, hard road."

"Skye is calling our manager," said Lucy.

"Good," Dr Rashid said. "Robyn needs to rest for a while, but I'll get you girls in to see her as soon as I can."

"Thank you so much," Iza said, wiping away the tears of relief that had gathered in her eyes.

Harper tumbled into the waiting area just as the doctor turned and walked back into the emergency room.

"Is she okay?" Harper demanded.

"Yeah, she will be," Lucy said. To her surprise, Harper responded by throwing herself into Lucy's arms and clinging tightly to her.

Lucy patted her back awkwardly. Was this just more Harper dramatics?

No; Harper was shaking.

"Are *you* okay?" Lucy asked quietly, so only the two of them could hear. "Where's Rafe?"

For a moment, Harper looked as though she might burst into tears, but instead she squared her shoulders and pasted a fake smile onto her face.

"Yeah, I'm fine," she said. "Rafe decided to just drop me off and head back. He hates hospitals."

Harper was a good liar, but Lucy knew her too well to be fooled. Something was wrong. This wasn't just about Robyn.

"How is Robyn?" Harper continued. "That's the only thing that matters."

"She's dehydrated and malnourished," Toni said. "Whatever Tomas gave her nearly did her in."

"Stupid cow," Harper said, wiping at her eyes. "I knew she was messed up. But I got..." Her lower lip quivered again as though she was only moments away from tears. "I got distracted. This is my fault."

"There wasn't anything you could have done," Skye broke in. "Not today. We all should have said something a long time ago."

"Yeah," Iza said. "It's no one's fault. We just have to help her now."

"It is someone's fault," Toni said, shaking her head. "It's Tomas Angerman's fault."

Before Lucy could reply, a pair of paramedics raced into the emergency unit, wheeling a stretcher at a dead run.

"Get the paddles," one of the medics yelled. "He's already crashed once. We got him back, but he's taci at best."

"There's significant internal bleeding," the other medic told Dr Rashid, who had come out of the ER to meet them. "Head trauma. Probable organ damage."

"Get me a neuro consult," Dr Rashid called to a nurse, falling in beside the stretcher as they disappeared down the hall into the ER.

Skye's mobile clattered from her fingers. She was chalk white. She'd clearly recognised the battered form on the stretcher, just as Lucy had.

It was Cesar.

"Was that..." Toni said, staring after the stretcher.

"Yeah," Iza said. "That's your gardener, isn't it, Skye? I wonder what happened to him?"

"Hit and run." One of the paramedics who'd brought Cesar in pushed back through the doors, looking exhausted. "A brutal one. Mowed him down right in the driveway of the house where the poor kid works. I hope we got there in time, but it's not good. If you know his next of kin, miss, you need to talk to the nurse right away."

"Oh my God." Harper's words were barely a whisper.

"That's awful," Toni said.

Skye was frozen, as though she'd been turned to stone at the sight of Cesar's prone body.

"Skye?" Lucy said, moving to the dark-haired girl's side. "Are you all right?"

Skye just shook her head.

No. She wasn't all right. Of course she wasn't. Lucy

couldn't imagine how Skye felt; the boy she loved was hurt – and badly so. But to the world, he was only her gardener. Could proud, image-conscious Skye really admit to the world that Cesar Delgado was more than just her employee?

Skye turned to look at Lucy with eyes that brimmed with tears.

"He... he looked dead, Lucy."

"But he's not," Lucy said, hoping that it was true. "They're trying to help him. And I think..." Someone had to say it to her, Lucy thought. "I think he needs you with him, don't you?"

Skye drew in a breath and then forced it out again, then another, as though each contraction of her lungs required intense concentration. Finally, she nodded. "I'm going to... I'm going in there. Please, just..." She clearly couldn't finish the thought.

"We'll be fine, Skye," Lucy said. "You have to go now. You'll never forgive yourself if you don't."

Skye nodded, scooped up her mobile and walked into the emergency ward without a backwards glance.

Harper was glad she had the Ladies to herself – she was a mess. She shook out the chignon she was trying to tie her hair up into and started again. Her locks were harsh and sticky with saltwater and sand and her hands were shaking so hard that she could barely keep a grip on the strands.

She clenched her fingers into fists for a moment, then shook them out. That was a little better.

She started again.. *Focus*, she thought. She just needed to focus.

Who was she kidding? She didn't need to focus. She needed to call the police and tell them what Rafe had done. What she and Rafe had done. It was just an accident. They'd understand that.

Or at least they would have, if she hadn't let Rafe drive away.

He must have been terrified, Harper thought, to do what he did. She'd felt like her brain had crumbled into dust when that horrible, smashing sound filled her ears, and she'd just been in the passenger seat. She couldn't imagine how Rafe felt.

But that didn't mean that running away was the answer.

What the hell was she going to do?

Her cell phone punctured the silence with a tinny refrain of 'I'll Cross the World'. She looked down at the screen. Unknown number. What if it was the police?

She thought about not answering. She thought about smashing the damn thing to bits.

Instead, she swiped the call to life.

"YOU BITCH."

The snarling voice was loud enough that she didn't even have to bring the phone to her ear.

"This is *not* the time, Tomas," she said.

"Oh, it's the time," he snarled back. "It's the last time

I'm going to ask you to hand over what's mine."

"I told you exactly what I was going to do if you came near Robyn again," Harper said, letting all of the pain and confusion and horror of her day burn into clean, righteous fury. "She's in the hospital, thanks to you. You're not going to turn a profit from nearly killing her. No. Way."

"I'm not the one you have to worry about, you stupid, stupid girl," he spat back. "Where do you think I get my product? The tooth fairy? You have no idea what you've put yourself in the middle of, Harper McKenzie. You don't mess with these people."

"And you don't mess with me," Harper said. And then she hung up.

She slid out of the Ladies and walked up the corridor, feeling as though she was slowly turning to stone. Tomas was right. She had no idea how big a mess she'd been letting herself in for when she signed up for *Project Next.* Maybe she should have just given up on Rafe and stayed at home.

No. Crush would never have happened if she'd stayed at home. And none of this trouble actually had anything to do with *Project Next.* This disaster was one hundred per cent Harper-made, from start to finish. She just hoped she could fix everything she'd broken.

He's going to die. He's going to die. He's going to die. He's going—

"Stop that," Skye ordered the frantic little voice in

the back of her head that was stuck in a loop of doom. Cesar wasn't going to die. Skye wasn't going to let him.

"He's *not* going to die," she insisted again. "He's not going to die."

She took a firmer grip on the horribly limp hand that she was holding and reached up to smooth his sweaty black hair away from the butterfly stitches that held a gash on his forehead together.

She willed herself to remember what it felt like when his big, calloused hand closed around hers, folding her fingers inside his and engulfing her hand with his own. Cesar liked to tease her for being cold in seventy-degree weather, but he was always ready to warm her icy hands in his own. He would do it again, she thought. Then she could forget the awful feeling of lifelessness in the hand she'd been gripping ever since they'd brought him back from six hours in surgery.

"Come on, C," she whispered. "You have to wake up. The doctor said you could. Now you just have to do it. I know you can. I know you. You don't give up."

The big hand didn't move. Skye shifted her fingers, searching for the light and rapid pulse at its base.

"Besides, if you don't wake up you'll never get to see the colours my mother turns when I tell her I'm leaving the heir to the Catch-22 empire and moving in with the gardener."

She squeezed his hand again, silently begging the pulse under her fingers to get stronger.

"That's right, I said moved in with. If I'm going to do this, I'm going to need somewhere to live, at least until my dad gets back from shooting. Because Mother is going to disown me. This is all your fault, you know. You're the one who made me want to be more than what she wants for me. You're just going to have to live with me taking over your bathroom," Skye scrubbed at the tears that burned at her eyes. "And don't go thinking you can get injured every time we have an argument," she said, forcing her voice to be cheerful. Hopeful. He had to hear her. He had to. "I'd already decided to leave Rafe this morning, before you got into this mess. I'm not doing this just because you went and got run over. But, C, oh, C, you have to wake up."

"I know my daughter is here." A familiar, brittle voice floated through the half-open door. "She sent me a text message telling me she was here with Cesar Delgado, though God knows why she'd be here with the gardener, really, but I *know* she's here and you need to tell me where to find her. Right. Now."

No way. Jennifer Owen had actually bothered to get in the car and come looking for her daughter? Skye had just assumed her mother would have something more important to do than to bother coming here.

"Ma'am." Another voice that must belong to the duty nurse said, "You'll have to check in with admitting."

"Do you know who I am?" Jennifer Owen's voice shrieked.

"No," the nurse said calmly. "I don't. I'm sure if you inform the front desk, however, they can use that information to help you track down your daughter."

Skye almost laughed out loud. Jennifer was going to have a heart attack if she kept this up. Or possibly kill someone. As much fun as it would be to watch, it was time to put a stop to this.

Skye stood and walked to the door.

"Mother," Skye said, keeping her voice low. "There are a lot of sick people here who need their rest. Please keep your voice down."

Jennifer Owen stormed up the corridor hissing, "Skye, what are you doing here? Did you know I've been dealing with the *police* all afternoon... *myself*? How could you?!"

"I've been a little busy, Mother," Skye said. "Cesar was badly hurt and he needed me here. You can go home. Cesar's parents are on their way from San Diego, and one of his family will give me a ride home when I'm ready."

"Cesar?" Jennifer Owen whined. "Why would Cesar need *you*? And why would the *gardener* be more important to you than your own family?"

"The gardener is not more important to me than my own family," Skye said, shocked at how little she cared about the sour expression on Jennifer's face. "But my *boyfriend* matters a great deal. He's badly hurt and he needs me."

"You aren't serious, Skye," Jennifer Owen sputtered.

"I know you've had your… dalliances, but your boyfriend is Rafe Jackson – *not* the boy who mows the lawn."

"No," Skye said firmly, standing a little taller as she repeated herself. "My boyfriend's name is Cesar Delgado. He happens to work for you, doing landscaping. Unlike Rafe Jackson, he loves me, and I love him. I'm not going to hide that from you any more, so you're just going to have to get used to it."

Jennifer Owen stepped closer, driving an icy glare into Skye that would have left her shaking, even a week earlier. "You listen to me, young lady," she began, but then a lower voice cut off her brewing diatribe with a word that was almost a groan.

"Skye?"

It was Cesar. Cesar was awake.

Skye didn't spare her mother another glance as she dashed back into Cesar's room, back into her chair beside his bed. She reached for Cesar's hand. The feeling of his fingers closing around her own was so perfect that she swore her heart actually skipped a beat. His grip was weak, but it was there. He was alive.

"Skye?" he said again, blinking blearily.

"I'm here, C," she said. "And I'm not going anywhere."

It was hours before Dr Rashid brought Lucy, Toni and Iza back to Robyn's room. Robyn was sitting up in bed. She still looked frighteningly pale and thin, but there was more life in her eyes than Lucy had seen for weeks.

"You're feeling better," Lucy said.

"Much," Robyn said. "Now I only want to die of embarrassment."

"Don't say things like that," Iza said. "You gave us a fright today, Robs."

"I know. I'm so, so, sorry. I can't imagine how you aren't laying into me," Robyn said, sniffing back tears. "I deserve it."

"Yep, you do," Toni said, grabbing a box of tissues and holding it out to Robyn. "But you're not the only one."

"She's right," Lucy said. "We all knew something was wrong. We shouldn't have let things get this far."

"You tried, Luce," Robyn sniffed. "I lied to you. I lied to all of you. And I would have kept it up too if this hadn't happened."

She blew her nose a few times on the tissue, sounding a lot like a mating duck. Iza giggled a little and Robyn looked embarrassed but then Toni pointedly took another tissue and blew her own nose even harder. Soon all four girls were laughing so hard that Lucy was finding it difficult to breathe.

"Where's Harper?" Toni said, when she'd finally recovered enough to speak.

"I don't know," Lucy admitted. "She was with us in the waiting room, but then she just took off and now she's not answering her phone. She drove back from the beach with Rafe and she seemed... I don't know. I think something dreadful might have happened between them on the way over."

"Hopefully she dumped the loser," Toni said. "He's no good for her."

"Yeah, but I don't think she's realised that yet." Lucy looked down at her phone again. It was almost half past eleven. Harper had been missing in action for nearly three hours. "Maybe I should head back to the house, you know? Check and see if she's there?"

"Don't go," Robyn said. "Knowing Harper she's just having a good sulk somewhere. She'll be back soon."

"I guess so," Lucy said, checking her phone again. She knew Robyn was right. But still, the hard knot of worry in the pit of Lucy's stomach refused to unwind.

"It'll be fine," Toni said. "We're all going to be okay now. Robs is getting help, and I'm—"

"Not going to get off with with our married manager any more?" Iza finished for her.

Toni stared at Iza, jaw dropped. Iza flushed a bit, but she didn't look away.

Finally Toni burst out laughing. "God, I was being such a massive idiot, wasn't I?" she said.

"That's one way of putting it," Robyn said dryly and then suddenly they were all off, a pile of giggles on the hospital bed.

"We'll be okay," Iza said firmly, grabbing Robyn's hand. "We'll be better than okay."

"I'll say," Toni said, looking past Lucy to the door

of the room with a huge grin on her face. "Some of us better than others."

"Huh?" Lucy twisted to follow Toni's gaze and saw Luke standing in the doorway.

"Um, hi, ladies," Luke said. "I hope, I mean... Robyn, I hope you're doing okay?"

"Oh yeah," Robyn said, smiling at him. "I'm much better, thanks, and I'm going to be fine. But I don't think you're here to check on me, are you, Luke?

"I... uh... no, I... I mean, I wanted to make sure you were okay. I mean, I saw the bit on the news and I was..."

"And you wanted to talk to Iza?" Toni suggested helpfully, visibly biting back a smile.

"Yes," he gulped, shooting her a grateful look. "Iz, can I talk to you for a second?"

Iza didn't say a word. She just kept staring at him. Perhaps Iza didn't actually want to talk to Luke. But then she jumped off the bed.

"Yes," she said in a clear, even voice that was distinctly un-Iza-like, given the circumstances. "Let's just go out in the hall a bit, shall we?"

Then she marched up to Luke, grabbed his hand and hauled him out of the room.

Lucy turned back to Toni and Robyn, amazed.

"I know, right?" Toni said, correctly reading the look on Lucy's face.

"Who is that girl, and what has she done with Iza?" Robyn added, leaning forwards. But she was grinning from ear to ear, and Lucy couldn't help joining her.

"You'd better take it easy and lie back down," Toni told Robyn. "I can't spy on them properly with you in the way."

Of course, that set them off all over again.

Iza could hardly believe it. Rather than simply collapsing in a puddle of nerves when Luke asked to speak to her, she'd got up and dragged him out into the hall. Just as though she was the sort of girl who pushed boys around all the time and always got what she wanted. And in the same afternoon that she'd put Ash in his place, as well. It was as though Harper McKenzie had suddenly possessed her body.

No, she thought. She wasn't becoming Harper at all. She was only realising that Iza Mazurczak had a voice of her own. She didn't need a piano to be heard.

But now came the tricky part – using that voice to convince Luke that she deserved another chance.

"Luke—" she began.

"Iz," he cut in. "I'm so glad you're okay. The piece that hit TMZ didn't say which of you was in the ambulance and I thought..."

"You were worried," she said. That meant he still cared. There was a chance.

"Worried?" He shook his head. "I was terrified. The thought that something had happened to you."

Iza reached out to grab his hand before the old shyness could stop her. "I'm so sorry, Luke."

"You don't have to apologise," he said, before she could finish. "You were in Vegas, you'd just won the show and we never talked about... I mean we never said we were exclusive. We've only been dating for a few months. I can't expect—"

"Yes, you can," Iza said. "And I do need to apologise. I messed up. I was so pleased that we'd won that I wasn't paying attention to what I was drinking and there were these guys getting me more drinks... I should have stuck with Lucy or Toni. Or I should have told those guys that I didn't want any more to drink. But I didn't, and then Lucy found me and she and Ash took me home. Together."

"I'm sorry you were alone," Luke said, shaking his head. "I should have been there."

"I should have taken care of myself," Iza said. "I'm perfectly capable of that. I think I know that now. But... Luke... I did kiss him. Ash, I mean. I was so beyond wasted that I don't really even remember it. I didn't mean for it to happen, and I'm so sorry and it's never going to happen again. But I don't want you to ever feel like you don't know everything."

Luke didn't say anything, so Iza pressed on.

"I understand if you don't want to be with me any more, but if you give me a second chance, I promise it will never happen again."

Luke was just standing there, staring at her. God, this was it. He was going to break up with her.

He kissed her.

Iza twined her arms around his neck and kissed him back with everything she had. He was kissing her, surely that meant—

"You forgive me?" she asked, pulling back just far enough to whisper into the thin space between their lips.

"You're my Iza," he said, kissing her again. "How could I not?"

The sound of clapping infiltrated Iza's bubble of happiness.

It was coming from inside Robyn's hospital room, Iza realised. Her ridiculous bandmates were applauding. Cheeky cows. Iza grinned against Luke's lips. His arms tightened around her. She could feel the laughter building in her chest, but she resisted the urge to giggle. She wanted to keep kissing Luke forever.

Toni's wolf whistle was the last straw. Iza buried her face in Luke's shoulder and shook with laughter. Thankfully, he was laughing just as hard.

"I guess I'll have to get used to an audience, if I'm going to date a rock star," he said, still chuckling and holding her close.

She hadn't known she'd made the decision until he said the words 'rock star'.

She pulled back to look him in the eye. "You're not going to have to get used to dating a rock star."

A stricken look flashed across his face and she hurried to clarify. "No, no, don't worry. I only mean I don't think

I want to be a rock star, that's all. I *definitely* want you to get used to dating me."

"What do you mean?" Luke asked. "What about Crush?"

"I love Crush," she said. "But I'm not sure this is the life I want. Especially after everything today... I don't know if I can keep up with something that's just not me. I want to play the piano on stage, but I want it to be in places like the Disney Concert Hall and I want to play things like Gershwin and Bach and Rachmaninov. I've been thinking... It'll mean going home for a while to finish school but I'd like, I mean... if you'd like it too, I'd like to come back to California, when I've done my exams. I want to get my music degree. What do you think?"

"I think I've always wanted a good excuse to see more than just the Royal Opera House in London, and visiting my girlfriend is probably the best one ever."

Iza launched herself back into his arms and kissed him until they were both completely, utterly, perfectly breathless.

Lucy and Toni and Robyn were grinning as madly as Iza knew she was, herself, when Iza walked back into the hospital room.

"Where'd lover boy go?" Toni asked. "It's no fun having just the one of you to tease."

"He'll be back," Iza said, biting her lip to keep from smiling like an idiot again. "He's gone to find some dinner for us all."

"So he's not upset then?" Robyn said.

"No." Iza shook her head. "When he saw on TMZ that one of us had been hurt and didn't know if it was me or not..."

"How massively romantic," Robyn sighed. "Sit; I want every single detail."

Lucy was texting. She looked up at Iza and smiled, but she was clearly distracted.

"What's wrong, Luce?" Toni asked, catching the look of concern.

"Harper's still not replying to me," Lucy said. "I'm worried. I don't know why, but I just..."

"I'm sure wherever Harper is, she's fine," Toni said. "It's Harper, after all. She can take care of herself."

17. TEENAGE TRAGEDY

Thank God for blind spots, Harper thought as she slid into the one in the corner of the entrance hall at Crush House, between the coat cupboard and the stairs. The last thing she needed was her complete breakdown being broadcast in the 'What happened next' episode of bloody *Project Next*.

She wished she'd never heard of the show. No, she wished she'd never met Rafe Jackson. If only she could take back the day in Year Nine when she'd let Rafe literally sweep her off her feet and carry her over a muddy puddle, when she and Lucy were trying to cross the rainy rugby pitch on their way home from school. If only she could go back and pick another route home. Or tell him to get lost when he picked her up and carried her away, leaving poor Lucy alone on the soggy pitch.

Why hadn't she been able to see it then? Why had she let him blind her to everything and everyone else?

Blind her to how often she was abandoning Lucy and her other friends after school in the hopes that he'd want to hang out with her after rugby training. Blind her to the fact the she'd nearly got Lucy killed trying to impress him.

But she wasn't going to let him blind her again. Not this time.

Harper longed to call Lucy. She wanted to think Lucy would understand, that she would help Harper find a way out of this mess. But Lucy didn't have any reason to be understanding. Not really. Lucy had told Harper that Rafe was dangerous. She'd begged her not to get in the car with him. And Harper had ignored her. Why should Lucy have any sympathy now?

Harper pulled out her mobile and switched it on. A tidal wave of text messages and voicemails burst through as the iPhone powered up – a dozen from Lucy, a few from Toni, one from Robyn and a couple from Iza. And about twenty from Tomas, devolving from threats to pleas to completely mad babbling.

She ignored them all and dialled a familiar number.

It rang eight times, then clicked to the answering machine.

"Hi, you've reached the McKenzies. We're out, and Harper is in Los Angeles being a rock star, so try our mobiles if you need one of us, otherwise, leave a message and we'll call you back!"

"Mom?" Harper said into her phone. "Dad? You there? Are you screening?"

Nothing. No one was home.

"I guess not," she said, trying not to sound like she was crying. "Just calling to... to say hi. Tell you about the show. We won, but you know that. I texted you. It was pretty great. Hope you managed to watch the final when it was on..."

She couldn't seem to form any other words without bursting into tears, so she just hung up. She could try her parents' mobiles, but they were probably busy. They might not even pick up and somehow that would be worse than not talking to them at all. She'd just have to deal with this herself. Just as she always did.

And the first thing she had to do was report Rafe Jackson to the police. She pulled herself to her feet and headed into the living room.

Harper had to clamp a hand over her mouth when she stepped into the room to stop herself from screaming.

The room was trashed. Holes had been gouged in the walls and stuffing had been torn from the sofa cushions. Chairs were overturned and tossed around at odd angles. The baby grand piano had been torn open and its strings had been ripped out.

Where do you think I get my product, Harper? The tooth fairy?

She'd known what Tomas had meant. He bought drugs from bad people. Dangerous people. She'd thought... She'd only meant to let Tomas stew a bit. Let him feel the panic for a day or two before she gave it back. Had she been wrong? Was she alone in the house with a criminal in search of drugs they thought she'd stolen?

She so, *so* couldn't deal with this on her own.

"Harper." She almost bolted before she recognised the voice. It was Rafe, calling to her from the garden.

"Rafe?" she called, climbing over the destroyed furniture to get to the door. "What are you doing here? Did you see who—"

The words dried up in Harper's throat as she stepped out onto the patio and saw the familiar red canvas bag in Rafe's hands. Tomas's stash.

"What are you doing with that, Rafe?" she asked, trying to sound calm despite the panic that was stabbing its way up her spine.

"It took me *ages* to find it, Harp," he whined, as though she'd somehow hid the little bag extra well just to annoy *him*. "If you'd just let me hide it in the first place, I wouldn't have had to rip the house apart like that."

"What?" Harper gasped. "You did this?"

"I had to," Rafe said, still sounding like a four year old. "I had to find it."

"Why?" Harper demanded. "What is wrong with you? Haven't you done enough damage today?"

"I had to show you," Rafe said.

He walked towards her, nearly stumbling into the pool as he went. He was wasted, Harper realised. Beyond wasted. How much of Tomas's stash was already coursing through Rafe's veins?

"I had to show you... You girls don't know how to deal with these things. I found it, didn't I? So will they. This way I'm the only one who knows, Harper. This way I can take care of you, and no one else has to know you kept all these drugs so long."

He tossed the red bag from hand to hand, like some kind of a crazy circus performer. "We can destroy it, you see. Together. I can protect you. Hiding drugs for someone, that's accessory after the fact, Harper. That's a crime. And a bad one, as well."

His smile glowed neon in the moonlight. "I'm pre-law at uni. Did you know that, Harp?"

Harper nodded, edging backwards towards the door. "But there's no way to prove I handled the drugs, Rafe. Tomas hid it here, that's all. That's all the police will think."

"You're wrong, Harper," Rafe insisted. "If they find this, you'll be in trouble. And Robyn will be in trouble. But I can help you. I will help you make Tomas and the drugs and all of it go away, and in return, you can tell them that you hit Cesar. It was an accident, but you panicked. Or," he said, brightening like he'd just had a brilliant idea, "you didn't even know you'd hit him! You thought you'd just scraped the garage or something and you're so sorry."

"Why can't you just say that?" Harper asked. "Why blame me?"

"You're a minor, Harp, and you'll pass a drugs test and you know I won't." He was begging now. "They probably wouldn't even punish you, not really. Me, I'd end up in jail. Real, adult jail. I wouldn't survive in prison, Harper."

"Rafe," Harper said slowly, "even if I didn't get charged with anything, it'd ruin things for us. Ruin Crush."

"So?" Rafe demanded. "It would ruin my *whole life.* Or get me killed in prison."

"You wouldn't get killed in prison, Rafe. You wouldn't go to prison. Your father would make sure of it."

"He doesn't care!" Rafe yelled. "Nobody cares. Nobody cares about me, apart from you."

He closed the distance between them before she had the chance to back away.

"I know you love me, Harper," he said, pulling her close, "and we could be together, if you help me. It wouldn't matter what happened to Crush then. You'd have me."

"It would *so* matter what happened to Crush," Harper said, pushing him away.

"Why?" he asked, looking puzzled. "You only started the band to get back together with me. Everyone knows that. You can have what you wanted, Harper. You can have me. All you have to do is say you were driving. That's all."

"No, Rafe," she said. "You might have been what I wanted, but not any more."

"No!" he shouted, stepping closer again. "You love me! I know you do!"

"I did," Harper agreed. "I really did. But you never loved me, Rafe. Not really. Not the way you were supposed to.

But there are people who do love me, people I love, who need me now. I have to call the police and tell them what you did."

Then she turned and walked away from him. The back door was only a few steps away. If she could just make it inside, she could get away. She was sure of it.

"No!" Rafe howled. "Please, Harper, don't leave me alone."

He sounded so pathetic.

Harper turned back to Rafe and her heart dropped straight through the white paving tiles below her.

He was holding Tomas's revolver.

"Oh, God, Rafe. Put that away. Please. You'll hurt one of us. Please."

"I don't want to hurt anyone," he whined. "I don't. You're making me. You won't help me. I don't have a choice."

"I'm sorry, Rafe. I can't do what you want me to do, but I can help you." She tried to take another step away from him, but she couldn't seem to convince her feet to move. "Just put that down and come in the house with me. This will go better if you call the police yourself."

"NO!"

His voice was so sharp, so loud, that she almost didn't hear the gunshot.

She looked down at the front of her white tank top and found it blooming with red. She hadn't thought fresh blood was that red. It was only that colour in movies. But that made sense. This couldn't be real blood.

Rafe was staring at her, practically hyperventilating.

"Rafe," Harper whispered, stumbling forwards, trying to stay on her feet. It didn't hurt, not really, but she just couldn't seem to move her feet properly. She was going to fall in the pool if she wasn't careful.

Rafe backed away from her, gun still dangling in his hand. "I'm so sorry," he babbled. "Oh, Harper, I didn't mean to... I didn't want to hurt you. But I can't go to the police. They can't know. *He* can't know. Can you imagine what he'd say? My father. Not that he'd be surprised; he always did say I was a disappointment. But I can't let him down him again, Harper. I can't. This way he'll never know. They'll see the drugs. Tomas's gun. It will look like you walked in on someone robbing the place. They'll never know. They never have to know."

Harper didn't try to reply. She couldn't. She wasn't there any more.

She was back at the beach. Rafe's arm was around her, dragging her towards the BMW. Lucy's hand was reaching out for hers. Lucy's voice...

Harper. Come with us. Please. He's had too much to drink.

But this time... this time Harper reached out and took Lucy's hand.

This time she let Lucy lead her to the SUV. Away from Rafe.

This time, a whole life was there, stretching out before her.

Touring with Crush.

Growing up.

Falling in love with someone who loved her in a way that Rafe Jackson would never begin to understand.

Travel.

Friends.

Sitting on a porch somewhere tropical with a grey-haired, wrinkled Lucy, playing Scrabble just as they had when they were Year Sevens at St Gabriel's. Still using only made-up words that made no sense to anyone but them. Still giggling madly the whole time, just like they had when they were only thirteen years old, sitting in the shade of the big old tree in the Goslings' garden.

She was still there, giggling with Lucy in a future they would never know, a life they would never share, when her eyes began to grow heavy and the world began to fade. Lucy's laughter grew softer. Her face less distinct.

It was getting so dark.

Then, there was nothing.

Harper McKenzie was dead.

18. I'll Cross the World (Reprise)

Lucy felt like she was having a nightmare, but she knew she wasn't. This was real life. She was sitting in the living room of the Crush house, clutching Toni and Iza's hands while an LAPD detective asked them questions.

"It looks like a break-in," Detective Hernandez said. "The house is in pretty bad shape and there was cash scattered around the patio. We found the gun in this, in the canyon below the house." He held up a red canvas bag.

"Tomas!" Toni gasped.

"You recognise it?" Detective Hernandez asked.

"There was a drug dealer named Tomas Angerman who gatecrashed a party here at the house about a week ago," Iza told him. "He got arrested. That bag is his."

"I think... I think Harper had taken his stash, hoping that he wouldn't be charged and keeping Crush from being involved... which it did," Lucy said. "She'd hidden it here."

"Check if he's still in custody," Detective Hernandez ordered the police officer writing it all down. "He may have come back for the stash. And if she interrupted him..."

"He killed her," Toni finished, eyes filling with tears again.

"I wish we had video evidence to back that up," Jason said, striding into the living room. He must have broken a dozen traffic laws, getting there so fast, Lucy thought. Less than twenty minutes had passed since Toni had called him.

"What do you mean?" Toni demanded. "Those bloody cameras are everywhere."

"And they were off last night," Jason said, dragging a hand through his hair. "Someone disconnected them from the wireless network at 9.14 p.m. After that we've got nothing."

"Tomas wouldn't have known how to do that," Lucy said. "Robyn might have shown him the blind spots, but he wouldn't have been able to turn off the cameras."

"*We* don't know how to turn off the cameras," Iza pointed out.

A flash of the look on Harper's face that afternoon when she'd rushed into the ER filled Lucy's mind. She'd been distraught. That had been clear. And she'd just got out of a car with Rafe.

A horrible thought shoved its way into Lucy's brain.

"I wonder if Rafe knows how," Lucy said.

Toni's jaw dropped a little.

Iza shook her head hard. "No way," she said. "Rafe is a jerk, but he wouldn't hurt Harper."

"Rafe?" Detective Hernandez asked.

"Rafe Jackson," Lucy said. "He and Harper... they used to date. They were... Well, something happened between them yesterday. Something that upset them both. She wouldn't tell me what."

"Rafe Jackson, as in son of Sir Peter Hanswell, lead singer of Winding Road and head of Catch-22?" Detective Hernandez asked, looking up at Jason for confirmation.

"That's him," Jason said grimly. "I don't know if Rafe would have been able to turn off the cameras, but it's possible. He and his girlfriend, Skye Owen, have been interning for me this summer. They know a lot about the mechanics of the show."

"Rafe and Harper had a..." Lucy hesitated, she needed the detectives to know the truth but it still felt wrong, sharing Harper's secrets. "Harper was still in love with him. They were together before he left for uni. She wanted him back. I think he may have still loved her as well. They were alone together driving to the hospital this afternoon, and afterwards Harper seemed shaken."

"Interesting." Detective Hernandez kept his expression carefully neutral, but his partner was scribbling notes furiously. "If you'll excuse us, we've got to make some calls."

Jason nodded as the detectives crossed out of the living room.

Lucy dragged in a shaky breath. Iza and Toni and Lucy hadn't let go of each other since their SUV had rolled up to the house in the dawn hours to the spinning red stain of police lights that painted the whole neighbourhood.

"I've got to call my grandmother again," Toni said. "She made me promise to check in every hour."

Toni didn't even pretend to complain about her grandmother's fussing. Lucy knew why. She could do with a bit of fussing herself, at the moment, but oddly, somehow, she also knew that she would be okay without it.

"Lucy!"

Alexander was striding into the house.

And her parents were right behind him.

"Mum?" she said, half wondering if she was hallucinating. "What are you doing here?"

"Alexander called us," Mum said, cautiously. As though she was afraid the wrong word would cause Lucy to crumble.

"How? I mean, we didn't know Harper was..." Lucy just couldn't say it.

"He called us days ago, long before any of this happened, sweetheart," Dad said, taking a step towards Lucy. "He called us when he discovered that we hadn't come to the final. He told us that he'd have plane tickets waiting for us at Heathrow, and we'd regret it more than we knew if we didn't use them."

"Of course, neither of us knew how much. If we hadn't come... if you'd been dealing with this alone, half a world away..." Mum shook her head. "I'd never have forgiven myself."

She stepped closer, coming almost close enough to touch Lucy, and then hesitating, as though she was afraid Lucy would push her away. "We should have... We shouldn't have let you go this long on your own. And your beautiful letter. We should have rung you then. We should have come to the show. We watched it, you know. Well, Emily turned it up so loud we didn't have much choice, but oh, Lucy... You were brilliant."

Mum was afraid, Lucy realised. And Dad was doing that same fidgeting thing that John always did when he was nervous. They were afraid that *Lucy* wouldn't forgive *them*. Just as afraid as Lucy had been that they'd never forgive her.

She felt like she'd never seen her parents before. They were suddenly so... not parent-like. She didn't know why she was surprised. They were human beings too, after all. It only made sense that they would be pretty much like all the other people she knew.

"Mum is right, Lucy," Dad said. "I still think we were right to want you to focus on your studies, but we should have listened to you when you tried so hard to tell us how much you wanted to do this. We should have talked about it, instead of just making a decision." He reached out and took Lucy's hand. "Most of all, we should have watched you play. You're spectacular, sweetheart. You really are."

"I'm so sorry, my darling," Mum said. "I'm so sorry it turned out this way. But we are so proud of you."

Then she threw her arms around Lucy and pulled her close.

Lucy let her head rest on her mum's shoulder. They were exactly the same height now. It was disconcerting, leaning down to her mother's shoulder, instead of being pulled upwards into her mother's embrace as she had been when she was small. But realising that she wasn't that little girl any more felt okay, like it was the real proof that she was the person she felt like she'd become this summer.

Wasn't that odd?

Harper would get it, Lucy thought. Harper would understand exactly what Lucy meant when she told her that it was only now, whilst getting a hug from her mum, that Lucy finally knew she'd grown up.

But Harper wouldn't understand, because Lucy would never be able to tell her – because Harper was dead.

That was when Lucy finally began to cry.

BONUS TRACK: BEGIN AT THE END

It had been Mum's suggestion for the girls to change out of their black clothes.

"Harper was too young and too lively for all this dreariness," Mum had said, shaking her head at the three downcast girls she was trying to coax some toast and coffee into before they set out for Harper's funeral. "A change of costume is in order, I think."

Dad had agreed.

Lucy was glad to ditch the stiff black dress and the dreadful black tights that had made her legs feel like chunks of wood.

Thankfully, Toni had thought to call Robyn to let her know, since she was coming from the rehab centre that her parents had helped her check into a few days after Harper died. She arrived at the cemetery looking like a spring day in a yellow dress with big green hoop earrings. Iza was wearing the shocking-pink mini with narrow stripes that Harper had always said made her look like a French starlet in a 1960s film. Toni sported a tomato-red sheath dress and oversized sunglasses, which made her look every inch the Hollywood bombshell.

Harper would have loved it.

She would have hated Lucy showing up to her funeral in purple Converse, Lucy thought, studying the way the bright high-tops contrasted the rich green of the grass beneath her feet. But she would have loved arguing with Lucy about it all day until Lucy finally gave up and admitted that the sparkly neon pink pumps that Harper would have wanted her to wear went much better with her short black and white polka-dot dress and three-quarter–length leggings. Then Harper would have laughed, looked at Lucy in the purple high–tops and said, “Oh whatever. The sneakers are more Lucy. Stick with those.”

Lucy could hear the conversation quite clearly, just as though Harper were still there, hiding somewhere inside Lucy’s head where no one else could hear her.

Just as Mum had said she would be.

Lucy had been trying and failing to sleep when her mum had slipped into her room in the hotel suite that Catch-22 had moved the girls and Lucy’s parents to the night after Harper died. Mum hadn’t said anything. She’d just crawled into Lucy’s bed and they’d lain there together, staring at the ceiling for a long, long time.

Then, just as Lucy had begun to drift off, Mum had whispered, "She'll always be with you, you know. Harper scared us with her recklessness, but she truly loved you, I think. And she made you who you are, in a lot of ways. Now you'll take everything you learned from her and live a life you can both be proud of."

And now, here Lucy was, watching two strange men in dark overalls pour dirt over a box that held her best friend's body and she could still hear Harper's voice. Just as if Harper were standing right beside her.

Harper would have loved the day. She would have loved the brilliant LA sunshine and the photographers capturing the moment for the newspapers. How she would have adored the idea of making the headlines. She'd have loved how the girls were making people whisper with their bright outfits glowing amongst the dreary black of the other mourners.

"Lucy?" Skye had come to stand next to her at the graveside.

Skye looked different. Older, Lucy thought, but not in a bad way. Confident. Grown up. Harper might have resented the fact that Skye Owen had come to her funeral, but Lucy was beginning to think they'd deeply misjudged Skye. In fact, Lucy was sure that Harper would have liked her eventually. If she'd had the chance.

But she never would. Not now.

"Hello, Skye," Lucy said. "How are you?"

"I'm all right," Skye said. "Better now that Cesar is off

the feeding tube. They're still not sure if he'll walk again, but there's no brain damage other than the short-term memory loss... He'll probably never remember getting hit, but the doctors say that's normal, with this kind of accident."

"I'm so sorry," Lucy said. "I mean, I'm so glad to hear he'll recover, but it's awful to think of him stuck in a wheelchair."

"He's alive," Skye said, a familiar gleam of determination in her eyes. "And I'm going to help him learn to walk again. I don't care what the doctors say."

Lucy believed she'd do it too. Skye Owen could do anything she put her mind to, Lucy thought. She was like Harper in that way.

"That's good," Lucy said. "Whether he can walk or not, at least you'll be together. I know how much he means to you."

"I know you do," Skye said. "Until two weeks ago, you were one of the only people who did. Thank you, Lucy."

"I didn't do anything," Lucy said. "You're the one who stood up to your mum."

Skye smiled wryly. "I should have done it a long time ago. I made a lot of decisions that day, Lucy. The day Cesar nearly died. One of them was that I don't want to be in the movie business. I don't think I ever did. I'm switching to a new major in the fall," she added. "Pre-med, so I can apply to medical school when I graduate."

Lucy thought about Skye helping Robyn on the beach.

She'd stayed calm as she checked the unconscious girl's pulse and airways, and kept her breathing while they waited for the ambulance. She'd probably saved Robyn's life.

"That's great, Skye," Lucy said. "I think you'll be an amazing doctor."

"Me too," Skye said. "My mother hates it though."

"She'll come round," Lucy replied. "Parents don't *always* know what the right thing is. They're only guessing, just like the rest of us."

"And..." Skye cleared her throat. Then cleared it again. She was nervous, Lucy realised. "I was wondering... I mean, you don't have to, but I was wondering... Can you do us a favour? Me and C?"

"Of course," Lucy said. "Anything. I mean, I'm driving to the airport with my mum and dad to go back to London since the tour has been cancelled. But if there's anything I can do before we leave, I'd be happy—"

Skye thrust a tiny blue hard drive into Lucy's hand.

"Just read that, and if you like it, give it to Alexander. Or Jason or... or someone else you trust."

"Is this Cesar's screenplay?" Lucy asked, stunned.

"Yeah," Skye said. "You said you wanted to read it, and now that I've thoroughly pissed off my mother, anyone else who might help us isn't going to take my calls and—"

"Of course," Lucy said. "But don't you want to—"

Skye shook her head. "I don't want my mom and her

cronies turning a profit on Cesar's talent. Not after the way she treated him. But I want Cesar to have his dream. Will you help?"

"Lucy!" Toni called. She stood in a cluster with Lucy's parents, Iza and Luke, and Robyn and her family. "We've got to go. We'll miss the plane!"

"Coming," Lucy called.

Then she turned back to Skye. "I'll read it, and I'll make sure Jason and Alexander do too. I'll help anyway I can."

"Thank you," Skye said. "I really... Thank you, Lucy. And not just for this, I mean..." She held out her hand to Lucy in a businesslike fashion. "Goodbye, Lucy."

Impulsively, Lucy reached out and pulled Skye into a hug.

"Goodbye, Skye."

Lucy looked up the sloped path that led towards the cemetery car park. Her parents were speaking to Alexander now. Luke and Iza had drawn themselves away from the others. Saying goodbye, Lucy thought. Poor things. At least it was temporary. Luke already had tickets to visit London in a month's time and, in less than a year, Iza hoped to be joining him at the University of Southern California.

Lucy really ought to go up there. Toni was right. It was time to go. Past time. But there was one last thing that Lucy needed to do. Instead of walking towards the cars, she turned and marched across the emerald grass towards Rafe Jackson, who stood rigid beside his father, just as he had throughout the service. To judge from Rafe's posture, it looked like Sir Peter might actually be secretly holding his son at gunpoint to keep him there.

"Rafe?" Lucy said.

"Hello, Lucy." It was Sir Peter who answered.

"Hello, Sir Peter," Lucy said. "I need a moment with Rafe, if you don't mind?"

"Of course," Sir Peter said, looking from Lucy to his son with a curious expression on his face. Then he turned to the Catch-22 executive he'd been chatting to.

"Shall we, Jack? I'll be at the car when you're finished, Rafe."

Lucy steeled herself as Sir Peter walked away. She wasn't exactly sure what she wanted to tell Rafe Jackson, but she was absolutely sure she couldn't just let him walk away and get on with his life, as though Harper had never existed.

As soon as Sir Peter was out of earshot, Rafe hissed, "What do you want, Lucy?"

His blank, distant expression had morphed into a hard-edged glare full of something... Not the anger she'd expected, though. No, it wasn't anger. It was fear. Rafe Jackson was *afraid* of her. Now why would that be?

"Don't worry, Rafe," Lucy said. "I only want to tell you something."

"Get on with it then," Rafe snapped.

"Just this," Lucy said. "I don't know what happened

to Harper, but I'm going to find out. The police might think that Tomas's supplier shot her when he was trying to get back his gear, but I don't think you believe that any more than I do."

"Why wouldn't I?" Rafe said. "She was messing about with drug dealers; it's hardly a stretch to think they killed her for it."

He looked down at the grave for the first time.

"If she'd just trusted me, this might not have happened," he said, bitterly.

Did he actually still resent Harper not letting him take Tomas's stash the night of the benefit? wondered Lucy. Surely not. Not even Rafe Jackson was that shallow. But then what was he talking about? What hadn't Harper trusted him with?

"Rafe," Lucy said, letting the acidic anger that had been eating away at her for days pour into her voice. "The house cameras were disconnected from the network before the killer entered the house. How could drug dealers know how to do that?"

Rafe's mouth opened, as though to speak. Then he closed it again. Then opened it. He looked like a not especially bright goldfish, Lucy thought absently. But more importantly, she'd clearly been right. Rafe Jackson *did* know something about Harper's death. Something he hadn't told the police.

"Something was wrong, Rafe," Lucy said. "The day Harper died. And it wasn't just Tomas and his drugs.

Something was wrong and whatever it was cost my best friend her life."

"Whatever, Lucy," Rafe said, his voice dropping into a quavering whine. "I don't know why you're making me talk about this. Not now. I loved Harper, you know. I don't need to imagine all the horrid things that might've happened to her."

"I don't know if you loved Harper or not," Lucy said, "but I do know this: I *will* find out what happened to her, Rafe. And I'll make sure that everyone else does too. I just thought you should know."

Lucy turned to walk away from him but he reached out and grabbed her arm, hard.

"Lucy," he said, sharply now. "Listen to me, you—"

"Rafe." A deeper voice cut through Rafe's panicked one. "I think your father was looking for you."

Rafe didn't let go of Lucy's arm as they both looked up to find Alexander walking towards them.

"I suggest you go find him," Alexander added. "Now."

"Goodbye for now, Rafe," Lucy said, trying to keep her own voice calm.

With a final dagger-sharp glare, Rafe dropped her arm and walked away.

"That boy is going to be trouble," Alexander observed. "I love Pete, but he didn't raise that child right."

Lucy wanted to tell Alexander exactly how much trouble Rafe had already been, but she wasn't sure how far to go. Sir Peter and Alexander were old friends, after all. Did he really want to know exactly how bad an apple Rafe Jackson really was?

"Jason tells me you're going home," Alexander said finally, as the silence stretched out around them.

"Yes. I'm going to finish school. I promised Mum and Dad."

"I understand." Alexander nodded, still staring out over the grave. "But when you're done, come back to LA and I'll find you a band."

"Really?" Lucy was stunned. "You will?"

"Of course," Alexander said. "You're not going to get away with slipping off to a middle-management job somewhere."

"That's... Thank you, Alexander," Lucy said. "And thank you for everything you taught me this summer. I couldn't have done this without you."

"You could have." Alexander shrugged. "You'll be a great drummer, someday, Lucille. Even without Crush. It's just too bad..."

"What?" Lucy asked.

"It's too bad you've got another year of school. Electric's drummer just dropped out and they're auditioning for a new one today. You'd be ideal."

Lucy shook her head. "I don't think Trent Eisner would be a big fan of that idea. I made a complete fool of myself with him after the Bowl."

"Jumping to conclusions isn't a useful habit, Lucille," Alexander said cryptically.

What did he mean by that? Could Trent have said something about her? No. He wouldn't have talked to Alexander about her. He wouldn't have talked about her at all. And even if he had, it didn't matter what Trent thought. Lucy was going home.

"I'll just have to take you up on that offer next year," she said firmly.

"Whatever you think is best," Alexander said. Then, with another of his brusque hugs, he was gone.

"What was that about?" Lucy's mum asked as they started up the hill towards the car park.

"Electric are auditioning new drummers today. He wanted me to try for it," Lucy said. Before her mum could reply, Lucy added, "But I told him that I needed to finish school first."

"Lucy," Toni cried, hanging back from Iza to fall in step with Lucy and her mother. "You should audition. I've just told Jason that I'll come back in two weeks to audition for this amazing new musical television show he's put me up for. He's pretty sure I'll get it. It would be so much fun if you were based here too. We could share an apartment, and then when Iza comes back for university, she can live with us as well. It'll be just like old times."

Lucy could just see the three of them in a little apartment somewhere in Hollywood, having a blast trying to cook for themselves and going to parties on the weekends. But she shook her head. "No, I'm sorry. I need to finish school. I promised Mum and Dad."

BONUS TRACK: Begin at the End

"I see," Lucy's mum said carefully, studying her daughter. "You really have grown up these past few months, haven't you, Lucy?"

"I guess so," Lucy said, turning back to look down at Harper's grave one last time.

"You need a moment alone?" her mum asked.

Lucy shook her head. "No, I'm ready to go."

Forty-five minutes later, Lucy sat in the crowded back seat of her parent's hire car, squeezed between Toni and Iza, staring out of the front window as they crawled through traffic, towards LAX.

Los Angeles seemed as reluctant to let her go as Lucy was to leave it. The traffic was getting worse every minute. Which was fine with Lucy, really. The closer they got to the airport, the worse Lucy seemed to feel.

Her head hurt. Her stomach was in knots. She felt like she was getting the flu.

What was wrong with her? And why did it feel like every centimetre closer to the airport was making it worse? It was as though the very idea of going home was actually killing her.

Maybe I shouldn't go back.

The moment the words formed themselves inside her head, her brain was convinced. She needed to stay. And she needed to get to the Electric audition.

Wait, Lucy thought. That wasn't what she needed at all. She needed to go home. She needed to finish school.

She needed to get out of the vortex of Hollywood. She tried to convince herself that she didn't need the music. What she needed was to get her life back under control.

But the thought just wouldn't go away. And worse, just thinking about turning around and going to the Electric audition made her feel better. Her stomach settled. Her head no longer hurt. Her skin stopped feeling too tight for her face. She felt... right.

"Mum," Lucy said slowly, still not quite believing she was really saying it out loud. She'd only just sorted things out with her parents. Did she want to ruin everything again?

But she couldn't shake the feeling that this was what she needed to do.

"Mum, I think... Would you guys be angry if I wanted to go to that Electric audition that Alexander mentioned?" Lucy blurted. "I know I said I'd go home and finish school, but I just... I think I need to do this. I tried not to, but I just... do."

Mum and Dad exchanged one of their secret parent-looks, silently comparing notes.

"You're sure," Dad said finally. "You're sure you want to do this?"

"Yes," Lucy said. "I don't know why. I just know I need to go back."

"And you promise, if you get the, ah..." Her mum searched for the word. "... gig – it is a *gig*, right?" She looked to Toni in the back seat who nodded, a big grin spreading across her face. "If you get the gig, you'll finish school while you're touring? They'll get you a tutor, won't they?" Mum continued.

"Yes, I'm sure they will!" Lucy said, hope swelling in her gut.

"Well, I guess we ought to hurry then, shouldn't we?" Mum said, a smile almost as wide as Toni's bursting from her lips.

"STEP ON IT!" Iza hooted, as Lucy's dad pulled into the exit lane, navigated the junction, and got on the freeway heading in the opposite direction.

Toni burst out laughing. "I think that's the biggest noise you've ever made, Iz."

"LUCY'S GONNA BE A ROCK STAR!" Iza shouted, not getting any quieter.

"Quite right!" Mum cried.

Lucy was so caught up in their excitement that she hardly realised that they were already zooming back the way they came.

"Wait, how do you know where to go?" Lucy asked her dad, who was suddenly driving as though he were in an action film.

"We asked Alexander," Toni said, still grinning. "While you were talking to Skye. Just in case. He told us they're holding the audition session at Troubadour."

Lucy looked from her parents to her friends, amazed. *They'd known*, she thought. They'd known what she needed to do all along. They'd just been waiting for her to realise it.

Then she burst into tears.

"Stop it!" Toni said. "Now you're just ruining your make-up."

"But you guys... You just... You guys!" Lucy babbled, incoherent with love for them all.

"Stop that right now," Toni said, though she had to wipe away a tear of her own. "And sit still. We need a repair job on that mascara if you're going to nail this audition."

"I'm calling Alexander," Iza said, actually bouncing with glee as she got out her phone. "To let him know you're coming."

"Do it!" Dad called, cutting up a Porsche as he slid into the fast lane. "We've got to get our girl on stage!"

Lucy burst into the matte-black and duct-tape world that was the backstage of the Troubadour club, zipping through the milling crowd of auditioning drummers like a tram on tracks. It was as though every nerve in her body had formed a straight line to the stage, with its big silver and white drum kit that read *Electric* across the kick drum.

"Alexander!" she called to her mentor, who stood at dead centre of the backstage chaos, directing traffic with his iPad in hand. "I'm here!"

"Good, because you're next!" Alexander said. "Go on, get up there."

BONUS TRACK: Begin at the End

Next? He wasn't serious. She wasn't ready. She wasn't warmed up. And Trent was up there. She hadn't even considered the fact that coming here meant seeing Trent until just now. Not to mention the part where getting this gig meant seeing Trent *every day*. What was she doing here? She wasn't ready for this. She'd never be ready for this.

"Lucy Gosling!" The stage manager read from his tablet. "Where is Lucy Gosling? We don't have all day, people."

Lucy knew she had to go on stage, but her feet weren't cooperating.

Then, for just a second, she was standing outside her house with Harper, the night they'd found out they were going to Los Angeles.

This is what you're meant to do. More than any of the rest of us, you belong up there on stage, on the drums. I can see it, and I hope you can see it too.

"LUCY GOSLING?" the stage manager called again.

This is what you're meant to do.

"Okay, Harper," Lucy whispered to herself. "Okay, let's do this."

And then she walked up on stage.

"Wooooo!"

Was that Mum back there cheering? It was. Toni and Iza were shushing her but they were completely failing in their attempts to make themselves invisible at the back of the club. Lucy didn't mind. She was just happy they were there at all.

"Lucy?"

Lucy felt a little breathless as she turned to look up at Trent Eisner. He wore rumpled cargo shorts, a black T-shirt and a pair of Birkenstocks that looked as though they might be older than Lucy. *Perfect*, Lucy thought. He looked perfect.

But she wasn't here to stare at a hot guy with her mouth hanging open like an idiot. She was here to play the drums.

Lucy opened her mouth to speak, but a squeaky, "Hi," was all that came out.

She caught a couple of covert raised eyebrows between the other band members and tried again.

"I mean, hello. I'm here to audition. For the drumming gig."

"I suggested it," Alexander said, stepping onto the stage behind her. "It seemed like kismet. Lucy being available at the same time Electric needed a new drummer. I think she'll have great chemistry with you guys."

"You're the *Project Next* winner, right?" said a short guy with hot-pink hair, who Lucy recognised as Rick Peterson, Electric's bassist. "That was harsh, what happened. Sorry, girl."

Lucy nodded, fighting back a flash of tears.

"Okay. Cool," Trent said slowly. "Let's try this. Lucy, you know our songs? We've been playing 'Storm the Gates' as the audition piece."

"I know it," Lucy said.

"Then let's do this thing," Trent replied, indicating the drum set.

Lucy picked up the drumsticks that lay on the stool and settled in behind the drums. She took a deep breath and rolled into the tricky, alternating beat of the throbbing ballad without a second thought.

It was easy. When had this become easy?

She was having too much fun to think about it now. She sank into the song and, just like some kind of warm ocean, it rolled over her head, dragging her down into its heart.

When the last note rang out from Trent's guitar, the silence that fell was almost painful. Lucy's hands itched to keep playing. Instead, she carefully put the sticks back where she'd found them and stepped away from the drum kit.

"Great work!" Rick crowed. "You're awesome."

"Thanks," Lucy said. "That was amazing. It was a real pleasure to play with you guys."

"Believe me, the pleasure was ours," said Lars Madison, the guitar player. "Right, Trent?"

Trent didn't reply to his bandmate. He just stood there staring at her, an unreadable expression on his face.

"Trent? Dude?" the guitarist tried again. "Earth to Trent."

Trent said nothing. He was probably trying to work out how to let her down gently, Lucy thought.

Suddenly, she just knew she couldn't handle another

rejection from Trent Eisner. Not today. Before he could say anything, Lucy jumped off the stage and ran past the tables at the front of the club, across the dance floor and out into the blinding Los Angeles sunlight.

Toni and Iza were on her heels, her mum and dad not far behind them.

"Don't mind that silly sod," Toni said. "You were brilliant up there, Lucy. Completely brilliant. If you don't get the gig just because he was too much of a wimp to ask you out, then he's an idiot."

"That boy wanted to ask you out?" Mum said. "The tall one who wouldn't say anything? That's why he's not going to pick you?"

"Yeah," Lucy choked out. "Sort of. It's complicated."

"Bastard," Mum declared stoutly.

Lucy stared at her mother in shock. She'd never heard Mum even come close to swearing before. Ever.

"I've half a mind to go in there and give him what for," Mum steamed. "You are *clearly* the perfect drummer for that band, and he wants to reject you because of a little romantic melodrama? Really, the nerve of—"

"Lucy!"

Trent was standing in the doorway of the club.

"You don't have to—" Dad began, but Lucy shook her head.

"I'm all right, Dad," she said.

Then she walked towards Trent.

"Hi," he said.

"Hi," she replied.

Trent stood there.

Lucy stood there.

They stared at each other.

This was so, so awkward.

"That was amazing, Lucy," he said, finally. The words were rushed, tumbling over each other. He was nervous, she realised.

The thought gave her the courage to nod in agreement. "It was," she managed to say. She took a deep breath. "I'd like the chance to do it again."

"The chance?" he said, bursting into a huge grin. "Do you think we'd let you get away after an audition like that? Oh no, you're going to be our drummer girl, Lucy Gosling. You have to be."

Lucy felt light-headed. She'd done it. He was offering her a place in Electric.

"But... Lucy," he said, his voice becoming serious again. "We need to talk first. About Blvd3."

Lucy had hoped he'd just let her pretend it had never happened. That she'd never lost her mind enough to think he wanted to date her.

"I'm so sorry, Trent," she said, hoping she didn't sound as though she was babbling. "I should never have... It was a mistake. I won't let it happen again. I promise."

"You're right. It was a mistake," he said, nodding slowly. "When you kissed me, I should have kissed you back."

Lucy's breakdancing stomach leaped just as though she were at the top of a rollercoaster.

"We had a moment, Lucy. The kind of moment you only get a few of in life," he continued. "I should have taken it, but I was too afraid of how it would feel if it went wrong. Of how badly I knew you could break my heart, if you wanted to. I even came to Vegas, you know. I watched you play in the final and, God, Lucy... you were incredible. I went there planning to... I don't know what I was planning to do, but I wanted to get that moment back. Then, when I saw you play up there, I knew you'd win and I chickened out. I thought I was doing the right thing – that anything between us was just going to be too hard. But I was wrong. I should have tried. And now... I just hope, someday, we'll find that moment again. I know it'll be even harder if that happens while we're both in the same band... but if I get that lucky again, I promise, I won't let anything stand in my way."

Lucy knew she was staring at him like an idiot, but she couldn't seem to do anything else.

"Lucy?" he said, humour starting to dance in his brown eyes as he took in her stunned face. "You okay in there?"

She managed to nod.

"And you forgive me for being an idiot and you'll join my band?" he continued.

She nodded again.

"Good." He grinned as if he'd just won the lottery.

"Well, I've got to tell a whole bunch of drummers they aren't getting a place in Electric today, so I'm going to go inside. I'll see you in there?"

She nodded again.

He strolled back into Troubadour, whistling to himself, and left Lucy standing on the pavement staring after him. She was going to be the drummer for Electric. And maybe, just maybe, someday she'd decide she wanted to kiss Trent Eisner again. And this time, he'd probably kiss her back.

"So?" Toni called. "What happened?"

Lucy turned to her friends and family and let the enormous smile that had been growing secretly, deep in her chest, bloom on her face. "I got it!"

Toni hooted with joy and swung Lucy off her feet in a spinning merry-go-round of a hug. Iza and Mum and Dad crowded in as well and the brilliant Los Angeles sunshine shone all around them like a spotlight as they hugged and patted and chattered their congratulations. But all Lucy could hear was the pounding of her own heart, beating steady and true.

Just like a drum.

Acknowledgements

Chasing your dreams long enough to catch them isn't easy, whether you want to write books or rock out on your drums with a band. Luckily for me, I've had a lot of help along the way.

First, I was born to a pair of great parents, who told me many stories and listened to all the stories I ever wanted to tell. Then I managed to acquire a wonderful assortment of friends who've stuck by me through the great times *and* the truly miserable ones. Without them, I could never have told Lucy's story – especially Janice, who has been a part of building Lucy's world from the very beginning.

As if great parents and great friends weren't enough, I've had more amazing teachers, professors and professional advisors than I can count or name here. In particular, Lucy would never have come to life if it weren't for Kemper Donovan, Jeff Norton, Emma Goldhawk and all the other wonderful people at Templar Publishing. Then there's Geoff Hollinger, who made it so much easier to write Trent by reminding me every day how it feels when your heart skips a bit every time the right guy smiles at you.

And last, but certainly not least, there's you. By reading this book, you've made Lucy's world bigger and richer. In short, you've helped me make Lucy Gosling's dreams come true! I do hope she'll return the favour.

About the author

Bridget Tyler began her writing career at the age of four with an epic poem about the Care Bears. Her grandfather was President of Oxford University Press in New York and later bought the children's list, filling Bridget's childhood home with classic British children's literature. This gave her the perfect tools to grow into a storyteller with a dry sense of humour and tragically confused spelling.

Bridget studied Dramatic Literature and Creative Writing at New York University and spent time at the London campus. During this time she travelled all over the UK, taking in as much of her adopted home as she could and developing a fondness for dark chocolate Digestives in the process.

After graduating, Bridget returned to her native California, where she worked as a feature film development executive and lived a fast-paced Hollywood lifestyle. After working with writers, she decided it was time to start spinning tales of her own and she began writing screenplays and magazine articles. She is now a writer for hit TV show *Burn Notice* and is co-producing a pilot (which she also wrote) with the producer of *The Walking Dead*.

Drummer Girl is Bridget's first novel.